Dedication

TO RAN.
ALWAYS.

I LOVE YOU.
Love always, your girl.

"Love to be real, it must cost—it must hurt—it must empty us of self."
— *Mother Teresa*

Prologue

Francesca

FACE TO FACE with the man I thought I was in love with, thought I knew, and fear has me frozen. Staring into his empty eyes, my life flashes through my mind like an old-time movie reel. The *tick, tick, tick* of the film keeping time with my heartbeat.

Tick . . . I was four years old when my mom was killed in a car accident.

Tick . . . Five when my dad partnered up with Joe Love and we all moved into the same building.

Tick . . . At seven the Loves claimed me as their Princess, daring anybody in school and out to mess with me.

Tick . . . By age ten they were my world.

Tick . . . We hit high school, our dynamic changed, and it was Deacon and I against the world.

Tick . . . Then he left me . . . for the first time, but not the last. He left me, and then I left him.

Tick . . . Now I need him . . . not for the first time, but if he doesn't hurry, it might be the last . . .

CHAPTER
One

DEACON

WHEN I WOKE up in bed with two Brazilian models that I didn't remember putting there, I realized it was time to pack it up and come home. After the win, I hung out in Brazil longer than I should have. Celebrating my victory or avoiding home, whatever.

Stalking into my office, heading straight to the cabinet where I keep the liquor, I pull down a glass and a bottle of whiskey, pouring a healthy amount into the tumbler. I toss it back in one gulp letting it set me on fire. Sucking in air through my teeth, I'm mid-pour on my second shot when I hear "Little Do You Know" filter throughout the room from the hidden speakers. Fucking perfect.

I walk over to the window, bringing the full-to-the-brim whiskey up to my lips and look out into the darkness, the picture of Frankie and I reflected in the glass. She is so fucking beautiful it sometimes takes my breath away. So sexy and elegant, the combination making for an incredible package, and the best thing is she doesn't act like it. She's not one of those women that are bitches feeling entitled because of how they look. She doesn't care about looks, hers or anyone else's. She's a good

2

time, and there's never been anything that my brothers and I felt we couldn't include her in—sports, drinking games, hell, we've even dragged her ass to the strip club with us on more than one occasion. Frankie is beautiful inside and out, absolute perfection, classy as fuck. That's my girl. Slowly sipping what's left of my drink, I think about the last time I spoke to her and her whispered words as she left the locker room, *"Little do you know."* Four words, one song that gave me more hope for us than I've had in the last few months.

Not that it matters because I'd never quit her. When I said I would go to war for her, I meant it. I'm just getting started. I'm brought from my thoughts by the sound of my phone. I glance over to see it skipping across my desk. When it dawns on me that it's "Fancy" coming from it, I can't get across the room fast enough. Once I reach my desk, I stop, my hand hovering over my phone lit up with a picture of Frankie dancing. All of a sudden a sick sense of déjà vu takes over me, and instantly I'm terrified to answer this fucking call, but I do. I have no choice.

"Princess?"

When I don't get an answer but can hear her breathing, panic spikes.

"Frankie!" I shout and then wait no more than a second before I'm frantically calling her name again. "Frankie! Don't fucking do this shit to me again, Princess!" Rounding my desk, I already have my keys in hand and I'm nearly to the front door when I hear her breathe out, "Andrew," right before the call is disconnected. This cannot be happening again. I'll kill him if he puts hands on her. Please fuck, let me get there in time. I'll fucking kill him.

Out the door in a matter of seconds, I don't even bother shutting it behind me. As I sprint to the Rover, I punch at the unlock button on the key fob, and then hit the button that will activate the gates. Yanking the door open and throwing myself behind the wheel and firing it up, I speed down my drive, lights not even factoring into my haste to get to Frankie. My thoughts are a jumbled mess as I take side streets at breakneck speeds, slowing but not stopping for stop signs and red lights. Grabbing the phone off the dash, I call Frankie.

"Come on, come on, come on. Pick up!" I shout. When it goes straight to voice mail after two rings, I bang a fist on the steering wheel in frustration. "Motherfucker!" I'm in such a fucking panic to get to her I can't even form a coherent thought. I should probably call someone, but I'm not sure who. Where the fuck are Reggie and Trent? Security detail, my ass! There's no time for anything else as I make a sharp turn onto Indie's street, plowing into three or five parked cars in the process and not giving a single fucking fuck.

I throw the Rover into park before it even comes to a stop, the front end buried in the trunk of a Honda parked at the curb. My anger and adrenaline hit an all-new high when I see Drew knock Frankie to the ground on Indie's front porch and then hurriedly drag her through the door. My vision is hazy with rage, my breath coming out in ragged puffs. I see red. Nothing but red as I vault over the fire hydrant and bushes that line the walkway to get to Frankie. This motherfucker has put hands on her for the last time. I'll make sure of that.

CHAPTER
Two

Francesca

"HELLO, FRANCESCA, AREN'T you excited to see me, darling?"

My eyes must be playing tricks on me. There is no possible way that Andrew is standing in front of me right now. Excited to see him? No, I don't think so. Shaking the fog that has taken up residence in my mind, the throbbing of my heart in my ears, I can once again hear Deacon shouting frantically for me through the phone line. So close, yet so far away.

Andrew reaches out and I watch in muted fear as he runs his fingertips down to my cold lifeless ones and takes the phone from my hand. He shakes his head as he thumbs the button, disconnecting the call. "Deacon—I should've known," a small, rueful smile touching his lips. "It was always him. It was always going to be. I did everything I could think of to keep you two apart, keep him out of our everyday lives, erase him from your skin," he says as he brushes the tattoo curling over my shoulder.

I flinch away from his touch and take a step back, stammering nervously, "Don't touch me. You—you shouldn't be here. I'm ca-calling the police." I can hear the terror in my voice. Feel

5

the trembling throughout my body screaming at me to run and get help, but I can't. It's as if I'm frozen from the inside out. My senses are all too acute, making me feel sick. The cloying smell of Andrew's cologne, pine and rosemary, a scent I used to love, now making my eyes tear and my throat close.

"Francesca, there's no need to call the police. They're already here," he tells me gently, almost eerily calm, pointing to a nondescript town car at the curb with two equally nondescript men sitting inside. They could be anyone. My eyes dart back to him when he starts talking again, "Well, marshals not police, but the law just the same. If you let me in, I can explain."

Let him in? Is he fucking insane? There's no way in hell that I'm letting him in this house. I need to figure out a way to get him out of the doorway so that I can slam and lock the door. My mind is racing, tuning out what he's saying. I'm brought back to reality when I hear "Whole Lotta Love" coming from my phone. I reach for it in desperation right before Andrew silences it and tucks it in his back pocket. Crying out in frustration, I lunge for it, but he grabs my wrists, squeezing tightly.

"Will you stop? With my luck he'll be pulling up in the next two damn minutes playing hero as per usual. I need to talk to you and get out of here before that happens."

He's exasperated. Getting more aggravated by the minute. I should be afraid, but I'm feeling braver than I was a moment ago. Maybe it's the knowledge that Andrew's right—any minute Deac will be pulling up with or without a police escort. He only lives about two miles from Indie's brownstone, and even as upset as he is with me, he'll be coming to save me.

"He'll kill you if he finds you here," I vow calmly and confidently. "He won't care who you supposedly have in that car." There is no way that I'm going to take his word on anything. Why would the marshals be here? Why would he know that? Where in the fuck are detectives Adams and Flores? They are supposed to be here any moment. That's the only reason Reggie

and Trent even left.

"I am well aware of that, hence the reason I would like to go inside. I don't have long anyway. This little visit is costing me dearly."

I open my mouth to speak when I hear the racing of an engine down the otherwise quiet street and the screeching of tires just before the crunch of metal as a vehicle crashes into another. I don't have time to see who it is before I am thrown to the ground by Andrew. My head smacks the cement hard, bouncing once with a painful thud, making me see stars. Blinking back the spots dancing in front of my eyes, it registers that I am being dragged through the door of Indie's house, the ground scraping the bare skin of my legs and across my back where my shirt has ridden up.

Once inside, Andrew is crouched down in front of me, swimming in and out of view. His lips are moving, but I can't hear what he's saying. I blink slowly and when I open my eyes again he's gone. Taking a deep breath, I roll over onto all fours and lift my head. I need to find where he went before he can do me any more harm. Out of the corner of my eye, I see movement. Slowly, I stand, placing my hands to my pounding head, willing the ringing in my ears to dissipate.

As the ringing fades, I'm startled to hear someone grunt in pain and the crunching of bone. As quickly as I can, I turn to the noise and see Deacon on top of Andrew, fists coming down fiercely and swiftly on his face. I open my mouth to scream for him to . . . what? To stop? Before I can even figure it out, two men come barreling through the door, sending me reeling back as they tackle Deacon. It's then that I find my voice and scream for *them* to stop. It makes absolutely no difference, as they're in no way strong enough to contain him.

I watch in horror and fascination as Deacon flings one man into the wall, the plaster cracking from the impact while the other one is trying with all of his might to put Deacon in some kind of hold. Shaking man two off like he's little more than a pesky child, he turns in my direction. Seeing that I'm up and still screaming, he shoots past the fallen men scooping me up, never breaking stride as he heads toward the open door. We make it to the threshold when I feel Deac tense. My eyes shooting to his face, I see him wince in pain. Putting me down gently, he twists at the waist, looking over his shoulder and then yanking the pronged wires of the Taser that one of the men had used to stop him from leaving.

Deacon flings them to the side and is about to lift me back up when Adams and Flores finally show up, guns drawn. Shaking uncontrollably, I start to sob in relief, falling into Deacon's chest, clinging to him as my legs give out. He puts his arms around me to keep me from falling, and brings his lips to my ear, talking to me softly, though I can't hear what he's saying over the sound of my own crying and chattering of my teeth. My head snaps up as I feel him being pulled from me, and I shake my head confused as I see Flores wrenching his arm behind his back.

"You're making a fucking mistake, you asshole! He attacked her again! Look at her legs, she's bleeding, you fuck!" Deacon's voice is booming, but he's cooperating and letting them cuff him. Why are they cuffing him?

"Why are you arresting him? What's going on? He was protecting me," I yell frantically to be heard over all the commotion in the front room and the sirens blaring outside. The tears are coming faster and faster, my head is still pounding and I fear I might pass out, my heart is beating so erratically. I'm jostled from behind when two medics make their way into the house and toward Andrew, slumped against the wall at an unnatural angle with blood covering his entire face, soaking through his white Oxford shirt nearly to the waist. I have no idea if he's even breathing. I should care. But I absolutely don't right now. This must be a dream. No, a nightmare. None of this can really be happening. Focused on Deacon, hands behind his back

arguing heatedly with Detective Flores, I stomp over and start yanking on his hands, at the two pairs of handcuffs they've had to use on him. I'm on the verge of a panic attack.

"You let him out of these right now, you're going to hurt him! He was helping me," I yell hysterically at the room as a whole. Tears fall faster and faster, my breath coming out in hiccupping gasps. "You can't take him, I won't let you. You'll ruin his career. He didn't do anything! Andrew hurt me first." My words are almost incoherent, and even though I realize they are, I don't care. I need them to listen to me and let him go. A hand on my shoulder halts my actions. I turn to see Detective Adams holstering her weapon, trying to lead me away from Deacon. I won't go. She can't make me; none of them can. It's then that I hear Deacon calling my name calmly.

"Princess, baby, deep breaths, okay?"

I circle around to face him, noticing for the first time that he's covered in blood. I search his face for an open wound before I realize that it must be Andrew's. Sniffling, I bury my face in his chest and let his soothing tone calm me.

"I need you to calm down for me, Frankie. You have to keep a straight head and make some phone calls, okay?" he says, not a hint of panic in his voice, only tenderness and worry. For me. Lips rolled in, I shake my head no and start sobbing all over again.

"Get him the hell out of here," one of the men who had attacked Deacon spits in disgust as he holds an ice pack to his shoulder. Whipping my head in his direction, I feel all of my fear turn into anger.

"Who the hell are you?" I demand, setting my feet wide and planting myself in Flores' path, which is funny because both he and Deacon tower over me and outweigh me by a lot. If he wants to take him out of here, me standing in front of him won't matter.

"I'm one of the U.S. Marshals that he went all Neanderthal

on, and I want him the fuck out of here now." Turning his back on me, he goes back to the medic who's tending to Andrew and the other man from the car who looks like he's just gone a few rounds with . . . well, a few rounds with Deacon.

My attention is brought back to Deacon and Flores when he starts moving him past me, reading Deac his Mirandas as they head toward the door. I scramble to catch up to them, still disbelieving that this is all happening.

Deacon looks back at me over his shoulder as he's led to the squad car at the curb, cameras and news crews already setting up.

"Frankie, you do not fucking stay here, do you hear me? You follow us to the station or go right to the gym and stay with one of my brothers. I need you to be somewhere safe; I don't give a fuck who those guys say they are. Do you understand?"

I nod my head yes and wrap my arms around myself as the cool wind whips my hair around my head as I walk behind them. As Flores is about to put Deacon in the back of the car, I rush forward and wedge myself in between him and the car door and pull his head down, putting my lips to his, kissing him softly. He stiffens before he kisses me back just as softly.

"It's all okay, baby. I promise. Just stay away from him until I can get out. Make the calls, Frankie. Sonny first—he'll call my lawyer—and then Mav." Every word is spoken against my lips, like he can't bear to pull away, same as me.

I sigh into his mouth on a shaky breath. "I will." Kissing him one last time, I step out of the way and watch as they push his head in and close the door. The screech of tires for the second time that night has me jumping in fear. Whirling toward the sound, I see Reggie and Trent running down the street to where I stand.

From the backseat and through the window I can hear Deacon scream, "Where in the motherfuck were you two?" just before Flores pulls away from the curb. Deacon is looking back

at me through the rear window of the cop car. I somehow manage to stay upright until the taillights disappear around the corner, and that's when my world goes black. I feel myself falling and he's not there to catch me.

CHAPTER
Three

DEACON

I CAN'T THINK of anything other than how I can keep Frankie safe from where I'm sitting. The pain in my shoulders from having my arms pulled behind me? Who gives a fuck? The spasms from the Taser? Nope. All I care about is the Princess. Now that my adrenaline is waning, my mind and blood feel sluggish. Probably after-effects from being tased as well. Shaking my head, I have to concentrate and think. What the fuck was Drew doing there now? Where the fuck had Reggie and Trent been? I swear to fuck I'm firing both of their asses if they don't have a good goddamn reason for leaving her alone, and even then I don't think I give a fuck. Drew. Reggie better make sure that she's not left anywhere near him. I don't know what kind of condition he's in, nor do I care. All I care about is Frankie being as far away from him as possible.

My head feels like it weighs a ton on my neck, and I let my head rest against the cold glass and catch Flores watching me in the review mirror. "Who were those guys that tased me? I heard one say something about being a marshal. That true?" I hope like fuck it isn't. The EWF lawyers are good, but I'm not sure they would be able to get me off for attacking U.S. Marshals.

The usually stoic detective sighs deeply. "They're both with the U.S. Marshals Service. Apparently they've had Mr. McAvoy under protection since the morning that Miss De Rosa was attacked." Glancing from the road back to meet my eyes in the mirror again, he looks as grim as I feel.

"You mean the morning after?" Looking to him for confirmation, he just stares back at me and I'm certain that he hadn't misspoken. "So, if they had Andrew, he couldn't have attacked her." It's not a question, and I'm not even sure I said it loud enough for him to hear. I fucked up. I fucked up big. I know it and so does Flores. Closing my eyes, I take a deep breath. "Well, good thing I didn't kill him then, huh?" Flores just grunts in response.

ONCE AT THE station, I'm placed in an interrogation room, the cuffs thankfully removed, locked in and left to wait. They offered me my phone call, but I turned it down. No use wasting that shit. Frankie and Reggie will handle all that, and Sonny and Mav will handle the rest. Resting my head in my hands, I tangle my fingers in the long strands and tug. I'm not worried about what will happen to me. I wasn't lying when I told Flashdance that I would go to prison for Frankie if it meant keeping her safe, but she's not safe from anything right now. If Andrew presses charges, I'm looking at the possibility of serious prison time. If he's not the one that attacked her that day, who the fuck did and why? Where are these motherfuckers with my answers? I stand abruptly, frustrated, the chair crashing to the floor behind me. Stalking to what I assume is one-way glass, I stare back at my own reflection and will myself to keep calm. My brothers won't let anything happen to Frankie if I get locked up. She'll be okay and that's all I really care about. I should care more about Drew's condition and what it means for me, but I don't. Whether he put hands on her or not, it was his fault she ended up in the hospital. He was her fucking fiancé and he should've protected her. So regardless of who actually hurt her, it was on him.

I look up at the sound of the door opening. The two men from Indie's who claimed they were marshals come in looking none too happy with me, Adams and Flores right behind them, none of their faces giving anything away. Fine. Whatever. I only want to know one thing anyway and the rest can wait until my lawyers get here.

"Sit down, Mr. Love. We have some questions for you," one of the suits says, indicating the toppled chair.

"Nah. I'm good. Where's Frankie?" I demand. I look to Adams and Flores because I'm certain that I won't be getting anywhere with the assholes.

"She's fine, went to the hospital with her bodyguard to be checked out, Mr. Love," Adams says to me. She knows me well enough from our few interactions that I won't cooperate with anyone before knowing Frankie is okay. I'm glad that she went to the hospital—she'll be safe there and she needs to get her head checked. It looked like she hit the ground pretty hard.

"Don't you want to know how Mr. McAvoy is?" suit number two asks, and he's visibly pissed.

Meeting his angry glare, I don't answer him, instead turning back to Adams. "Are my lawyers on their way?" Her mouth opens to answer me, but she's cut off by number one.

"Lawyers? Get into this kind of trouble often that you have a team of lawyers just waiting for you to call?" he sneers. Not giving in to his taunts, I ignore him and lean against the wall in silence. Now that I've been assured that Frankie is safe and being cared for at the hospital, I have all the time in the world to wait on the cavalry. I just hope to fuck they're ready to do battle.

CHAPTER
Four

FIVE HOURS LATER, I'm finally released, the marshals not pressing charges . . . yet. And Andrew's condition still not known. They'll pull me back in once they find out how he fared and if his punk ass wants to charge me. I honestly can't even think about all of that right now. I just want to get to Frankie and find out if she's okay; I'll deal with the consequences of my actions later. Crawling in the back of Bo's blacked out Rover with my dad, I duck and dodge the cameras flashing, reporters yelling shit from every corner of the parking lot. My lawyers and the EWF are adamant that I speak to no one, not that I have to be convinced of that shit.

Pop looks over at me his face pinched in worry. "Deacon, this is serious, son. What were you thinking?" He sounds so disappointed, and that's a new one on me.

"I wasn't thinking, Pop. I saw him knock her to the ground and then drag her into the house, and I just reacted." Shaking my head, I beg for him to understand. "He was standing over her and her eyes were closed and I just snapped. I thought back to her lying there in that hospital bed, machines keeping her alive, and I fucking snapped." I scrub my hands down my face and back through my hair. "Is she okay? They released her without any problems?"

He nods. "She has a slight concussion. Reggie has her at

your place. He said he'd wake her up every little while until you got there." On a deep sigh he squeezes my leg. "Guy is meeting with Derek and the rest of the board at EWF headquarters this afternoon. They'll probably postpone the fight until all of this is cleared up. You need to be prepared though, Deacon." He pauses before going on grimly, "They might not let you fight for the title after this. We're going to have to do whatever they say, kiss whomever's ass they tell us to."

I just nod, staring out at the city flashing by in a blur. "Does she know that he didn't attack her that day, that he was in protective custody?" My voice is flat. If she knows, what will that mean for us? Will she go back to him? Will she despise me for hurting him? And what the fuck happens if I killed him? I'm pretty sure I didn't, but I'm not a hundred percent certain. A somewhat innocent man, dead at my hands? Could she get past that? Could I?

"No. According to Adams, they can't even put the details of the story on the news. No names or anything because of the case. After though . . ." he trails off.

"I don't want anyone telling her that it wasn't Drew. At least until after all of this shit blows over. I don't care how we do it, but I don't want her knowing. Especially if he dies."

Huffing out a breath, Pop looks at me like I'm crazy—and I probably am. "Deacon, you can't keep that from her. I won't lie to her, son," he states adamantly.

"I'm not asking you to lie to her, I'm just asking you to not offer up any unsolicited fucking information, Pop." Swinging my gaze back to him, "Can you please just do that for me? You and I are the only ones who know aside from the cops and our lawyers. I just need to get us through this and then I'll tell her. I promise."

I'VE BEEN AT the station all night, so as soon as we get back to my house, I take the stairs two at a time, eager to check on my girl and then jump in the shower. Once on the landing, I turn toward her room and open the door, peeking in only to find it empty. Fuck, I hope that she didn't talk Reggie into taking her somewhere else. Dead cell phone in hand, I head for my room to plug it in before I go looking for answers. As I step foot into the room, my eyes are instantly drawn to the bed and the tiny form curled up on the left side, *her* side of the bed. Walking silently over the hardwood floors to where she lies, I brush the hair from her face, reach for her hand, and place a kiss to my spot on the inside of her wrist, careful not to wake her.

"I just woke her about fifteen minutes ago; she's fine, Deacon. A little shook up and worried as hell about you, but okay," comes from the loveseat tucked in the corner. Glancing over, I see Reggie sitting there, keeping vigil, his brown skin paler than I've ever seen it.

I nod curtly. "Thanks, you can go, I've got her," I wave him off dismissively.

"Deacon, bro, I—"

I hold up my hand stopping him. I don't have the energy to get into it with him right now. The way I'm feeling, I really will fire his ass. "Not now, Reg. We'll talk later." My need to be near my girl supersedes everything else right now. He must realize it because I hear the door close behind him just as I'm crawling in beside her. Slowly, gently, I pull her into me and wrap around her, breathing her in. Every part of me needs every part of her right now. I pull the covers over us and kiss her temple before laying my head on the pillow next to hers.

"I'm sorry I wasn't there sooner, baby. I came as fast as I could. I'm so fucking sorry you got hurt again," I whisper to her sleeping form. "He won't hurt you ever again."

I'm awoken from a deep sleep by Frankie thrashing wildly, yelling incoherently, both of us covered in her sweat. I try to catch a flailing arm but end up catching an elbow in the eye as she whimpers, "Please stop. Don't hurt me." Then on a guttural moan she cries, "He's not here. Please he isn't here. I don't have what you want." My heart breaks listening to my girl begging for mercy. Breaks and makes me want to kill people. Gathering her in close to me, I talk to her in soothing tones, doing my best to make sure she hears me over her own plaintive wails and pleading.

"Frankie, it's me. Everything is okay; you're safe, baby. You're safe. Hear me, Princess. Feel me. Listen to my voice and come back to me. Nobody is here but me, baby." Rocking her back and forth gently, I can feel the tension draining out of her little by little. Her trembling body presses into me as I kiss her head, her cheek. Wrapping her in love and soothing her the only way I can. How have I not known she has nightmares like this? How in the fuck have I not realized she has been suffering in silence? Am I that blind that I haven't seen how deeply affected she is? To think Frankie has been suffering, been hurting from something nobody but she could see . . . I feel like shit. My heart swells at the thought that she felt safe with me before, safe enough to lay these demons to rest for the time being. And it shatters me to hear I'm no longer that anchor, that balm. I make a vow to myself to be that safe place for her again. I just never realized she was struggling this deeply with what happened to her that night.

Finally, she quiets in my arms and falls back to sleep cuddled into my chest, her head tucked under my chin as I trail my hand over her hair and down her back over and over, calming us both. There's no way I'm going back to sleep now. Staring at the ceiling, I think about how right she feels in my arms, how I've missed this, missed her. I think about all that still needs to be done before I can claim my girl fully. We have to get past all of this shit with Drew, figure out how much to tell her, how much to keep from her so she doesn't worry any more than she already will. We have one more fight, *the* fight, and I won't do it without her by my side. I said I would wait, do it right, but its four months away. Four months might as well be four fucking years. There is no way I'm waiting anymore.

She's about to be wooed whether she wants to be or not. I'm coming for my girl, guns blazing. It's time to go to war.

I'M ON THE phone with Guy, reassuring him Frankie is fine, that I won't let anything happen to her, and listen as he goes on about how much shit I'm in with the EWF. I had been riding a fine line with them as it was, and now add to that these fucking charges hanging over my head and they're pissed as hell. After telling him that I'm willing to do whatever they ask, jump through as many hoops as they want, I disconnect the call and head up to wake the Princess. Slowly making my way to the bed, I notice the dark circles under her eyes. She slept so fitfully last night I didn't even bother waking her when I finally got out of bed a few hours ago.

She's been asleep off and on for almost eighteen hours now. I need for her to wake and eat something and then it's time to break the news to her. Her hair is a mess but looks so gorgeous spread across my pillow, so right. Gently I sit next to her and brush the hair off her face, letting my fingers tangle in the golden mass. My lips find their way to her mouth and I kiss her softly. She makes a quiet mewling sound and snuggles into me. Jesus fuck, what I wouldn't give to be able to wake her up like I used to. My mouth on her clit, teeth nipping, tongue and fingers taking turns stroking the inside of her beautiful fucking pussy as she rides my face, my hand, even in her sleep. She would wake up on a gasp, clutching at my head, pulling my hair, begging me not to stop. The taste of her exploding on my tongue almost enough to make me come. Without even realizing, I've slipped my hand into the front of my sweats taking hold of my now rock hard cock at the thought, the memories of how good things were with us. As I stroke up and over the crown, I pull the covers back and look at my gorgeous girl, asleep in nothing but one of my t-shirts, her tan legs bare, the shirt riding up exposing her barely-there red thong. Groaning, I give my dick one final squeeze before removing my hand. Quietly, so I don't scare her, I lean in and kiss the dark circles under each eye and then bring my lips to her ear,

"Frankie, baby, wake up. It's almost dinner time, you need to eat."

Her face scrunches up as she reaches for the covers. Not finding them, she slowly opens her eyes, "Deac, you're okay?" she asks softly, scooting over to me groggily and placing her head in my lap. I do my best to make my cock not seem so hard, but it's no use. Her lashes flutter and she gazes down at her semi-naked form and then I see her gaze go to the bulge dangerously close to poking her in the cheek and then up at me. All I can do is smile shamelessly at her.

"It can't be helped so don't even bother giving me shit for it. I know a way to fix it if it's bothering you, though." Frankie looks up at me and I can see the need in her eyes. So many days, nights, and mornings, I saw that same look. Growling low in my throat, I tell her now what I did then, "You keep looking at me like that, Princess, and you're gonna get fucked."

I mean it just as much now as I did then. I watch as she exhales deeply, a shiver taking over her body as soon as the breath makes it past her lips. My eyes leave her face long enough to notice that her nipples are hard beneath the soft fabric of my shirt, that she has her thighs pressed together tightly like she's either trying to create friction or stop them from opening to me in invitation.

Turning her face deeper into my lap, her lips nearly

touching my cock through the cotton of my pants, she whispers, "Love me, Deac. Love me until I can't think about anything else, anyone else. Make me feel good. Make me forget, please. I just need . . . you." Every word is whispered across my cock, her warm breath turning me to steel. I don't give her any time to change her mind, because although I'm aware now is not the time for this, I can't say no. I won't say no. I need to be inside her more than I need my next fucking breath.

My hand trembles a bit as I let the backs of my fingers trail over her cheek, down her neck, until I'm encircling her throat possessively. I can feel her gaze on me as I hold her in place with one hand while I let the other trail down her stomach, smiling when her muscles shudder as I pass over them. I slip in between her thighs and nudge them apart, groaning in approval as she lets them fall to the sides, leaving her wide open for me.

"You remember whose this is?" I ask in a gravelly voice as I slip my hand into her panties and cup her pussy, letting the heat and wetness slick over my fingers before I brush them lightly over her lips and her clit where I press down and wait for her to answer. Never taking my eyes off of my big hand inside those tiny fucking panties, I press harder when she doesn't answer right away. "Do you need me to remind you, Frankie? Do you need me to show you who this belongs to?"

She shakes her head no but that's not what she says, the word "yes" like a plea as it leaves her mouth, her back arching, putting my hand tighter against her, my fingers flexing against her throat and into her pussy. I loosen my hold on her neck when she moves her head trying to burrow deeper into my lap. My whole body jolts when she opens her mouth on my cock, breathing over the wet spot she created in the fabric. Surging forward, I encourage her to do it again, and she does. It's so fucking hot I'm afraid I'll come. Fuck me if I care right now though. Our eyes crash together and I'm certain that mine are as glazed over in lust as hers are. There's no way they aren't.

Dipping my fingers farther, I let one slide deep into her, once, twice, twisting on the third, drawing a moan from her that vibrates against my cock. Wrist and palm rubbing against her clit as I thrust and twist over and over, her panting like a fucking inferno against the dampened head of my dick through the layers separating us. She's so close, I can feel it, smell it. I bring her closer before pulling my hand from where it's nestled, causing her to throw her head back in frustration, her legs scissoring, searching for release. I throw my leg over hers to stop her movement and bring my fingers to her lips, painting them with her wetness before slipping them inside her mouth. "Suck, Frankie. Taste what's mine. Taste how sweet you are, for me. Only for me," I rasp. Watching as her lips close around them, her tongue gliding over and around as I push them further into her hot mouth and pull out. My control at its breaking point, I take my fingers from her mouth, untangling us enough to lay her out under me. I rise up on my knees in between her spread legs and take a second to look at her. Her skin is flushed with want, just how I like it, her blue eyes flames. She lights me up. Every bit of her sets me afire just by being. I love this woman fiercely. I love her like no one ever can, and right now I'm going to show her. I'm going to fuck her until she believes in my love. Fuck her into remembering. Fuck her like I hate her. Fuck her to claim her because she's mine. She. Is. Mine. I can't be without her again.

Not able to wait any longer, I grab the hem of her shirt and pull it over her head, tossing it to the side, leaving her in nothing but that scrap of lace covering what I need inside of. There are twin bows on each of her hips; that's all that's standing between me and her sweet, sweet cunt and I want them gone. Tugging first one and then the other, I smile at her pleading moan as she plants her feet and lifts so I can get rid of the barrier completely. She sighs, her eyes closed tight, bottom lip clamped in between her teeth as she waits me out. As much as I would like to draw this out, there's no way I can. Straightening, I push my

pants and boxer briefs down and get them just past my ass when Frankie uses her feet to shove them down further, the two of us working together until they hit the floor. She's reaching for me, pulling at me desperately, and that's all it takes to push me right over the fucking edge. Hooking her legs behind her knees, draping them over my forearms as I pull her forward until her ass settles against my thighs, the head of my cock glides through her glistening pussy lips and then back down. The sight mesmerizes me. She's so fucking wet for me, it coats my cock from base to tip as I repeat the path it just took. I glance up and see that she's watching, just as enthralled as I am. "You like that, Princess, hmmm? You like seeing your come all over my dick? I fucking love it. I love knowing that I make you so wet that it covers me. I can smell it on me and I haven't even fucked you yet."

Opening her legs wider to give her a better view, I push forward and slide over her pussy again, lifting her and pulling her forward to create more friction. Her legs tremble. "Please, please, please," she begs.

"Whose pussy is this?" I hiss in between clenched teeth. Fighting the need to slam into her.

"Yours. It's your pussy, only yours. Yours, yours, yours," she chants, closer and closer to losing her fucking mind with wanting to come. That's all it takes. I throw one of her legs over my shoulder and grab the base of my cock and press against her slit, letting her swallow me up. The muscles of her pussy grabbing at me, clenching my length, encouraging me, welcoming me. She's so much tighter than I remember. Never did I think that was possible.

"This pussy was made for me. Mmmmmm, so fucking tight around my cock, Frankie. So fucking tight," I murmur as I surge forward, bottoming out before pulling all the way out and doing it again. I should be gentle—she has a damn concussion for fuck's sake—but I can't. I just fucking can't. My blood sizzles with my need to fuck her stupid.

"Deacon, please. Oh fuck, please. Fuck me. Show me I'm yours. I'm so close. So close," she cries out in pleasure as I palm one of her tits roughly. Squeezing it, I use it for leverage to hammer into her. Hard, deep thrusts. Sinking into her over and over as my name falls from her lips in gasps. I feel her orgasm rolling through her and slow my movements, making her look at me with wide eyes. She whimpers and rolls her hips trying to make me finish her off.

"You want to come, baby?"

She nods, writhing beneath me as I slowly slide in and out, *just the tip*, torturing us both. I let her legs fall and pull out of her completely. "Roll over, Princess." She looks at me a little dazed, so I repeat myself, "Roll over. I want that ass in the air." As she untangles herself from me to do as I ask, I groan when she flashes that pink at me dripping with her arousal. Jesus fuck, this woman.

I settle behind Frankie and waste no time entering her, pulling back on her hips making us both groan as her ass slaps against my stomach. Nudging her legs wider, I grab a fistful of her hair and pull her upright, my other hand wrapping around her throat as I fuck into her. Her back is arched, which lets me hit her at the perfect angle. Using her hair and my hold on her throat, I pound into her mercilessly. I feel my balls tightening, the pulsing warning me that I'm close. I release her throat, dropping my hand to her clit. She bucks against me when I flick over it and then alternate rubbing just how she likes it, the way that gets her off. I give it a soft slap. "You're gonna come all over my cock, Frankie. Then I'm going to come so fucking hard, so fucking deep in this perfect," *Slam* "Tight," *Slam* "Wet," *Slam, slam* "Pussy." *Slam* "Your cunt is fucking heaven and I love it. I love that I get to make it dirty because it's mine." Biting down on her shoulder, I slam into her one last time, pushing down forcefully with my palm on her clit, and she shatters around me. Her orgasm so fucking intense it takes me right along with her, my vision wavering. I release her hair and she flops forward, her ass and back a vision in front of me that I can't ignore. My hands curve over and up her rounded ass as I rock slowly, still semi-hard. Leaning forward, I place kisses across her back, over the lacy ink.

"You okay, baby? Did I hurt you? Your head?" I ask, massaging her scalp gently, still inside of her.

She shakes her head. "You didn't hurt me. You fucked me sleepy though," she says, laughing softly. Pulling out of the warmth of her body, I place a kiss on each of her ass cheeks before padding to the bathroom to grab a towel to clean her up. As I make my way back to the bed, I realize that she's already asleep. Chuckling to myself, I gently wipe away my mess, tossing the towel in the hamper before I climb into bed next to her and pull the covers over us both. Frankie sighs deeply and turns toward me, nuzzling her face into my neck. I pull her tighter. The food can wait. The bullshit can wait. This right here, my girl in my arms, is all that fucking matters right now. This can't wait.

CHAPTER
Five

I WAKE UP disoriented and hungry as hell. My eyes slowly adjust to the complete darkness in the room. Careful not to wake Frankie up, I reach for my phone and see that it's nearly midnight. Holy fuck, I can't believe everyone left us alone for this long. There's a quiet knock on the door—I spoke too soon. Quickly pulling the comforter up to be sure Frankie is completely covered, I slip out of bed and pull on my discarded sweatpants and pad over to the door, opening it to see who the fuck is here this late.

"Hey, brother, I just got back from dropping Pop off. Just checking to see if you need anything and to see if the Princess is doing okay." Mav looks tired and worried. He's been working his ass off trying to make sure this doesn't all turn into a bigger clusterfuck than it already is.

"Why was Pop still here?" I ask as I lead him down the stairs to the kitchen.

"Everyone has been here all day. Guy and Pop got here after the meeting over at EWF. Neither one of them wants to let her, fuck, even you, out of their sight."

"How did that go?" I ask hesitantly. He sighs loudly,

"Could've gone worse, little brother. Could've gone better too, but it is what it is. All we can do is wait and see what charges you face, if any, and what happens with Drew." Nodding my head in understanding, I turn and start rummaging in the fridge, pulling stuff out to make omelets.

"You eating, bro?" I call from inside the freezer, taking stock.

"You got any of that jarred queso shit you love so much?"

My head pops around the open door, "Is that a trick question? Of course I do. It's in the pantry. Grab the bread out of there too," I call after him as he saunters to the huge butler's pantry.

"Just let me go wake Frankie up. Start making some potatoes. Don't forget the oil this time, dumb ass," I yell to him from the foot of the stairs. My feet don't even hit the third step when Frankie comes into view at the top, standing on the landing in nothing but my t-shirt. The smile that takes over my face at seeing her is easy. Those smiles have been few and far between lately.

"Hey, Princess. I was just coming to get you. You hungry?"

Her eyes dart away from me and she nods. The fuck? She better not start this shit. I'm well aware that having sex didn't just fix all of our problems, but I thought it would at least put us in a better place. Maybe she needs fucked again to help her along to my way of thinking. At that thought, I let my gaze roam over her, sexy red painted toes, bare legs tanned and toned and slightly fucking scraped up, that dip in her waist that shows off the curve in her hips, and that damn bubble ass. I need in that ass. My eyes make it all the way up to the words inside a bearded silhouette—"She Liked the B so She Stayed for the D"—covering her tits, and finally to her face flushed from my eye fucking. I smirk knowingly. I refuse to make this easy on her. I've been too easy for too long now. She's about to get the full Deacon effect from here on out. "Can you walk?"

She looks at me confused. "Yes, why wouldn't I be able to walk?" Her brows are drawn low in confusion.

I let the smirk through again and shrug. "We fucked like

beasts just a little bit ago, baby. You fell asleep about fifteen seconds later, so I'm pretty sure I wore your ass out," I say smugly. Frankie blinks slowly. Ignoring me, she starts down the stairs—on shaky legs. When she reaches the bottom, I offer her my hand, which she takes, much to my surprise. I can't resist and pull her into my chest, placing a kiss to my spot before dropping her hand and wrapping my arms around her. All the playfulness leaves my body when I hear her sniff back tears, tears that are making a track down my chest.

"Ahhhh, baby. You know I can't handle you crying. What's wrong?" I ask, placing a kiss to the top of her head, swaying back and forth, hoping to soothe her. Frankie pushes away from me and wipes the tears left on her face.

"Nothing, I just—it was nice to forget everything while we were up there." She points behind her to the staircase and my room. "I didn't have to think about anything but the way you make me feel, and it's been so long since that's all I had to do that I just feel a little overwhelmed right now." Shrugging, she puffs out a little laugh, "Then you go ahead and hit me with all of that 'Deacon' and it's like a fucking tsunami." As she says that, her stomach lets out a loud growl.

"When's the last time you ate, Princess?"

"What day is it?" she asks me. I'm pretty sure she's serious.

"Come on, Sleeping Beauty. Let's feed you. We have a shit ton to talk about."

"Can we talk now, about last night?" Frankie asks quietly, tugging on my hand. "They wouldn't tell me anything at the hospital and Detective Adams just said that you were fine, just answering some questions. I don't even know where the hell they took Andrew." She says, hiccupping back tears.

"Hey, shhhh. Look at me." I murmur, pulling her back into my arms. When her eyes are focused on me I do my best to ease her worries, "I'm here right? They didn't throw me in jail. And most importantly you're fine." Smiling reassuringly, "The rest can wait, yeah?" When she nods I take her hand, pulling her behind me, "Come on, we'll eat and talk."

We walk to the kitchen, and she stops on the way to put the sound system on. I'm surprised she hadn't done it sooner; it's usually the first thing she does the minute she walks in the house. Maverick smiles at her as she strolls in, tugging the shirt down her legs. I forgot he was even here.

"Hey, Princess. You feeling better? You look better," he says, glaring at me. She looks like she's been fucked. Her hair is all sexed up and she has beard burn on her neck. I just grin and help her onto the stool at the island.

I place a kiss on her wrist, then lean in and whisper against her ear, "As soon as my brother leaves, we'll talk about us. And how as soon as I get you back upstairs, I'm going to take you again so all you have room for in that beautiful head of yours is me. Same as your pretty, little pussy." She gasps and I laugh. It thrills the fuck out of me that I can still shock her. My hand brushes lightly over her head and her soft hair. I freeze when I feel a large bump and she winces away from my touch. "Shit, I'm sorry, baby. Did I hurt you?" I lift my chin toward the ceiling indicating that I mean when I had fistfuls of her hair in bed.

"I didn't notice at the time," Frankie says softly.

I search her face, looking for signs that she's lying to me. Satisfied that she's not, I ask, "Do you have any pain pills or anything from the hospital?"

"No, I didn't want them. I'll take some Tylenol. I need to eat something first though."

Mav walks over to where she sits, sliding onto the stool next to her with the bottle of medicine and a glass of orange juice, "Cook for us, chef Deacon, we're hungry." Lazy ass, he knows how to make a damn omelet.

"Garbage omelet, okay, Princess? Or do you want something else?" I ask, pulling pans and turning to the stove to fire up the bacon. Glancing over my shoulder for her answer, she nods and goes back to Mav, the two of them playing with the iPad that controls my whole damn house now. TVs, stereo system, alarm, thermostat, everything. I love it . . . when I can find the fucking thing. One of them raises the volume on the song being played, Alabama Shakes, that's gotta be my girl, she loves them. The muscle in my jaw starts ticking as I think about her being hurt by that fucker. "What did they say at the hospital, Frankie?"

"A mild concussion. They just did some tests, told me what to watch out for and sent me home. They wanted me to stay for observation, but I needed to be out of there. I needed to be here." She says it so softly that I almost don't hear her over the popping bacon in the pan, but I *hear* her.

"You're okay though, right? Should you have stayed?" I ask sternly.

"No, I'm fine. Tired and a little sore, but other than that, I'll be okay," Frankie assures us. Flipping the omelets, I set each of the burners to low as I grab plates and silverware and pop bread in the toaster. I take a minute to gather my thoughts. I have a million fucking questions for her, but I have no clue where to start and I need to be easy with her and not get all worked up. Easier said than done.

Bringing everything over to where they sit, heads bent together over the tablet, I take it from them and replace it with their plates when they look up at me all indignant. "You two wanna eat or what?" I ask, my brow raised.

"Thank you, Deac."

"Yeah, thanks, fucker face."

The Princess snorts out a laugh, "Good one, Mav!" and high fives him.

"If you two are finished being cute . . ." I say, trying to hide my amusement. I miss this. The Princess and her Loves just hanging out, busting each other's balls.

They both grin and dig into their food. I eat standing across

from them so that I can actually see her face while we talk about everything that's been going on.

"How long have you been getting shit from him, Frankie?" I'm careful to not use *his* name.

I watch as she stiffens, her fork frozen in front of her open mouth.

"Since right after that night. That's when the phone calls started, then the letters and pictures," she says in a resigned voice before taking her bite, eyes cast down.

Every cell in my body, every muscle, every bit of every-fucking-thing inside me goes molten with anger, rage, an unnamable feeling that takes over and makes me see red. The air around us crackles with my fury.

Out of the corner of my eye, I see Mav staring at her, mouth agape before saying, "Oh shit," as he soundlessly slips off of his stool and takes his plate with him into the other room. Frankie sits, squirming on her seat, still avoiding eye contact.

My hands tremble with the need to crush her to me. I'm not sure whether I want to shake the shit out of her or bend her over my knee and spank her. I have to have misheard her. As calmly as I possibly can, I push my plate aside. "I'm sorry. I didn't hear you. For a minute there I thought you said that you've been harassed with letters, pictures, and phone calls for months. Months where you were in my bed, in my arms. Months where you kept your fears from me while we told each other that we loved one another. Months where I could've made sure you were safe, where you didn't have to be afraid. Fucking months where you were my girl and you denied me the chance to take care of you." My voice is raised louder than I intend, my fists clenched so tight they're starting to cramp in protest. The simple task of breathing a huge fucking chore right now as I struggle to regulate it and my out of control heart rate. "Now, please. *Please*, tell me that I misunderstood what you said because I know in my fucking heart you wouldn't keep something that fucking big from me. Not my girl, not my best friend, the woman I love, would die for, kill for." Looking at her imploringly, I see the truth. The tears in her eyes, running down her face, all the answer I need. Before I have a chance to rein it in, my arm sweeps everything off the island in a deafening crash of broken glass and clattering cutlery. The Princess jumps, stunned, and sits back in her seat, eyes screwed tightly shut. Head hanging down, I grip the edge of the granite countertop and concentrate on breathing in and out.

Maverick comes skidding to a stop in the doorway but halts his advance when without raising my head, I point for him to leave. Once he's turned and left, I stand straight and make my way around to where Frankie is, sobbing into her hands. It kills me to see her like this. That I'm a part of this pain. Wordlessly, I scoop her up in my arms and cradle her to my chest. The muscle in my jaw jumps in time with my racing heart as I walk her up the stairs and into my room. Instead of going straight to the bed, where I would like to take this for the next few hours just so I can love on her, I head to the sectional in my office, the one that faces the fireplace so that I can see our story spread out in front of me on my mantel, hanging on my wall. It calms me and reminds me *who* I'm dealing with, *who* I have in my arms. She would never hurt me on purpose. She's always been in my corner, loved me even when it should have been impossible to do. There was a reason she kept this from me, from all of us, and I'm about to find out what.

Settling us into the supple leather, I position her on my lap with her legs draped over me to the side and her head cradled in the crook of my arm so that I can look at her while we discuss this. Though right now her face is still buried between my neck and shoulder. I let my head fall to the back of the couch and release a deep breath. My eyes close and I focus on the music filtering around the room, letting it wash over me as I hold my girl and let her cry while I run my hands up and down her back, doing my best to soothe her. The words of the song penetrate the numb feeling taking over my mind.

"Who sings this?" I ask softly, trailing my fingers over her bare thigh.

Her normally raspy voice is now hoarse from crying. "Sam Smith and John Legend," she sniffles. Nodding I go back to listening and stroking over her, waiting.

I've stalled long enough. "Why didn't you tell me, Frankie? Why didn't you tell anyone?" She sighs loudly, accepting that she can't get out of this.

"At first I didn't tell you because things were so strained between us and you had the guys with me all the time anyway, so I didn't think I should bother you with it." She plucks at the strings on the throw pillow as she talks to me. I open my mouth to argue, but she goes on, "Then we were together and even though they were still coming, I felt safe. I knew no harm would come to me when I was with you. Plus you were training for your big comeback." Glancing up at me, I watch as she gathers her confidence and melts back into my arms a bit more. "Then we weren't together anymore and I was terrified. All the time I was scared, but I couldn't tell you because you would've fixed it and doing that would interfere with your matches."

"The fights, Frankie? That's why you didn't fucking tell me? None of that matters more than you!" I say completely exasperated.

Her head bobs in agreement. "I know that, Deac. I know that you would have done anything to make it all go away." She brushes a tear gliding down her cheek before going on, "I had no doubt you would protect me, but I couldn't do that to you. I had already taken so much from you. You were busting ass try-ing to make your way back into the standings, training harder than I'd ever seen you train, and if I said a single word about any of it, you would've dropped everything you have been working for and rescued me." I watch as her eyes dart away. "So instead

I made sure I was never alone, and I kept everything he sent for the detectives."

My teeth ached from grinding them together while she spoke. "Why didn't you tell one of my brothers or Reggie? Fuck, your dad even, Princess," I bite out. I can't understand why the fuck she would shoulder this. That she has been going through this alone and that I've been clueless to it eats at me.

"Every one of them would have told you," she says quietly as I push the hair off of her forehead and tuck it behind her ear. "I wanted to tell you so bad, Deac. Every day I wanted to just run to you, admit everything, and beg you to make it go away. I needed you, more than I ever have before, and I couldn't go to you." Her voice is full of anguish; it's like a punch to the face.

"No, it's not that you couldn't; it's that you wouldn't. No matter what, Princess, I told you that nothing would ever come between us. We're a part of each other, remember? That's never gonna change." She gives me a watery smile, reaching out to finger my chain and the charm lying against my chest.

"I love when you wear this. You have the tattoo, but it always makes my heart smile when I see your half of the coin around your neck." Her thumb brushes over the letters engraved into the metal while I watch her.

"Frankie, don't keep shit from me. Not to protect me, not because you think it's what's best. You're what's best for me. You being safe and happy and whole. That's what I need, you feel me?" With a finger under her chin, I force her to look at me. "You feel me?" I repeat. I need her to understand that even now, when I'm not sure where we stand, that she comes first. Her eyes dart over my face before settling on my unblinking gaze.

"I feel you, Deac," Frankie answers softly, putting her lips over the Mizpah charm and then curling into me quietly. "Can we talk more later? I just want to sleep now. I'm so tired again."

I stand with her still in my arms, her head against my chest and go into the bedroom. Laying her in the bed and crawling behind her, tucking her against me. "Sleep, baby. The rest can wait for now." Raising her wrist, I place a kiss first on the other half of the charm dangling from her bracelet and then to my spot.

Tomorrow. Tomorrow I'll break the news to her.

"PRINCESS. JONES." I greet them both with what I think is my most disarming smile. I'm going to need all the help I can get when I drop this bomb on them.

"Morning, Deac," Frankie says, returning my smile, happy to see me.

"Why the fuck are you smiling like that? What do you want?" Indie looks at me through narrowed, suspicious eyes and then turns to Frankie. "What does he want? Look at him, he's totally trying to use his swoony shit on us." Crossing her arms, she covers the "I'm a Vagitarian" scrawled across her chest and cocks her eyebrow. "You can save all that nonsense; it won't work here. Your bad boy hotness and bedroom eyes have no effect on me." She indicates Frankie with a tilt of her chin. "It may work on this one but not me. Whatever you want, stop being a cuntasaurus and just say it."

The fuck? What did she just call me? Taken aback, I forget for a second what I came in here to tell them as I listen to Frankie laugh at Indie's antics. Then I remember that I have news. Big news. News that affects us all and that I'm kinda dreading telling them. There's gonna be dramatics, I'm sure. I have nothing prepped, no speech practiced to ease them into what I'm about to say, so I just cut to the chase. "Indie, your place isn't safe enough for you two right now. You're both moving in here until all of this shit blows over. We'll all go pack up your shit as soon as my brothers wake up." There, it's done. I give them a nod and reach into the cabinet for my coffee cup, filling it up as I count down in my head for the detonation I'm certain is coming.

"You must be out of your motherfucking mind if you think I'm moving in here with you two. Especially if you're using that smile on her!" she accuses. "Frankie won't last five minutes against it and I'm not gonna be locked away while you two are going at it like rabbits all over the damn place, and I know that's what you'll do," she huffs out. "The way you're looking at her, even now, with me in the room, tells me you want to bend her over something and would probably let me watch just so you could get at her." Indie turns to Frankie and says reassuringly, "Not that I would watch, because as hot as you are, you're like a sister to me and it would just be a little too weird." I'm fighting back my laugh and doing my damnedest to smother my smile, but she's fucking crazy. Bat shit crazy. She turns her attention back to me, "So the answer is no. Fuck no. Hell to the fuck to the no even."

"Fine, you can stay at my place then," Maverick says from where he's leaning against the doorframe, startling us all. I look back at Indie, my brows raised. Well, this just got interesting.

"There ya go, Jones. Problem solved," I tell her mockingly and smile at the wide open mouth and stunned look on her face at Mav's solution. Swinging my gaze to Frankie, it's my turn to cross my arms over my chest and widen my stance in preparation for a fight. "I'm not taking no for an answer, Princess. You can't keep shit from me if you're in my house where I can make sure that you're safe. This is—"

"Okay, Deacon," Frankie says simply. No arguing, no pouting. Just, "okay," before she goes back to her coffee and the iPad in front of her. I look around the room in confusion. Mav and Indie are in a heated discussion, so they don't even realize that my girl clearly hit her head harder than they thought.

"I don't mean for the night, Princess. I mean you're moving in for the next few months or however long it takes for the case to go to trial." I say it slowly so there's not any room for misinterpretation. She looks up at me and nods.

"Okay. Do I have to go with or can I stay he—?" Shaking her head as she's speaking, she changes her mind midsentence, "No, I'll go. I don't want Reggie and Trent packing my panties and stuff." Slipping off the stool, she leaves me standing in the kitchen completely stunned by how easy that was. I was prepared to use force if necessary. I'm a little worried that I didn't have to resort to underhandedness to get her to agree.

Frankie turns at the door. "I'll be ready in just a minute, Deacon. Indie, are you coming with us?" she asks her pain in the ass friend.

"No, I guess I'm going to stay over at Mav's. We'll go and get my stuff later. I have a consult for an engagement party in a little while." Indie snaps her fingers and turns to me, "Speaking of parties, we gotta get started on Frankie's, Deacon!"

Just as I'm about to agree with her, Frankie says, "Not this year. I want to skip the big party. I would much rather do an intimate dinner, just you, our dads, and my Loves, if you guys don't mind. We can even celebrate yours and mine together." She doesn't wait for us to answer before leaving the kitchen.

I watch her leave and then turn to Indie, "You heard her. Do you want me to handle it or are you going to so that you can charge me a million dollars?" I deadpan.

Indie snickers, "I'll do it and I'll only bill you a half mil, no worries."

The women in my life are gonna be the fucking death of me, I swear.

CHAPTER
Six

IT DOESN'T TAKE us long to pack all Frankie's stuff up and get it loaded into our two vehicles. From the bedroom where she's doing a final check to make sure she didn't forget anything, I hear her phone start playing the song that I loathe because it means Flashdance is calling. Good, I can't wait for her to tell him that she's moving in with me. Hands in my pockets, I walk to her room and lean against the door, watching as she paces, hands flying as she speaks in rapid Spanish. She doesn't sound happy and when she says in English, "It's not your decision or any of your business where I stay, Cristiano. I'll be in the studio later for tonight's class," Frankie disconnects the call, no good-bye or anything.

"Problems with Flashdance, Princess?" I ask, trying to keep the smug smile off my face since I can't possibly keep it out of my voice. She spins and huffs out an exasperated breath,

"He's pissed, wants me to stay at his place." Her hands are planted on her hips and she's biting the inside of her lower lip in concentration. I'm not sure what the fuck she's concentrating so hard on—his place isn't a choice. Not now or ever.

I bark out a laugh. "Yeah, no. That's not gonna happen," I say as I scoop up the duffel bag she has by the door. "You ready to go?" I glance up and she's still just standing there, pissed. "What? You want to go stay with him? Tell me you're fucking

38

joking, Frankie." I toss her bag onto the bed and stalk to the middle of the room, stopping when I'm within a foot of where she is. "Tell me that's where you'd rather be and I'll take you there," I lie. Blatantly.

Shaking her head she snorts, "You're a terrible fucking liar, Deacon." She reaches up and yanks her hair out of the hair tie binding it and rubs at her temples. "I just want to feel like I'm in control of my own life for five minutes. With you barking orders at me and me knowing that I have no choice, no say in anything because nowhere is safe for me, I'm just a little overwhelmed, a little pissy."

I take a step forward closing the distance between us and take her gently in my arms. Spearing my fingers through her hair, I tilt her head so that her forehead is resting against my chest and begin to massage.

"Does your head hurt?" I ask softly as I rub circles into her scalp and down to her neck and shoulders where I knead and continue the path back up into her loose hair. She nods against me and sighs in relief as the tension gradually leaves her body. "I'm sorry, Princess. It's always been my way to take charge when it comes to you. Nobody can ever take care of you like I can and will. It's your choice though—I don't want you to feel like a prisoner. I only want to keep you safe." I place kisses on her lowered head and when she looks up at me, I drag my hands through her hair one last time before linking them at the small of her back.

"I know where I need to be. Where I want to be," she murmurs in her soft rasp.

Nodding, I bring my hand up and brush aside the hair that's constantly hiding her blues from me and tuck it behind her ear. As I drop my hand, she grabs it and holds it to her cheek for a second and then she places a kiss to the inside of my wrist just like I always do to her. Pussy that I am when it comes to Frankie, it makes my heart speed up before it settles into a steady tempo. Looking her in the eyes, I take the hand holding my much larger one and flip it so that I can put my lips on her, same as she did to me. She smiles that smile at me. The one that always does my shit in.

"Let's go then." Fingers laced with hers, I get the bag from the bed and lead us out of the house. On the porch, I turn to her and hold out my hand for the keys. When she hands them over, I lock up, and as I'm giving them back to her, my eye catches on the gold heart-shaped key chain. "That's nice, where did it come from?" Flipping the key chain open, she reveals that it's a locket with her initials on one side and a picture of her and her mom on the other.

"Don't get mad. I couldn't get rid of it, it's the only thing I have of my mom and me. Andrew gave it to me right before my birthday, an early gift." She takes one last look at the tiny cut-out of their smiling faces before snapping it closed and tossing the keys into her purse. Reggie clears his throat from the bottom of the stairs reminding me that he's there.

"You two have everything?" he asks in that unnaturally deep voice of his. I look to Frankie for an answer.

"Yes, let's move me into your house," she says as she descends the steps.

I love the sound of that more than I should. Eye on the prize, asshole. Stick and move. Stick and motherfucking move.

WE WEREN'T BACK at my house for more than ten minutes when Frankie says that she's going to lie down before her class tonight. She looks beat down. Beautiful, but exhausted. I stand at the base of the stairs and watch as she makes her way up, waiting to see which way she turns. Left toward my room or right to hers. When she goes left I can't help the grin that splits my face. I can't put the armbar to her just yet with the fight and everything else going on, but that one turn feels like a small victory. I wasn't bullshitting when I said I was done waiting. I accept that it has to be small wins here and there though and not a complete TKO. I can live with that. As long as I get moments like we had today and her sleeping in my bed even if I'm not in it.

Smile on my face, I head to the den where Sonny and Reggie are having what appears to be a serious discussion. It's about to get a whole lot more fucking serious. I have yet to talk to him about where the hell they were when Drew managed to get to Frankie and I'm done with the radio silence and letting everyone avoid it. Shit is gonna get hashed out. Now.

"Where's Trent?" I ask curtly. Sonny and Reggie both raise their heads, looking at me warily. I'm incapable of being rational when it comes to Frankie and they're both aware of it. They're a little nervous right now, rightly so.

"I sent him with Mav and Indie to get her things and take them back to his place. I didn't want them at her house alone, just in case," my brother tells me in a placating tone. He better talk sweet to me—shit's about to get ugly. I can feel it.

"So *now* everyone wants to do their job? Now that it's too late?" I stare pointedly at Reggie who shifts uncomfortably.

"It wasn't like that. Dial it down a notch, brother," Sonny warns.

"No? Then how was it?" My gaze bounces between Sonny and Reggie waiting for one of them to speak up. Clearly Sonny is already aware of what went down. The fact that Reg is still sitting here and not fired should reassure me about his actions that night, but all of a sudden I'm ready for a fight. I know that my older brother would have handed him his ass and his walking papers if he thought he was liable.

"Why don't you sit down and let Reggie explain?" he suggests.

Folding my arms over my chest, my feet planted wide, I shake my head no.

"Nah, I'm good. I'm ready for one of you to explain to me how Drew was able to put hands on Frankie though."

My brother nods to Reggie, indicating that he should go ahead with his story. Any second now my molars are going to be nothing but dust, I'm grinding them so hard. I can't help it though; I'm heated all over again just thinking about getting that phone call. The fear it was happening again, and that this time she wouldn't survive it.

Reggie leans forward, folding his nearly seven-foot frame in half as he places his forearms on his knees, his fingers clasped loosely and dangling. Head bent, he lets out a deep breath and then meets my glare.

"That night, I sent Trent on an errand while I stayed with Frankie. He was gone about fifteen minutes when I got a phone call saying that he got pulled over and that they were giving him a hard time about the piece in the glove box. He told them it was registered to me and that he didn't even know it was in there. They told him unless he could verify that it wasn't his weapon that they were taking his ass in." Shaking his head he goes on, "The Princess hasn't been alone for a single minute since you've been gone. I've slept there every night and the only reason I left her alone right then was because she told me that the detectives were on their way there. Any minute they would be pulling up. I asked Trent where he was, he wasn't even a mile away. I figured I'd show them my registration and get our asses back." He lets loose a bitter laugh. "When I got there it was like a fucking circus. Nothing they did or said made any sense to me and I challenged them at every turn. I kept thinking that something wasn't right, this should've been routine. I had all of my paperwork in order, nothing that should have caused any issues. After dealing with their bullshit and them asking about my military background, I knew they were stalling." He looks

up at me, "I handed them my gun, told them to keep it, told Trent to leave the truck and we jumped in Frankie's Rover and got the fuck out of there. I got played. I'm not sure why, but I did. They played me and by the time we pulled up to the house, it was too late." Sighing heavily he stands. "You love her, I get it, but I do too and I never want to see her get hurt again. If I could have stopped it, I would have killed him the moment I opened the door and asked questions later. I've slept at Indie's since that night Frankie had a panic attack and I felt like she was keeping more from us all. Been by her side when she needed a friend and took care of her when you couldn't. I got played, bro." Lifting his hands palm up, he shrugs. "Do what you need to, but I would lay down my life for her. Believe that. And right now, she needs all of us."

Unblinking, I process everything he's told me while he and Sonny stand staring at me, waiting to see how this is going to play out. "Did you know about the letters and the phone calls?" I ask them both.

Reggie shakes his head no as does Sonny. "I had a feeling that she was hiding something, but I wasn't sure what it was. To be honest, I thought it had to do with that punk, Flashdance. I figured she didn't want me reporting back to you, which I was, and that's what she was being secretive about. I brought it up briefly with Sonny and he said to keep a closer eye on her, and I did."

Sonny stands. "If we had known what was really going on, Deac, we would have told you. I want to win the title too, but not at Frankie's expense. We wouldn't have kept that from you, and that's probably why she never said anything to Reggie." I huff out a breath and nod in agreement. He's right about that. The Princess is stubborn as shit, always has been. She would suffer in silence instead of taking the risk of telling them and them in turn telling me. She knows I would have forfeited every single fight I had slated if I knew she needed me. I raise my chin in acknowledgment.

"It's more serious than she was letting on, D," Reggie admits reluctantly.

"How do you mean?" Confused, I wait for him to explain to me how it could be any worse.

"While you two were inside Indie's place packing, I grabbed the mail, and there was a letter in there." He shifts, reaching into his back pocket, handing me a Ziploc bag with what looks like a greeting card.

"What is this?" I demand as I take it from him. He has a tissue in the baggie that I use to slip it out of it's cheery looking purple envelope. There's no stamp, no return address, just Frankie's name and address. Carefully I unfold the slip of paper.

Francesca,

Hope that you have healed from the last time we saw one another. I will take great joy in hurting you again, this time while your fiancé watches. Maybe the taste of your blood will make him talk.

See you soon, darlin'

My insides quake with the fury I feel. The muscles in my jaw tick and bulge, my molars being ground to nothing as I try to get my composure. Handing the envelope to Sonny who was standing beside me quietly, waiting to read, I turn to Reggie.

"She's staying here, but we'll be at the gym a lot over the next few months. Frankie is not to be left alone for any reason. I don't care if someone is being hauled off to jail by their dick, she is not to be left alone at any time for any motherfucking reason." My voice is a little shaky with my rage. "Get this to Adams immediately. We'll have everything forwarded here. But I don't want shit like this getting into Frankie's hands." I glance over Sonny who nods, his face flushed with his own anger. Narrowing my eyes in warning, "I swear to fuck, Reggie, someone better be with her every second of every fucking day. You're my friend, my brother, and we've been through a lot together, but she's my

girl and she'll come first every fucking time," I state simply.

Reggie nods, "As it should be, bro. I promise, it will never happen again. I'll call in some of the other guys we've worked with in the past too. We'll have this place swarming with Jarheads," he jokes, trying to lighten up the tension in the room.

I stick my hand out and we shake, and then he pulls me in for that man hug slap thing and that's the end of it. Sonny pops in a DVD of Rude Awakening's last fight and we all sit there silently watching, pissed off and on edge over the letter. My brother must have recognized my need for some normalcy to decompress after that shit. I refuse to believe that we can't keep her safe. I'll hire a fucking army if I have to.

CHAPTER
Seven

FRANKIE'S BEEN AT my place almost a week now, and although she sleeps in my bed every night, in my arms, all we've done is sleep. Something isn't quite right with my girl at the moment and I can't figure out what the fuck it is. I've been in the gym no less than ten hours a day, but tonight, I'm taking the night off to have dinner with Frankie. No brothers, no security, just us. I'll cook for her; maybe that will help me get her out of her panties. Lying next to her every night, waking up tangled in each other, and I'm a walking fucking hard on. Who the fuck am I kidding? I was hard a lot even when I could take her whenever I wanted. All she has to do is walk into a room and I go solid. I'm like a damn thirteen-year-old punk again. It's worse now though because I have no place to put that raging hard on except my own hand, and that's only fun while you're doing it.

Reaching her studio, I look through the glass partition and see that she's in the middle of a class. My heart stutters then stops before it takes off at a punishing pace when I see her. The first thing I notice is that she isn't dancing with Flashdance. No, he's hovering in the corner by the music system eyeing Frankie and the guy she *is* dancing with. I've not seen him before and he's definitely a pro and not one of her students. She brings in different dancers all the time to help with choreography and shit, but I bet that Cristiano is pissed as hell that she's brought

someone in to help with what looks like the Tango—their specialty. They've won more awards in Latin dancing for their Tango than any other form of dance when they were partners. Turning my attention back to the Princess, I lean against the glass, my arms raised, gripping the ledge above my head. Watching her dance with another man is like the sweetest fucking form of torture. She's incredible, sensual, so goddamn sexy. Frankie dances like I fight. All heart, with everything that she is, because it matters. It's who she is.

She has on a black dress that is slit high in the thigh, and with every kick, I catch a glimpse of black lace panties. Jesus fuck. Whoever this guy is, he's good. I want to fucking kill him right now for having his hands all over—and I mean all the fuck over—my girl, but he's got talent. I watch as she flicks her feet in between his legs, her movements clean and precise. He pushes her away and spins her back into him, lifting her so that his face is pressed against her chest before sliding her down his front all the way into a split on the floor. Grabbing her by the wrists, he pulls her back into his hold and then spins and dips her around the floor in a wide circle as the class watches. I'm worried about her head when I watch the Tango King twirl her away and then back into his arms, her leg wrapped high around his waist as he bends to the floor.

I can't take any more and am about to walk away when I realize that Frankie is looking right at me. My gaze locks on to hers, and I watch, more turned on than I should be, as her back is pressed to his front, his hands curved around her ribs, brushing the underside of her tits as he buries his face in her neck swaying them back and forth, and all the while she's watching me. Her eyes blue flames pinning me to the spot and lighting my ass up. It's like she's beckoning to me. Telling me that she sees me and that her every movement is done with me in mind. One of his hands travels right up the center of her, palm flat, and then encircles her throat gently, eliciting a growl from me.

Shaking my head no, she tosses his hand away forcefully as she turns into his hold, breaking our eye contact. I can't watch anymore. I'm so hard I could probably fuck her through the wall. Looking to where Flashdance is still standing, I smile when I catch him glaring at me. He's not dumb. He's aware of what just went on between Frankie and I. What he doesn't know is that little eye fucking she gave me is gonna get her fucked. Tonight. Smirk firmly in place, I poke my head in the studio just as they take their bows.

"Frankie!" I call out, stopping her. Slowly she turns to face me just as Cristiano makes it to her side, placing a proprietary hand on the small of her back. She glances at him and smiles but steps away, breaking contact, his hand falling away in the process.

"Yes?" she asks a little breathlessly.

"As soon as this class is over I'm taking you home." *And fucking you until you can't walk* is implied in my tone. Although I don't say the words, she knows. She can feel it and when she nods her head in acceptance, I grin wickedly at her and then turn it up a notch when I look into the furious face of Cristiano. Motherfucker looks about one word away from a stroke. Let me see what I can do to help that along. "Oh, and Princess, love the black lace. It's my favorite on you."

BACK AT MY place, it takes me nearly an hour to get rid of Reggie, Trent, and my pain in the dick brothers. When I finally do, I head for the kitchen and start pulling stuff out for dinner. Everything prepped for our meal, I wait on the Princess to finish with her shower. I can't stop myself from thinking about her, naked, wet, flushed from the heat of the water. Groaning, I slide my hand into the front of my low slung sweatpants and

squeeze my cock roughly, willing myself into control. I'm startled from my nasty thoughts when I hear what sounds like a
woman moaning throughout the kitchen. The fuck? Turning,
I see Frankie walking in with the iPad, controlling the sound
system.

"This is straight up porn music, you know that, right?" I
ask, causing her steps to falter. "You trying to seduce me with
dirty music, Princess?" The flush starts at her chest and inches
up her neck to her cheeks. Following its path, my gaze lingers on
her mouth and her lip caught in between her teeth. "What song
is this? It's about to get you fucked." There will be no bullshit
between us tonight. I'm just telling her how it is. My mouth and
my cock are on the same page, and they both want Frankie.

"'Wa-waiting Game,'" she stammers making her way slowly to where I'm leaning against the counter, my hand still tucked
into the front of my sweats and boxer briefs, holding on to my
cock. Placing the iPad down, she looks at me through lust glazed
eyes. "Are you cooking?" She's trying to change the subject. It
won't work. I'm too fucking worked up.

"Later. Who were you dancing with today?"

"Oh." She's thrown off by *my* abrupt change in topic. *Little
does she know.* "That was Roman. He and I bounce ideas for choreography off of each other all the time and he needed me to
help him out." She glances down at the hand in my waistband
and quickly back up. Snaking my arm out, I hook her around
the waist and pull her to me, swinging Frankie onto the counter
and stepping in between her legs in one quick, fluid motion.
Soft, tiny hands find my bare shoulders to steady herself and I
use it to my advantage and push in a little closer. Close enough
to see the navy flecks in her crystalline eyes and the rapid pulse
in her throat. Pressing my lips to that spot, I smile against her
coconut-scented skin when she gasps. I love that no matter how
many times we've done this, my lips on her elicit that same reaction. Every. Time. Dragging my lips up until I end at her ear,

"Does dancing with him make you hot?" I breathe against her.

"No." Her answer is nothing more than an exhale.

"Mmmm, no? Watching you with him made me hot. Not as hot as you eye fucking me while he touched me though." Pressing in even tighter, I can feel the heat of her pussy against my bare skin. Taking my hands, I place them on her knees. She glances down, watching as they make a path inward to her thighs. Pressing and kneading, my fingertips nearly touching her pussy through the thin cotton of her shorts. Never stopping, I drag my callused touch back to her knees where I begin the journey all over again, this time grazing against her clit in the softest touch. A touch that sets her legs to tremble and me to rock my hips forward, digging my now solid cock into the cabinet. The bite of wood not affecting me in the least. Frankie's breath catches when I use a fingernail to trace over her, pressing the material into her wetness. I groan when I realize that she isn't wearing anything under the tiny bottoms. Eyes clashing, "I never thought I would enjoy watching another man with his hands on you. I think it was knowing that the whole time he touched you, you wanted it to be me. You were thinking about me fucking you. Weren't you?" My hands are still roaming over her and into those barely-there shorts. With every pass of my fingers over the damp lips of her pussy, of her clit, she arches into my touch a little more. "Weren't you, Frankie? You were imagining that those hands all over you were mine. That it was my cock pressed into your back." I lean back so that I can see her face clearly. "Tell me you wanted me, Frankie. I want to hear you say it," I demand softly while my fingers continue their sweetly torturous path.

"Deacon, we can't keep doing thi—ahhhh," she moans as I dip my thumb into her, running it back up her slit then out to drag the wetness along her thigh to her knee.

"Yes. We can," I inform her as I bend and lick the trail I left, sucking at her soft skin along the way. Reveling in the

way her legs quiver under my lips and her nails dig into my shoulders. Once I reach her center, she tenses in anticipation, her breath held waiting for my next move. Instead of putting my mouth where we both want it, I place a kiss on the inside of each thigh, nipping and then soothing. "Tell me that you wanted me, Frankie. And that you want me now, and I'll give you what you want. What we both want." Placing another kiss to her sex-scented skin, I wait her out, hovering over her pussy, breathing the scent of her arousal. Jesus fuck, if she doesn't say yes . . . running my nose over her clit, she clutches my head, pulling the hair from its tie. She'll say yes.

"I wanted you. All I could think about was you inside of me, your hands on me. You understand my body, what I want, everything I need. I need you now." I can't see her face, but I can hear the heat in her words, the carnality in her rasp. "Fuck me, please. Dirty like you used to, Deac. Like if you didn't claim me you would die, I would die. Please?" she begs as she writhes, trying to put her sweet cunt closer to my face. Growling, I yank her shorts down her legs and over her feet, tossing them somewhere behind me. Frankie starts to lie back when I still her with my hands against her spine. The granite is too hard and cold for what I have in mind. Placing her legs over my shoulders, my palms flat against the center of her back, I stand, bringing her with me, perfectly aligning her pussy and my mouth. Placing a kiss right to her center, I turn to the wall closest to us and make my way over.

"Deacon," she moans, tightening her hold on me. "I'm going to fall," she says halfheartedly.

Glancing up from in between her legs, "Do you trust me?" I ask. When she hesitates and I see that little flicker of doubt shadow her eyes, I die a little inside. "Do you trust me to keep you safe, Princess?" I clarify. She nods that she does and that's all the encouragement I need. I press her back against the wall, holding her there as I delve into her pussy. Her soft moan echoes the ones coming from the speakers, fueling me. With my hands under her ass, I hoist her a bit higher and nuzzle right into her heat, her wetness on my face, clinging to the stubble of my beard. Groaning, I pull her clit into my mouth and release it with an audible pop before I press my tongue deep into her, spearing in and out, mimicking what my cock is aching to do. I hum low in my throat while my mouth covers her, the vibrations making her call out my name and clutch the long strands of my hair as she grinds into my face.

I smile against her glistening lips and pull back just far enough to blow a soft breath over her and watch as her pussy quivers, her body begging me for release just as her words are. "Don't tease me, Deacon. I want to come, please let me come," she pleads.

"You want to come all over my face, baby? Do it. Come all over my face and then I'm going to make you come all over my cock. Over." I lick right through her center and flick my tongue around her clit. "And over." My tongue flattens on her again as I use my beard to rasp against her and almost come all over myself at the low throaty sound she makes. "And over. Until you can't stand. Until you can't take it anymore and you beg me to stop just so I can start again. I'll fuck you dirty, Princess. I'll fuck you dirty until we're both clean." I never remove my mouth, every word uttered against her pussy while she grinds against me, my words bringing her closer. I won't be able to take much more of this. I need to be buried inside my girl—now. I stop teasing her and fuck her with my tongue, my lips, my beard, and when she comes, it's long and loud and fucking hot as hell. Flicking over her one last time, I don't give her a chance to come down from the high she's on, sliding her down so that her legs are wrapped around my waist instead of my head. As quickly as I can, I turn us toward the media room, the closest to us and therefore perfect. Reaching down, I hit the recline button on the overstuffed chair and untangle her legs from around

me and place her in the center of it. My hands braced on the arms, I lean over her and place a kiss on her open mouth, the taste of her pussy dancing over both of our tongues as they meet. Lifting her arms over her head, I reach for the hem of her shirt and pull it off, using it to wipe the wetness covering my face. Smirking, I let my eyes take in the flush covering her body and the beard burn on her thighs. "You look so fucking beautiful like this, Frankie. Spread open for me, fucked, wet, and ready." I can't take my eyes off of all she's offering. She reaches out and tugs on the elastic waistband of my sweats.

"I want these off. Now," she insists.

"Yes, ma'am," I salute her and do as I'm told, making her smile. I need those lips wrapped around my cock.

Climbing onto the chair, I place my knees on either of her hips and stretch, sliding my dick in between her tits. Frankie doesn't hesitate, pushing them together, and takes the tip of me into her mouth when I push through the tunnel she's created for me. I do it one more time before straightening my legs, gripping the back of the chair as I thrust into Frankie's mouth. We moan in unison, her hands clasping my ass and pulling me further in. My head falls back on my shoulders as I fuck her mouth, pushing her head farther and farther into the chair back with every thrust. "I've missed this mouth. God, I've fucking missed it. You suck me so fucking good, Princess. This mouth is mine," I tell her as I jerk my hips forward, triggering her gag reflex a little but not pulling back. "That pussy that I'm about to tear the fuck up is mine. And that tight little ass is mine too."

I go to pull out and Frankie pulls me back in, hollowing out her cheeks and swallowing my whole length to my balls. Jesus fuck, when did she learn to do that? Growling, I do my best not to come. I feel a trickle of sweat making its way down my spine as I fight it. Pushing me back so that she can take a breath, I hop off the chair and bring her with me, spinning us so that her back is to me and I'm now the one sitting in the chair.

My hands on her waist, I guide her backwards into my lap and onto my waiting cock. "That's it, baby. Slow and easy. You're so fucking tight." Frankie whimpers as I stretch her. She lowers herself further. With my hands under her ass, I spread her wider in order to take more of me then lift her back up, groaning at the way she grips me before easing down again. The need to claim her is too much. My hand travels up her body over her tits to her throat, encircling it gently, possessively. "I'm the only one that's allowed to hold you here," I remind her of Roman doing the same while they were dancing. "You're mine, and no one will ever know that kind of possession but me." I punctuate my words by thrusting hard and deep, consumed completely by her pussy. Her breath catches as I rock into her while I pull her back to meet my demanding thrusts without actually pulling out. I'm afforded a full body view when I lean back into the chair. The flush on her skin, her perfect tits with nipples pulled tight, her ink, and that beautiful pussy swallowing my cock over and over.

She wants it dirty, but I'm so far gone I'm fighting coming with every move I make. Grabbing her hand, I bring it up and put her middle finger into my mouth, wetting it. "Help me make you come, Frankie. I want to watch you play with your pussy while I fuck you," I command while I guide her hand to her clit. "Show me how you made yourself come when I wasn't there to do it for you." Frankie leans into me, turning her face into my neck, mouth open against my skin.

"It was never the same," she pants. "I rubbed and fingered myself, always thinking about you and pretending it was you and it never felt the same." Her words are like a fist around my balls, my orgasm hovering just at the precipice. Snarling, I roll my hips, angling hers so that I'm hitting her sweet spot and I watch her finger slide over and around her clit, wet and languid before both of our movements turn frantic.

"Jesus fuck, Princess," I moan as I pound into her with

rapid fire thrusts, our skin slapping out a tempo that fills the room, our breathing and low moans joining. "You own me, Princess. Fuck, do you own me, this pussy was made for my cock, made for me to fuck." I feel her orgasm pulling me under, squeezing almost to the point of pain before rippling around my shaft. "That's it, baby, come for me. Come all over me." I let go of her hips just long enough to spread her legs wider over my thighs allowing me to get even deeper, and that pushes us both over the edge.

Frankie cries out, my name like a prayer on her lips over and over as I come so hard my vision goes hazy. My movements slow, and grunting, I thrust one final time before I still. Pulling her hand away from where we're still joined, I bring it up to my mouth, placing a kiss to her wrist, the scent of us on her fingers is the sexiest thing I've ever smelled. I drop her hand and wrap my arms around her as she snuggles into me, placing small pecks on my neck and shoulder. We sit like that, quietly stroking, coming down from an incredible high, allowing our breathing and rapid heartbeats to slow to normal. After a few minutes, I gather Frankie up in my arms, tucking her under my chin as I lower the chair and stand.

"Where are we going?" she asks, her voice heavy with sleep.

"To bed, baby. You wore my ass out." I chuckle as I make my way to our room, leaving our clothes. I'll get them later. Once upstairs I lay her down in the bed, crawling in after her, pulling the blanket around us. This is where I'm happiest, not in the Cage, or the gym. Right here, wrapped around my girl. My arm around her waist, I tug her closer and place a kiss to her head, inhaling the smell of us in her hair, on her skin. Frankie sighs, deeply, content, and then again with a resigned air. "What are you thinking so hard about, Frankie?" Voice quiet, I run my fingers up and down her arm soothingly.

"We can't keep doing this, Deac. We're not resolving any of our issues. I can't think. The minute you put your hands on me, I'm done. I can't remember what I need to protect myself from or why I'm angry, hurt, whatever. All I can think about is your touch and what it does to me. What it means to me," she says softly. "I love you so much it hurts. It physically hurts me because I am terrified of the power you have over me." I do my best to not interrupt her. I feel like she needs to get this out, for her. I just continue stroking over her, letting her talk, listening. "You have the power to shatter me, Deacon. I ran to protect you from the danger following me, but also to protect me, from you." She laces our fingers together. "I can't be without you, I don't want to be, but I want to go slow. I need to go slow. You're too much . . . of everything. It's a lot for me." Frankie brings our joined hands up to her mouth and brushes a kiss across my knuckles. "I don't want you to ever feel trapped or obligated to love me. I wouldn't survive that either. It would hurt me worse than walking away." I open my mouth to say that it's not even a possibility when she turns in my arms so that we're looking at each other. "Can you do that for me? I know slow isn't your style—you're all in, all the way—but I need this. I'm still uncertain of so much, I—I just . . . please?" she begs.

Tangling my hands in her hair, I tip her head back so that I can see her better. My lips touch first her forehead, her eyes flutter closed, and I kiss each eyelid then her nose, finally making my way to her mouth. Softly, reverently, I kiss her, swiping my tongue along her pouty lower lip before pulling away. "I'll take this as slow as you want me to as long as I don't have to share you, Frankie. Hell, we can even go on dates if you want, all proper and shit. I'm done sharing you with Flashdance though. That shit is done." There's an edge in my voice that I can't help. That I won't hide.

"Deacon, you have never had to share me with him. He's a friend, nothing more. I don't have room for anyone else in my heart," she reassures me with her words and a soft kiss to my chin.

My hair falls in a curtain around us when I look down at her. "Whether you have room or not, I've had to share you with him. He's been able to talk to you, laugh with you, put his fucking hands on you, all while I watched. Wishing things were different and that you could let go of your anger long enough to see that it was bullshit. It *is* bullshit, Princess. So don't tell me that I didn't have to share you," I say harshly.

I don't mean to lose my temper, but it's like she's blind to him and what their friendship does to me. I know she doesn't see it and isn't trying to hurt me but she needs to understand that she is. Frankie is the only one capable of hurting me. The only fucking one. So while I'm willing to go slow for her because I understand her fear when it comes to the power our feelings give us over one another, I won't be going slow so that Cristiano has a chance to talk her into something safer. Fuck what she says, I have a dick, same as him, and I know where the fuck he wants to put it, and that shit ain't never gonna happen again. Trying to lighten the mood—I hate bringing this shit to our bed, always have—I ask, "Does going slow mean no more fucking and separate bedrooms?" My hands full of her ass, I squeeze and give her a suggestive look.

Frankie laughs and slaps my chest. "You're a beast. Yes, taking it slow means no sex and separate rooms. We need to be sure about what we want," she tells me resolutely.

"Oh, I'm sure I want you to put out on the first date," I tease, slapping her ass. I'm not sure why, but she seems to be pushing this slow thing like I'm going to change my mind about her and I don't like it. I'll have to do my best to prove to her that I'm in this. "Because, I'm a sure thing." Winking I wrap her arms around me, returning mine to where they were, and pull her in tight. "No more talking, it's making me hard. I have an early gym time, and you're keeping me awake with your glorious pussy and awesome fucking rack. I think they got bigger," I tease, kind of, as I rub my chest on hers, brushing against taut nipples and eliciting her gasp. Groaning, I tighten my hold on her ass. "Sleep, you fucking minx, unless you want to put it on me again." I'm only half kidding. Maybe not even half. Or not one fucking bit.

"Goodnight, Deacon."

"Goodnight Princess."

CHAPTER
Eight

SONNY AND I walk onto the gym floor after being in the weight room for the last three hours. My legs feel like jelly, my arms like lead, but I love it. It feels like winning, like accomplishment. Still not sure if they'll even let me fight, but I'll be ready regardless. We head toward the mats for a little cool down when I see Reggie and Frankie standing with my pop and two suits. Frankie's arms are crossed over her chest, her posture rigid. She's pissed. I'm about to walk over when I catch a glimpse of the men they're talking to. Fucking hell, I'm a dead man. It's the marshals and I'd bet money that they just told Frankie that Drew wasn't the one to attack her. Certain it's true when I make eye contact with Pop and he shakes his head at me as if to say, "I told you this was a shit idea." I knew it and I'd planned on telling her. I can't even remember why I didn't want her to know. Jesus fuck, would I ever not fuck up with her?

My dad waves me over. There are a million other places I would rather be right now. "Who are the guys with Pop?" Sonny asks as he follows me over to where they all stand waiting for me.

"That would be asshole one and asshole two, better known as the marshals I knuckled up at Indie's place," I admit to him flatly.

"Wait, what? I thought you just roughed Drew up. What

were marshals doing there?" Hand on my arm he stops us, waiting for an answer. I just look him in the eyes and wait for it to sink in. Jameson is smart; it doesn't take long. "Holy shit, he was in protective custody." Eyes narrowed, "Did you know and not tell anyone?"

Dragging my hands through my loose hair, I scrape it into a bun. "I didn't find out until after I beat the shit out of everyone."

"And you didn't tell us why?" he demands

"Fuck, Sonny, I don't know. I had a lot of shit going on? I was worried she'd go back to him? Afraid I might have killed his ass? Take your pick." His mouth is hanging open in astonishment, making me want to hit him. "Not my smartest move, but it's done now, so you can lock your shit up, I don't need it."

"Oh, you're not gonna get it from me. Did you see the Princess?" He jerks his chin in her direction. "She's gonna hand you your fucking ass." Shaking his head, he stalks off toward them, leaving me to follow after him.

"Mr. Love, just the man we want to see," suit number one booms.

When I don't answer him, my pop speaks up, "Deacon, this is Deputy Baird and his partner, Deputy Riley. They need to speak to you." I look over at Frankie, she's glaring daggers straight through me.

"Princess, I—"

She raises her hand to shut me up. "I don't even want to hear it." Turning to the deputies, "When you're finished speaking to him, is there any way that I can see Andrew? Is it safe?"

"You're shitting me, right? You're gonna go and see him?" I huff, "This is the fucking reason I didn't tell you." Turning away from her and her anger, "Un-fucking-believable," I mutter, disgusted with the whole situation.

"Deacon, that's enough," Pop warns.

"Are you guys arresting me? Because if not, I don't have shit to say without my lawyers present." Stubbornly I meet their gaze. They've fucked my day enough; I'm not going to make this easy on them.

"We just wanted to go over Mr. McAvoy's condition and ask you a couple questions," Deputy Riley tells me. He doesn't like me, but he doesn't hate me as much as his partner. That much is obvious.

"Are you charging me with something? Did Andrew decide to press charges?" His name tastes like shit leaving my mouth.

"No, he's decided not to, as have we, considering the circumstances."

I nod begrudgingly. They could have really screwed me. I should be grateful, but all I can think about is Frankie going to see Drew. "What do you need with me then?" If they aren't charging me, what the hell do they want? "Any questions you have will have to go through my lawyers," I inform them again.

"We just wanted to let you know that Mr. McAvoy wasn't pressing charges, and we'll get in contact with the lawyers for the rest." He turns to Frankie, "And to offer Miss De Rosa the option of being under our protection." He pulls a card out of his pocket and hands it to her. "You really should consider it. These men don't want to go to prison and they don't care what it takes to stay out. Unfortunately you know that all too well," he says sympathetically and I snap.

"Yeah, she does know too well because your boy, Drew, is a fucking pussy and left her to fend for herself while he saved his own ass. You tell him I said he's a coward and he's lucky that she survived." My chest heaves in anger. I feel my brother and Pop come up beside me.

"Deacon, he wasn't the one who—" The fuck? Whirling around, I cut Frankie off.

"Don't you fucking dare defend him. He left you, alone and vulnerable in a house he didn't feel was safe for his ass to be in," I roar. When she flinches and Sonny moves to stand between us, I realize it's time for me to get the fuck out. I can't do this with her right now. My brother places a hand to my chest and pushes me back a step, but I swat it away. "He may have not have been the one to put hands on you that day, Frankie, but he *is* the reason you were lying in that hospital bed, fighting for your life. Never forget that shit; God knows I never will. Maybe we should ask the cops for the pictures they took of you, every cut and scrape, busted up face and body. Would that convince you that all of this is his fucking fault?" Hands trembling in rage, I ignore the tears streaming down her face. "I sat there with you, wishing and praying to a God I'm not sure even fucking exists to not take you from me, so don't you ever defend him to me again."

Sonny blocks her from my view. "Why don't you go hit the shower? We can deal with all of this later, all right?" He's not really asking, but he doesn't have to; I'm aware I need to go get my mind right. I hate myself for yelling at her like that; it wasn't right to treat her that way, but fuck me, was she serious?

IN THE LOCKER room, my hair damp and loose, towel slung low on my hips, I stand in front of the vending machine staring vacantly when I hear the door creak open. "Deacon, are you alone?' Frankie calls out, her voice extra raspy, extra fucking sexy. I'm pissed at her and still she affects me.

"I'm alone. I don't want to do this right now though, Frankie. Have one of the guys take you home," I bite out, never turning to look at her.

"I'm not here to fight. I just wanted to come in here and apologize to you." That catches my attention. Slowly I face her, eyebrows raised.

"You were right—I should never have defended him. He doesn't deserve it, not for a second. Andrew left me there to my own devices, just like you said. I still want to go and talk to him though. Ask him why, get some closure." Hands tucked into the pocket of her 'Frankie's Place' hoodie, she shrugs. "I'm confused, and pissed that you didn't tell me. I didn't even know that you were possibly facing charges still." The confusion in her voice is evident. "Why didn't you tell me about any of it, Deacon? Honestly, I'm trying to not be angry, but you make it so hard sometimes."

Can't deny that. Right now though, the only thing that I can focus on is the fact that she said she's still going to see him.

"Princess," I start as I walk over to the bench that runs down the center of the room, straddling it, the anger I feel being replaced by exasperation, a little bit of desperation even. "I was afraid," I admit quietly. I feel like a pussy even acknowledging it, but it's the truth.

Eyebrows creased in confusion, "Afraid of what, Deac?"

"Of you going back to him mostly." Meeting her gaze, I shrug.

"You didn't tell me that he wasn't the one that attacked me, you let me think these last few days that I was finally safe, because you were scared I'd take him back?" When she says it like that, it sounds like a dick move on my part. I don't bother answering. "I was leaving him that night, for you. Why would I take him back?" That's the first time she's said that to me and I'd never been sure.

"Never knew why you were leaving; I had hoped, but you never said."

Head down, staring at her feet, she shakes her head. "How could you not have known?" I can barely hear her she's so quiet. When she looks at me again, I'm not sure what she's feeling. There's a myriad of emotions flashing in her eyes, across her face. "Did you not know how much I loved you, still love you?" I nod that I did. Because I did. No matter if we were together or not, I knew she loved me, even if she pushed me away.

"Then how could you think so little of me, of my feelings?" Tears in her eyes again, she blows out a breath. "Clearly our need to take it slow is very real."

At this moment, I agree with her. I never thought that the day would come where I needed to be away from Frankie in order to clear my head, get my shit straight, but it has, and I do. "I think you're right," I say resolutely, meeting her gaze. "It's pretty obvious that our communication is shit. You're pissed at me for keeping things from you when for months you were doing the same thing." My eyes roam her face, touching on the tears I can see hovering on her lashes and the sadness pulling at her mouth. "We're either in this all the way or not at all, and right now, I feel like we're in different corners, fighting each other, and I need a minute."

"So, what does that even mean, Deacon?"

Hands clenched in the towel hanging around my neck, I blow out an agitated breath. "It means . . . fuck, I don't know what it means. I guess it means I need a fucking break," I bite out more harshly than I intended.

She blinks slowly, digesting what I just said, and in a daze, walks out of the locker room all kinds of upset and beat down. I can't even go after her, although part of me wants to. A greater part . . . doesn't.

"Fuck."

CHAPTER
Nine

QUIETLY, I MAKE my way into the kitchen from the garage. It's nearly one in the morning and I don't want to wake Frankie. Just as I'm placing my keys and wallet in the bowl, "I didn't think that you were coming home." There's so much in her tone. Accusations, questions, hurt, hope. I can't even bear to hear all of it right now. I've spent the last several hours at the gym beating the hell out of myself and thinking about this morning, and the more I thought about our conversation, the madder I got. The madder I got, the more the need to be away from her grew.

"I'm home. Just need to get packed; I've got a flight to catch in a couple of hours." I make my way past her and fight the need to touch her, to hold her, to shake her for making me feel this way.

Taken aback, she looks at me, confusion clouding her eyes. "A flight? Where are you going?"

"I've got a meeting with the EWF in California in a couple days. Gonna get there early and get some training in with my buddies on base. Might stay a few days after I see what the Federation has to say." Not making eye contact, I start up the stairs. I can feel her watching me as I take them two at a time.

"Can I come with?" Frankie asks hesitantly from the foot of the staircase.

At the landing, I turn and look down at my girl. Big, comfy sweater hanging off one shoulder, fuzzy socks hiding her legs from me, stopping just above her knees. Blue eyes watching me, lip pulled between her teeth, and hands playing with the hem of her top. I shake my head to rid myself of the thoughts running through my mind, the first being, "Get inside her. Now," and focus on the mad I've been letting fester all damn day.

"Nah, not this time. I need a minute to get my shit straight. You go ahead and see Drew. I'll be back soon." I fight to keep the bitterness out of my tone, but I'm shit at hiding my feelings, especially from her. She hears it—there's no way she can miss it. Pivoting, I head into my bedroom. It's just a matter of time before she comes at me, demanding an explanation. Duffel on the bed, I start grabbing up clothes, rolling them tight, and putting them in the bag on autopilot.

"You're mad because I want to go and talk to him, so you're punishing me by leaving me alone here?" she asks incredulously.

"Not mad, Princess, just got shit to do. And I'm not leaving you alone. Reggie, Trent, Bo, and a couple other guys that Reg called will all be here with you." Brushing past, I grab my shit out of the bathroom.

"You *are* mad. Why can't you just admit it? I told you I wasn't going back to him. I only want to talk to him, Deacon, not suck his di—"

"Stop. Just fucking stop," my voice raised to drown out what she's saying. "I don't want to talk about it. You want to go see him, go. I don't have to like it. In fact, I won't. I'm not gonna hash this shit out with you again." I say that, but I can't stop from doing exactly that. Throwing my toiletry bag on the bed, I spin to face her. "You almost fucking died, Frankie. Died. And again, while he may not have been the one to physically hurt you, it's his fault. So excuse the fuck out of me if I'm a little fucking pissed that you want to be anywhere near him." I huff out a disgusted breath and cross to my closet, only to turn

and stalk back to where she stands. Stopping directly in front of her. Close enough to reach out and touch her. Far enough that I won't.

"Tell me why. Why do you need to see him?" I demand. "Make me understand so that I'm not so fucking heated, Frankie. Because right now I just don't fucking get it. I don't get it. I don't like it. And I sure as fuck am not going to sit here with my dick in my hand while you go and get your closure or whatever bullshit you need." Not waiting for an answer, I grab up my stuff and slam out of the room. Whatever I don't have I can buy. I'm madder than I should be, but I can't help it. Some of it is jealousy, I know. But the majority of it is plain ass pissed the fuck off. Instead of waiting and letting her explain, I bail. I can't hear it right now. Not with my head where it's at. So now it's me who's running like a pussy, but I need a minute and there's no way I'm getting it with her in the same fucking zip code, let alone house.

SAN DIEGO IS where I was stationed while I was in the Marines. My pop and Guy opened a gym less than a mile from the base while I was in boot camp, offering free membership to anyone active duty and discounted to retired military. It's my favorite of all our gyms and where I did a lot of my early training. Walking through the doors at six A.M. after a red-eye feels like coming home in a way. Even at this early hour, the gym is busy. I scan the floor as I make my way to the reception desk before I hit the stairs and the apartment that we keep atop the gym for when we're in town. Mav and Sonny will be meeting me here later today, as they opted to take a flight at a more reasonable hour.

"Hey, Jodi, I'm heading up to the apartment. I'll be in town for the next few days at least if anyone is looking for me," I say, reaching for the mail addressed to me that's kept in a slot behind her. Her eyes light up as they run over me from head to toe. *Fuck.*

"I'm glad you're back. Things are always more interesting when you're around." Smiling coyly, "I'm off at seven. Want me to come up?" she asks hopefully. Jodi is beyond hot and whenever I'm in town we hook up. A lot. She's down for anything and knows that I'm not looking for more than a quick fuck. I hope to hell she doesn't get all fucking weird on me now.

"As tempting as that offer is," I lie, "I have to pass, Jo. I have a girl now." Doesn't matter that we aren't in a great place at the moment, she's mine and I'm hers, no matter how pissed I am at her frustrating ass.

Jodi lets a surprised laugh slip past her lips before she catches herself. "Oh, shit. You're serious, aren't you?" Her eyes are about to bug out of her damn head. "If I didn't know you better I'd swear that you were full of shit. But I give amazing head, so you must be telling the truth," she teases. I just shake my head and laugh.

"Yeah, I'm serious. We cool?" Eyebrows raised questioningly, I feel like an ass when she's now the one laughing.

"Uhhh, yeah. We're cool, you wanker. I'm happy for you. It's about damn time," Jodi chides, throwing me a hip bump. "So do I know her? Please don't say it's that fecking Veronica whore." She pins me with crazy eyes. Her posh English accent going out the door and replaced with something decidedly *not* posh. "I may have to cut you and then blow you anyway just because it's her. That would make it funny."

My shit mood forgotten, I give her a hug, laughing my ass off. "Nah, you can keep the 'in your face' blow job . . . it's definitely not Veronica. It's Frankie." Releasing her I take a step back just in time to catch her reaction to that news.

She smiles and says, "Always has been."

I nod and agree, "Yeah, it has. Anyways, I'm here. Let the boys know if you see any of my crew, yeah? Especially Leo."

"You got it. Now get out of here with your tempting off-the-market ass before I knock you down and rape your face." Throwing me a wink, she goes back to her work.

"See ya around, Jodi," I call as I head for the door that will take me to the apartment and to bed. Alone.

My brothers arrive by early afternoon, banging around and being pains in the ass to make sure I'm awake. "I'm up, you dumb fuckers," I yell, climbing out of bed and pulling on the sweats I had thrown over the chair. Striding into the living room, I find Mav and Sonny sitting on the couch and eyeing me expectantly. "You just get in?" I ask them, running my fingers through my tangled hair, pulling it into a messy knot on the top of my head.

"Yeah, Pops told us to get here, so we got here," Mav says as he shoves a bite of bagel into his mouth.

Sonny looks over the brim of his coffee cup at me; I would kill for a cup of that right now. "You want to tell us why we're here instead of our home base?" he asks in that calm tone of his.

Adjusting myself in my sweats, I go to the kitchen, avoiding his probing gaze, and pour a cup of coffee, adding cream and sugar. Fuck it. I lean back against the counter and watch him across the breakfast bar. "I just needed to get away, Sonny. There was too much going on and I needed out." The steam from my mug feels good against my face as I blow on the hot brew. "Plus, I have the meeting with the EWF, and being here gives me a chance to go at some fresh sparring partners. I'm sure Leo has some guys."

I'm avoiding the real reason. My brothers aren't stupid though. They're both just looking at me, patiently waiting for me to cut the shit and just say it. It pisses me off. "What?" I demand as they watch me silently. "For fuck's sake. What do you want me to say? You want to hear that I'm pissed at Frankie? That I don't want to be in the same room with her right now because I'm afraid that I want to shake some sense into her?" My voice rises with each word before I'm shouting across the kitchen at them. I would never touch her, and they know that. "I just . . . I just don't get what the fuck she's thinking and I need a minute to wrap my head around everything."

What I don't tell them is that I'm scared. Scared that I'll lose her to him. Scared that I hurt him as much as I wanted to, or not enough, and that she'll be angry with me. Shit, I'm scared that they'll take her away and put her in protective custody with him somewhere and I won't be able to find her. I don't tell them all that though. That's my shit to work through. The real reason I had to fly nearly two thousand miles away to think. I'm not good at dealing with this shit and I should've stayed to work through it all. But I didn't and now I'm here and I need to find a way to man up and get past it.

"I don't blame you, Deacon," Sonny says, interrupting my thoughts.

Eyes narrowed, I wait for him to elaborate or to get all sentimental or shit on me with that one, but he doesn't. He shakes his head a little and goes on, "She's dead wrong on this, and I don't blame you for needing a little bit of a breather. You're volatile on your best day. You'd tear the damn city apart if you had to sit there while she went to see him. I would've suggested training here if you hadn't. I just needed to hear you admit that it was all too much for you."

I glance over at Mav who is tapping out a beat on his knee, not saying anything.

"Just say it, Maverick. I can see that you want to. You think I'm being stupid, don't you?"

Curling his nose at me, he blows out a breath. "Yeah, I do. She just wants answers. How can you not see that?" His exasperation with the two of us is obvious. "You, I'm not surprised at." He jerks his chin in my direction. "You have tunnel vision when it comes to the Princess. You see her and you want nothing from the outside world to get near her unless you say so. You've always been like that, it's just gotten worse." Pointing a finger at Sonny, "You though I am shocked at. You are usually the voice of reason for this one," Mav says, flicking his thumb over his shoulder where I sit. "I can't handle two reckless brothers. That's all your area, not mine," he tells Sonny defiantly.

The sound of my phone breaks the sudden silence that settled over us after Mav's little speech. Scooping it up off the counter,

Frankie: I hope you landed safely xoxo

My lip kicks up in a small smile without me even thinking about it. As mad as I am, I love the fuck out of this woman. It's why she's able to piss me off like she does. Love her or not, I'm not ready to talk to her. I'm bitter and anything I say now would be out of anger. That will only hurt us both even more. I shoot back,

Me: Yeah, I'm here

Right before I'm about to tuck it in my pocket, it pings again.

Frankie: I'm glad. I'm here when you want to talk

Me : K

Locking the phone, I toss it back onto the counter. It's going to take everything in me to not cave and just go back home to her.

"I'm gonna hit the shower; meet you downstairs in twenty?" I ask as I head to the bathroom. I need a minute away from their observant stares and Mav's judgey ass. This isn't about him. It's about me. It's about Frankie and the fact that she has the ability to wreck me. She may not do it on purpose, but regardless, it wouldn't be hard to do.

AFTER FIVE DAYS, I'm ready to be home. I'm not any less moody here than I was there. I'm still ass hurt over Frankie wanting to talk to that asshole, and although I came here to be away from her so that I can get my thoughts in order, it's just not happening. Something's gotta fucking give. San Diego is usually one of my favorite cities to visit. Great friends, good eats, and our gym is low key with some stellar sparring talent. Not this trip though. No, this trip is fucking torture. The meeting didn't go all that well with the EWF. They're stoked that Andrew isn't pressing charges, but the press surrounding the whole thing isn't great since so much of it has to be kept out of the media. All they see is some ragey fucking MMA fighter who beat up his girlfriend's ex-fiancé. Nobody has the particulars. At least I'm able to say it was in self-defense and that I was protecting Frankie. Even with that, they're still up in the air on if they're going to let me have my go at the strap or if they're just going to postpone it until the shitstorm settles a bit. Either way, I'm fucked and left kissing their asses and meeting their every demand. I don't kiss ass well. Well, I do, just not like this and not theirs. The ping of my phone interrupts me from my thoughts.

Frankie: How are things with the federation? Anything I can do?

The Princess has texted me every day that I've been gone. I'm still mad though, and even though it kills me to be away from her, I need to be. She's not aware of the extent of the bullshit I'm dealing with over the Andrew debacle. I don't want her to worry or feel guilty, so I've asked everyone to just keep her out of it.

Me: OK

Frankie: You coming home now?

With my thumbs hovering above the keyboard, I want to ask her if she still plans on going to see that fucker, but I don't have the energy to deal with that shit right now and I have to be in the gym in a few minutes.

Me: Not yet.

Frankie: OK. I canceled my classes tonight so I'm home if you feel like talking later.

Why the hell did she cancel her classes? That's not like her at all. I've seen her dance with sprains, colds, the flu, even broken bones. I don't ask why though; it would be too easy. I care too much, even now when I don't want to.

Me: OK

Not waiting for a response, I turn the phone to silent and pocket it. I've got the next four hours at the gym to try and figure out my girl and what the hell my next move is.

Less than ten minutes later, I bound down the steps and enter the gym. Sonny and Mav are already down here working on getting together some sparring partners and maybe a little impromptu Cage match while we're here. We used to do them all the time, but it's hard now that I'm pro. There are so many rules and waivers involved it just becomes too much. I hope they can get it figured out though. It would be a good time, like bringing it all back to my roots. I reach the bottom of the stairs and swing the door open, running right into my boy, Leo. I went through basic with him and two tours.

"What's up, my brotha?" he asks, raising his arm for a fist bump. "I was just coming up to get your lazy ass. Your brothers have been busting their balls all morning trying to line up sparring partners that are willing to take on 'The Hitman,'" he says mockingly.

"Shut up, dick. Why don't you bring your ass in the ring and let me take you to the mats?"

He scoffs, "Bitch, please, I'm not stupid. One time in the Cage with you was more than enough. I'm not as dumb as YOU look, fucker."

Both of us laughing, we go over to where my brothers are standing, handing out what I assume are waivers to spar and to absolve the gym of any liability that me hurting anyone might incur. The struggle is real, apparently.

"You two got anyone good for me to beat up?" I yell to them.

"Just do your warm up and wait in the ring, punk!" Sonny tells me, a shit-eating grin on his usually stoic face.

"Dude, your brother is actually smiling. I almost didn't recognize his serious ass."

"Shocking, right? He must've gotten laid last night. Come help me stretch before I whoop some pussy's ass." Leo follows behind me chuckling deeply as we walk into the Cage, letting the door clang shut behind us.

"Same as always?" he asks. Nodding yes, we settle into what is our usual routine whenever I'm in town. Leo is a few years older than me. He enlisted later in life when he couldn't afford to pay for him and his little brother to go to college after their dad split. He took my young, rough ass under his wing and became like another brother to me. Him and Reggie both. I had a lot of anger that I'd been working through when I signed up. Fighting had always been my outlet, but I needed more and

I didn't know exactly what. The Marines gave me purpose and something to be proud of. Plus, I still found time and willing participants to fight with on base. Leo had been my trainer then, having been a boxer at one time himself, with a degree in Sports Medicine.

"So the Title, huh, man? That's big time, you ready?" he questions as he pulls on my outstretched arm, stretching me as far as I can go before releasing.

"Yeah, I'm ready. Been ready. I just hope that they let me fight. I'm tired of all the bullshit that they're putting me through already, and it's just started."

With a low grunt, he agrees. "Why are they still fucking with you? The guy's not pressing charges, right?" he asks.

I can't tell him everything, although I want to. "It's a little more complicated than that. I just have to ride it out and keep my nose clean and be in the best shape of my fucking life when they say it's go time, ya know?"

Leo nods in understanding and hands me a jump rope. Skipping out a sequence of fast, fast, slow, I listen while he watches me.

"So what's going on with you and Frankie? Jodi told me that you and her finally got together and yet here you are, alone. Not like you, buddy." He smiles at me as if to say I'm losing my touch.

"That's complicated too," I huff out. It only makes his grin that much bigger. I'm gonna hit him.

"So the Hitman is having trouble with the ladies, huh? Never thought I'd see the day."

"You're not seeing it now, fucker. I'm just taking a minute to get my shit straight with the fight end, then I'll go home and get shit straight with my girl," my breath coming out in short pants now. "Stick and move. Stick and motherfucking move."

"Good. I'm glad to see something I tried teaching you and that hard head of yours stuck. You can't be anyone until you're someone. Accomplish what you set out to do, my brother. The rest will fall into place," Leo tells me sagely.

The guy is an old soul. He used to have these little fucking adages and pieces of wisdom he was always dropping on me. We all made fun of him for it and it's how he got the call sign Yoda. Half the time we had no goddamn clue what he was saying to us. I shake my head and toss my rope aside, dropping to do some more stretches when Sonny whistles loudly through the gym. I glance up and he makes a motion with his hand indicating that they're ready.

"You hanging out or do you have to get back?" I ask Leo, handing him my gloves to help me with.

"Nope, I don't have to be on base for a few hours yet. I want to stay and watch you beat some poor dude's ass before I leave." Laughing, he slaps my hands away and exits the Cage just as Sonny, Mav, and some huge, young kid with a fresh buzz cut that screams "new recruit" enter. I look over at Leo and he shrugs. And so it begins. Stick and move. Stick and motherfucking move.

CHAPTER
Ten

"DEACON! WHAT THE fuck are you doing, bro? Sonny sees that shit and he's gonna flip the hell out. What're ya thinking?" Leo asks incredulously.

The answer is I'm not. I can't think of anything other than Frankie and that fucking asshole, Drew. I've never held on to a mad this long when it's come to Frankie. Not even with all of the Flashdance bullshit. And that's another thing eating away at me. Where the fuck is he while I'm a couple thousand miles away? You know damn well he's not just sitting back doing nothing when he knows Frankie is alone. My only saving grace is that Reggie's there and can't stand Cristiano any more than I can. I'm not worried about Frankie either—there's no way she's fucking around with him. But the thought of Flashdance there with her has me pissed off. And not necessarily *at* her, just with the situation. I'm a fucking mess.

I reach out a hand to help my sparring partner up. "Sorry, man. You okay?"

He nods as he rubs at the shoulder I nearly popped out of joint. "I'm okay, I think I'm done for the day though," he tells me as he leaves the Cage.

"Where were you, Hitman?" Leo hands me a towel, watching me.

"Fuck if I know. I was in my head, acting on autopilot," I

tell him, swiping the towel over my face.

"If Sonny were to see that shit, he'd have both of our asses. He barely trusts me with you as it is," he says, half jokingly.

"And that's the truth. I think I'm done for the day too. I have to get my mind right, Yoda. All of this shit with Frankie is fucking with me bad. I've never had such a problem disconnecting. Especially when I step into the Cage," I say in disgust.

Leo scoffs. "That's because you've never given a shit."

He's right, I haven't. But I do now. Too much. "What the fuck am I gonna do with her, bro? I'm still so mad I don't even want to speak to her, yet all I want is to hear her voice because it's the only thing that anchors me." Shaking my head, "I get all fired up, can't fucking think straight, and she's the one that calms the chaos. Ya know?"

"I do. You have to make a decision. Choose a side, brother." Smiling like that's all there is to it. "Do you want to call it quits with her? Where's your head?" Leo questions.

"No. No, I just don't want to be near her right now. She let me down and I'm not sure what to do with that," I admit.

"You know what you want, and you have a right to be upset. Just make sure this is the battle you want to wage and what you hope to achieve by fighting." I tell him the very basics of what's going on with her. I never could keep anything from him. "So now we both know that you're going home to her when this is all said and done and you're finished being pissed. But you need to allow yourself to just be pissed, stop pussy footing around it so that you can move past it." Leo claps a hand on my shoulder. "And don't ever put a sparring partner in an armbar like that again or I'm gonna snitch on you to your brother," he jokes.

"Just remember, bro, snitches get stitches." I toss him to the side and exit the Cage, laughing my ass off as he hurls good-natured insults at my retreating back.

TWELVE. TWELVE DAYS I've been away from the Princess. And I've felt every single one of them. Her texts still come every day, sometimes they're just song titles, other times random shit, but they're not coming as frequently. At first, at any given time of the day, I could look at my phone and see something from her, but after my lack of response, she's down to just two a day. I always read them. Always. I just don't always respond, instead keeping busy at the gym. Mr. New Recruit turned out to be a great sparring partner. Tough, willing, and able to take a punch.

I'm hurting her, but I can't stop. I can't fucking get over her going to see Andrew. I talked it out with Yoda . . . again, and he said I need to stop punishing the two of us, but fuck if I can find it in me to do that just yet.

A knock at the apartment door pulls me out of my head. I throw the door open to find Jodi on the other side.

"Your phone broke?" she asks.

"No, I forgot to turn it back on after my workout. What's up?" I ask, moving back so that she can enter. When she doesn't, I just raise my eyebrows in question.

"I can't stay, I just got on, but your mates want you to meet them down at the Sandbox. They called and asked me to deliver the message when they couldn't get a hold of you."

I look down at my watch and see that it's only ten P.M. and my gym time isn't until noon tomorrow. Plenty of time to have a couple of drinks and still be in top form when my brother gets his hands on me. I usually don't drink when I'm training this hard, but after the goodnight text from Frankie, I need a distraction.

Frankie: I miss you. I wish you would come home or at least call me. xoxo

"Thanks, Jo," I call to her retreating back. Hand raised in the air, she gives me a little finger wave.

Stepping into the foyer, I snatch my keys, wallet, and phone out of the bowl on the side table and head back out. As I walk past the reception area, Jodi calls out, "Oi, you going out to a Marine bar wearing a pink shirt?" I glance down before looking over at her.

"I'm more than man enough to rock pink. Plus, the ladies dig a man in pink." I toss her a wink and a wave and continue out the front door. Ignoring her yell to stay away from the ladies and *their* pink.

The bar is packed when I walk in. There's a band playing in the corner, writhing bodies taking up every square inch of the dance floor, and not an empty seat in the house. Not stopping, I head to the back of the room where I'm sure I'll find the guys at a secluded table. A round of catcalls and whistles rip through the air when they spot me. I lift my chin in greeting at the men I used to spend so much time with. Men I've trained with, fought beside. Braedon, Eddie, Cisco, and some guy I don't know nod back, and Leo kicks a chair out for me.

"Well, don't you look pretty with your pink shirt and your hair in a bun?" Snickering at himself, he signals for the waitress to come over.

"Don't be mad that this is the only pink you've seen in a while, bro."

The table erupts in a chorus of laughter as I give the girl my order and kick back on the legs of my chair, smiling at Leo.

"Yeah, well, we can't all be in complicated relationships with our hot as hell best friend. Can we?" he snipes.

"Wait! You're fucking Frankie?" Braedon groans. "You were supposed to hook me up with her, you asshole!"

I snort out a laugh. "There was no way in fuck I was ever letting you get anywhere near her, dude. Ever."

Cisco looks at him like he's lost his damn mind. "Really?

You honestly thought that would happen?" He looks so dumb-founded I can't help but snicker.

"Why not?" Braedon asks, offended. "Hitman let me take her out once when she came to visit," he says in total indignation.

"He let you give her a ride back to base because he had been drinking. That's not taking her out—that's playing taxi." The whole table is laughing now, remembering the night Leo is talking about except the one guy sitting with us I don't recognize. I'm just about to ask Leo who he is when he speaks up.

"So Frankie is a girl then?"

Braedon turns wide eyes on him. "Oh, yeah. She's a girl. A dancer. With the hottest ass and ra—" I smack him upside the head before he can finish.

"No talking about my girl's ass or her rack, fucker," I bite out, shooting him a warning look before turning back to the new guy.

"Like a stripper?" he asks, clearly intrigued.

Eddie bites back a laugh. "No, man. Like a legit dancer. Try not to piss the Hitman off before we even introduce your ass."

Looking embarrassed, he raises his hand in surrender. "No disrespect, bro. Nothing wrong with dating a stripper. I think they even wrote a song about it or some shit."

The table breaks out into laughter at his rambling to cover his ass.

"Since she's not a stripper, it's all good." I smile and reach a hand out, "Deacon. The boys call me the Hitman, but either is fine."

His hand stills before reaching mine. "Like the fighter?" Groans from the guys drown out whatever else he's saying.

"Fucking hell, Tommy. Don't feed that massive fucking ego of his."

"Wow. I'm a huge fan. I didn't even recognize you with clothes on." The hoots and hollers only get louder and more obnoxious. "I mean with a shirt on. No, not a shirt, it's just that I would recognize your body anywhere—I'm going to shut up now." Tommy bends and thunks his head against the table in embarrassment.

Eddie elbows him in the ribs. "You all done now or do you want to crawl under the table and get reacquainted with his body?" This kid is never gonna live this shit down.

He's saved by the cocktail waitress with the next round. They quiet down to just an occasional chuckle at Tommy's expense while she doles out everyone's drinks. Once she leaves, Leo raises his bottle. "To the Hitman and his recognizable 'body,' it's good have you back, brother." We clink bottles and let out a loud, "OORAH!"

WAY TOO MANY drinks later, we're sitting in the same place we've been all night, shooting the shit, telling stories about missions gone bad, brothers we lost, pranks we pulled, and Sergeant Major fucking Fraterelli. How a hardass like me survived him I'll never understand. Leo is right in the middle of telling a story about Braedon nearly pissing his pants when Fraterelli made me climb into the boxing ring with him one day just to prove to everyone that I wasn't as tough as I thought. He was right. Chuckling as Leo stands on his chair and animatedly embellishes the fuck out of the story, at least from what I remember, I down a shot and let it work its magic. Coursing through my bloodstream, I feel the effects of it and the eight others before. Body feeling weightless, eyes at half-mast, I let the numbness takeover. The chaos in my head quiets for the first time since I've been here. I'll need to call a cab, but this little reprieve from my thoughts and all of the fucked up feelings that go with them is worth it.

I lean back in my chair, feet planted wide, to listen to the rest of the story. My head falls back as I bark out a laugh at Eddie laughing so hard he shoots beer out of his nose.

"You boys sure are rowdy tonight," the hot blonde suddenly standing next to my chair teases, then glances my way with "fuck me" eyes for days. Her skirt is short, barely covering her ass and her shirt is cut low. Low enough to let me know that her tits are fake and she's not wearing anything under it. She reaches out and runs a hand over my stubbled cheek and points to my hair. "Man bun, huh? You're definitely not a Marine then."

I smirk. "Once a Marine always a Marine, honey."

The boy's slur out a little "OORAH." Her peach tinted lips spread into a smile as she sits in my lap, pressing her tits into my chest, leaning in. "I'm Lisa," she whispers, flicking her tongue against my lobe then sitting back a little, not so subtly grinding her ass into my cock as she does. I don't introduce myself. She doesn't really care what my name is anyway, just how good I'll fuck her. How many times I'll make her come. Chicks like this are all the same. Just looking for a Soldier to show them some glory. She'll drop to her knees on the dirty bar floor and be calling me Sir, all I have to do is pop my fly. I know her type. I've fucked her type more times than I can count.

The band breaks, the bartender throwing on the sound system in their absence. "I Belong to You" by Lenny Kravitz fills the room, making me smile as I think about how I played it for Frankie before everything went to shit. Lisa squeals excitedly and straddles my lap, throwing her arms around my neck, rolling her hips, thrusting out a lap dance to the beat of the song. I glance down to where we're connected and see that her skirt is now bunched around her waist, flashing her purple panties at me with every gyration. My dick hardens, which only makes her work me over even more. Pressing down so that my fly hits her clit with every movement.

Another time, another place, I would have taken her up on

her very blatant offer, probably in the fucking bathroom before the song ended. Hell, right here in a bar full of people with my boys sitting at the table. That's not the man I'm trying to be anymore though. Regardless what my cock thinks. I don't even miss that guy. All the nameless faces and meaningless fucks were fun, but nothing compared to what I have with Frankie. Once you get a piece of something real, bury yourself so deep inside of it that you don't recognize who you are anymore without her . . . there's no coming back from that. I don't want to come back from that. Ever.

Without warning, I stand, nearly dumping the chick on her ass. Saluting the table as a whole, I walk out of the bar, never glancing back. Behind me is my past, some of it good, some of it . . . not so much. I need to go after my future. I need to go home to my girl.

CHAPTER
Eleven

I WASN'T ABLE to get a flight out of Cali until later the next day, my brothers flying back with me. As much as I want to get home, I can wait on a commercial flight. I'm not Kanye. Thank fuck.

I didn't bother telling Frankie when she texted me that I'm coming home.

Frankie: Morning. Miss You. We need to talk. Xo

Me: Miss you

That was it. Short and simple. I don't want to be mad at her anymore. I'm sick as fuck of feeling this way. I just want to love her. Learn to be the man that she needs and deserves. All this relationship shit is hard. I see now how so many marriages end in divorce. People just too damn tired of fighting, of losing, of being beat down. We're not those people. I'll never stop fighting for her. I know in my heart, in my fucking soul, that I will never love another woman. I'm not even talking about not being *able* to love another woman *as much*, I mean straight up, I will never love anyone else as long as I live. I'm certain of it. She can take that shit to the fucking bank.

I had the whole plane ride to think about all of our shit. I still don't like her going to see Drew, but if she's determined to see him, I won't stop her. She can bet her sweet ass that Reg will be in the fucking room with them though. I want to know every single word said. I have no shame when it comes to Frankie, and I'll do whatever it takes. I understand what I have to do to make this work now. I'm not stupid enough to think that it will be easy to give my girl the attention she needs while I'm training for the biggest fight of my career, but I will make it happen. My stick and move mentality, still firmly in place, just needs some fucking adjustments.

We touch down at Midway just after eleven P.M., Bo there, waiting to take us home.

"What up, my man?" I greet him as I climb into the backseat. Mav pushes me in so that I almost fall on my face. Kicking at him, I ask Bo. "Everything okay at the house?" Reggie would've called if there was something up, but being back in the city with my girl, knowing that I'm close, has me anxious.

"Yeah, been pretty quiet. Nobody has left all that much really," he reports as he heads for the expressway.

"Good. Drop me off first. You can just go home after you drop these fools at their place."

Bo glances at me in the rearview. "You sure? I don't mind coming back once I leave them."

"Nah, I'm sure. It's late." He nods in agreement.

Sonny cranks the rearview mirror to face him and pins me with a stern gaze. "You realize your ass is in the gym early as hell tomorrow right? All this flying back and forth shit doesn't get you any breaks."

Inwardly I groan, but I know better than to challenge him on it. "Yeah, I got it, Jameson. I'll be there at ten." There's no way that's gonna fly, but I try and elbow Mav in the ribs when he snickers. He knows it ain't happening either.

"You wish, little brother. Seven A.M. gym time and if you're even a minute late, I'm coming after you."

"Sonny, by the time you get home, you won't be getting very much sleep. You're gonna be all cranky and shit," I tease knowing damn well that my older brother could go without sleeping ever again and still function like the upstanding fucking citizen he is.

"Seven, Deac," he says flatly before twisting the mirror back to its original position.

My head hits the rest behind me. I push the brim of my baseball cap up and rough my hands over my face and beard in exhaustion. I just want to get home, crawl into bed beside Frankie, and sleep for a month. I haven't slept for shit since I've been gone and I'm aware that it's because I wasn't wrapped around the Princess.

"Hey, what went on at the bar last night? Leo said for the first time since he's known you that you turned down free pussy," Mav asks, head cocked and eyebrows raised in question.

"Same shit as usual, dude. Chick looking to get fucked. Thought about it for half a second and then realized where I needed to be." Yanking the bill of my hat over my eyes, I'm hoping he gets the hint that I'm done talking about it. Apparently, he doesn't realize that's what it means. He for sure doesn't give a shit.

"What do you mean you thought about it? Frankie isn't just one of your gir—"

"You can shut the fuck up before you get hit, Maverick. I *thought* about it because I'm a guy. A guy who hasn't gotten any ass in almost two weeks. Thinking about *maybe* getting your dick wet isn't the same as actually doing it, for one. And for two, I would never cheat on Frankie." He should know this.

"What about Brazil?" Sonny asks solemnly from his seat up front.

Jackknifing to an upright position, I whip my cap off. "What about Brazil, bro?" I demand, the muscle in my jaw starting to tick in time with my heart. "What about it?" I repeat, hitting the back of his chair, insisting he answer me.

"The two girls, Deacon," he tells me, exasperated, as Mav just sits there watching us finish what he started.

"I'm not even sure I did anything with them, Sonny." He turns and just looks at me in that silent way of his and I know that I did. My brother wouldn't lie to me about it. Not about something this important. "Fuck," I hiss out under my breath. I had hoped that I couldn't remember any of it because nothing went down. "Well, it shouldn't fucking count if you don't remember it." That's bullshit; I'm not fooling anyone with that excuse. Complete and total bullshit, but it's what I need to tell myself. What I need to tell them.

"Maybe it shouldn't, but it does," Mav adds.

"We weren't together then. We had been broken up for months and her coming to see me before the fight fucked with my head. I was drinking way too much and you know it. We weren't together," I say again quietly. My voice thick with regret.

"And you are now? How is now any different, Deac?" Sonny questions.

"Now is different because I know that she's at home, at my home, in my bed. Waiting for me. She's where she's supposed to be and I don't plan on letting either one of us forget that again. I'm going home. To her."

I don't realize that we've arrived until the truck rocks to a stop. Popping the door, I grab my duffel. "I'll see you guys in the gym at seven."

Just as I'm jumping down, Sonny says, "I'm certain that you love her. I see how much every time you look at her, Deacon. Don't throw that away. You'll never find it again. Trust me," he says cryptically. I glance at Mav who shakes his head, and I nod that I understand, exiting the truck and shooting them a wave as Bo heads back down the drive.

I don't even have to bother with trying to find my keys. As soon as my foot hits the top step, the front door swings open and

Reggie is standing there waiting for me. He's as bad as Sonny. Neither of these motherfuckers sleep.

"How was the flight, brotha?" he asks, stepping out of the way so that I can enter.

"Better than the car ride home," I grit out, passing him.

He cocks a brow questioningly.

"Nothing, Reg. My brothers just rode my ass the whole way and I'm beat. I need to be at the gym by seven. I told Bo to just go home after dropping the assholes off." Turning to the stairs, "I just want to get my hands on Frankie and get some sleep."

I'm three steps up when he calls out to me in a loud whisper, "Yo, Deac." Pivoting I turn to face him. "She's not alone," he says, scratching the underside of his chin with the back of his fingers. "I told Bo to let you know, he must have forgot."

Stunned, I walk down the steps I just went up. "Are they in my room?" I bite out through gritted teeth, my blood getting ready to sear my veins. He nods that they are. "They went up a little while ago, Frankie wasn't feeling well again and didn't want to be alone. It's the third time this week." The concern is evident in his voice. He needs to be concerned with keeping me from killing someone.

"You didn't think the fact that she's sleeping with someone else in my bed was something that you should have maybe fucking called and told me?" I bark at him in disgust. "Is it Flashdance? I swear to fuck, I'll kill him." Spinning, I take the stairs two at a time in my haste to get up there and just start wrecking shit.

"Whoa, Deac, wait!" he whisper-shouts, clamping a beefy hand on my shoulder to stop my progress. "You thought she was up here with Flashdance and I didn't call you? Brother, I would have kicked his pretty boy ass before he made it through the front door. But he's been around. Calling and popping up at the studio. Frankie hasn't been alone with him much though aside from whatever classes they're teaching."

"I figured his ass would make sure he was around since I was gone. I fucking knew it! Is that why she canceled her classes?" I bite out.

"Not sure, bro."

"So it's not, Flashdance up there, right?"

Chuckling he gives me a little shake. "Indie has been staying here since you've been gone, but lately she's been sleeping in the room with her. Frankie asked her to." Letting his arm drop he shakes his head at me. "I just wanted to give you a heads up because I'm not a hundred percent on how those two roll and what you might find going in there, ya know? But they're chicks, so it's cool, right? I never even thought to call you about them sleeping in the same room together." His brows are drawn in thought. "I guess since Indie swings both ways I should have though, huh?"

The relief that washes over me is so immense it almost makes me weak. "Motherfucker, I almost went in there and started knocking heads," hitting him in the arm hard enough to make him stumble.

Rubbing at the spot, "Sorry, bro," he says on a laugh. "I didn't mean to get you all worked up. I never even thought about it, honestly." Sobering, he says, "We do need to talk about what's been going on while you've been gone . . . it's serious shit. Nothing that I can't handle though. And trust we won't let Frankie out of our sight, but I want to bring you up to speed so that you're on the same page." He waves me off, "Now go to bed and try not to wake up the girls while you're up there, they've had a rough couple days. Everything else will wait 'til tomorrow."

Throwing one more shot to his arm, I start back up the stairs, but turn back to Reggie, "Did she go see him?" I question, although I'm not sure I want to know the answer.

"Who? Drew? No, never even mentioned it after you left."

My heart rate slowing to a normal rhythm, I nod, thanking

him because I needed to hear it. He's right, we can talk later about all the other shit. I head to my room. If I have to, I'll sleep in Frankie's bedroom tonight, but I need to go put eyes on her at least. I want nothing more than to climb into bed with her, fuck it if Indie is in there. If I can, I'm climbing in with both of them. Indie can be pissed about it all she wants . . . in the morning.

Quietly opening the door, I slip in and walk over to the bed. She's lying on her side of the bed facing me. Hands tucked under her cheek, hair splayed out across the pillows. Careful not to wake her, I squat next to the bed and brush the hair off her face, just taking a moment to watch her sleep. I glance next to her to where Indie is sound asleep in my spot, arm curled around my girl. I've never been jealous of Indie before. I am now. Not because she's in bed spooning my girl, but because I'm not. Knowing that there's no room for my ass, I place a kiss to Frankie's head. Rising, I leave the room as quietly as I entered.

Once in her room, I strip down to my boxer briefs, climb into bed, and bury my face in the pillow that still smells faintly of the Princess. It's as close as I'll get to being in bed with her tonight.

The next morning the alarm goes off at a quarter to six. Hitting the shower, I groan at the lack of sleep I got the night before and the fact that I'll probably be in the gym hitting it hard for the next ten hours. I don't mind the beating I'm going to take, but I mind waiting so long to connect with Frankie. There's no way Frankie is going to be up before I leave and I'm not sure I'll see her until I get home tonight if she doesn't come into the gym. After being gone for so long I just want to get my hands on my girl. Tell her I missed her and that there won't be anymore running. From either of us.

Snatching up my duffel, I grab clothes from it so that I don't have to wake the girls by going into my room. Five minutes later, I'm out the door, making plans for the talk I'll be having with Frankie tonight. After I catch up with Reg and find out what went down while I wasn't here. Where I should have been.

I SMELL HER before I actually see her. She's walking toward me at a clipped pace, Flashdance right fucking behind her calling her name. Turning so that I'm facing her fully, I let my eyes sweep down her front looking for an injury, that's how flustered she seems.

"Princess?" I question, taking a step in her direction, my heart starting to beat faster. She's making me nervous. Finally she's in front of me and I can see the wild look in her eyes. The rapidly beating pulse at her throat. I'm just about to pull her to me when Cristiano reaches out and tugs on her arm to stop her. Frankie comes to a halt and glances back at him and shakes her head no and he drops his hold. "What the fuck is going on?" I demand as my brothers and Pop stop what they're doing and come to my side, followed by Guy.

"Deac, I need to speak to you. All of you really." Her voice is so shaky, so timid, I'm not sure what to think. Something isn't right though. Nodding, I take the towel that Sonny hands me, wiping it over my face I sling it around my neck and wait her out. Just when I think that she's not going to say shit, she blurts out in a rush, "I'm going to Spain with Cristiano." The silence is deafening. Deafening and all-consuming, as is the rage that starts from deep within and then explodes from my every pore, working its way out of my mouth.

"The fuck you are. The. Fuck. You. Are," I grit out between clenched teeth.

Everyone starts talking at once around me, everyone but Frankie, who hasn't broken eye contact. The pleading look in her eyes undoes me. What is she begging me for? My blessing? Not gonna fucking happen and she knows it. It's gotta be something else. I've been gone for two weeks. Two fucking weeks that she texted me daily, not once mentioning that she was getting back together with him and for damn sure not anything about Spain. I'm trying to get a grip on the situation, but I can't. She's not fucking going anywhere though, I do know that. Especially with this asshole.

I watch as she walks just a little closer before stopping and swallowing. Guy and my brothers are still talking over one another, getting louder and louder by the second. Slicing my hand through the air to silence them and their questions, I look to her for answers.

"I'm not safe, Deac. They're getting desperate. I'm not sure if Reggie has told you anything about what happened while you were gone." When I shake my head no, she continues, "They tried to ki-kill Andrew," her voice thick with tears. "They didn't find what they're looking for. It's just a matter of time before they come looking for me again and I'm not hard to find. I won't survive that again, Deacon. I won't." The tears are flowing now, the fear palpable, visible in the way her body trembles. This is my girl and she's terrified. Why the fuck didn't anyone tell me? My eyes dart over every inch of her, willing my mind to form a plan. I'll die for her, that's not even a question, but there's no way she's leaving. Not with him. Not with anyone.

"No," slips past my lips. It's firm and succinct. No room for argument as I meet her gaze head on.

"Dea—"

"I said no, Frankie," I interject, shaking my head.

"But Deacon, you don—"

"You are not fucking leaving with him. He cannot keep you saf—"

"I'm pregnant, Deacon," she shouts, silencing me. "I'm pregnant." This time it's said on an expelled breath before her hand quickly covers her mouth.

Not stopping to even let what she said sink in, I retort, "Baby's not his." I say it so calmly you would think that my blood isn't racing through my veins. Like my heart isn't about to shoot right out of my throat. Like it's just her and I in the room and we don't have an audience. Like my girl isn't standing in front of me telling me that she's pregnant with my baby, and it *is* my baby, and leaving with another man. As I'm about to tell her again, Flashdance, who I'm about to start calling Death Wish, opens his fucking mouth.

"How are you so sure that she's not carrying my baby? How dare you just assume that everything is about you all the time? Who's to say that isn't my chi—"

My arm shoots out and I point at him in warning, satisfied when he flinches at my swift movement. "You shut your fucking mouth right now. If Frankie's pregnant, it's my baby." Bringing my eyes back to hers, I lock on those blues. "Even if it weren't mine, it would be. You feel me?" The words aren't for him and she knows it. Her face softens and she nods once, telling me all I need to know. Not that I ever thought differently. Without looking away, "Give us a minute alone." As my brothers and dad shuffle past, they each kiss the Princess swiftly on the cheek, her dad lingers, pulling her into a tight embrace and whispering softly to her in Italian. Finally, they all make it out the door, leaving just Frankie and I . . . and Cristiano. "Tell him to go back to his place, Frankie." My tone leaves no room for misinterpretation. I'm giving her the chance to handle this before I do. She swallows and holds my gaze.

"I'm sorry. Go home, Cristiano."

"Are you sure, mi amor?" he asks haltingly.

"Yes, I'm sure."

"All right, I'll stop by your place later tonight. You shouldn—"

"No, Cristiano. Go home. To Spain," Frankie says gently.

My lips kick up in a slow smile, the tension in my shoulders easing as I hear what she's saying. I watch as she takes a deep breath and turns to face him.

"I've let you stay too long. I knew what you wanted. What you hoped for. And I let you stay anyway. I'm sorry for that. You didn't deserve for me to let you think we could be more. I missed our connection, dancing with you, and I was selfish." She steps closer and reaches for his hand and it takes everything in me to not growl like some kind of fucking beast. "I hope that you can forgive me and believe me when I tell you that I never intended to make you believe that we could be more." Eyes cast down, "He's the other half of me, he always has been. Always will be. I've been unfair to you both because of my fears."

My shoulders bunch as he places a finger under her chin to force her to look at him.

"I knew. I always knew. I just hoped I could be enough to change your mind even if I couldn't change your heart." I watch, dangerously close to losing my cool as he places his lips to her forehead. "I will go back, but please understand that you can come to me at any time and I will take care of you. When he hurts you . . . I will be waiting to welcome you, to love you and your baby." Without another word he turns and strides out of the weight room.

Every fiber of my being wants to celebrate the fact that he is gone and that *she* had been the one to send him away. I hold back because although Frankie was gentle, it still hurt her to hurt him. Fuck him though with his little parting dig about me hurting her and being there to take care of my kid. Over my fucking dead body. She's my woman and that's my baby. Holy shit.

"I'm going to be a dad," I whisper reverently. In awe. In fear. She turns to me and smiles softly, questioningly, tears spilling over to dance down her face. I reach my hand out and pull her to me. When she's flush against my body, I place a kiss against her head, before leaning back to kiss the trail of tears on her cheeks. Gripping her torso, my thumbs settling just under her breasts, I lift her, resting my forehead against her belly, her hands going to my shoulders. I take a deep breath and let the moment wash over me. A baby. I never thought . . . a baby. Smiling, I place small kisses to her stomach and then slowly lower her back down, letting every part of her slide against me until her feet touch the ground. I'm just about to start hitting her with a barrage of questions when there's a knock at the door.

"Sorry to interrupt you guys, but Frankie's appointment is here and you have a phone call from the Federation holding, Deacon," Julia, our receptionist, says.   Nodding we signal that we're coming.

"We'll talk as soon as we get home, yeah?" I don't want to wait, but I clearly have no choice, and this isn't really the place anyway.

"I'd like that," Frankie says quietly as I drop my arms and walk her to the door.

Stopping, I place a kiss to her wrist. "I'm gonna be a dad," I say with my lips pressed against her soft skin. The awe is still very much apparent in my words as a smile, this one bigger than the last, creeps across my face. Jesus fuck, we're having a baby.

CHAPTER
Twelve

REGGIE BROUGHT THE Princess back to the house a while ago now. I had to sit in on a conference call with the head honchos at EWF before I could pack it up for the day and go home to my girl. I tell Mav to pick Indie up and let the boys know they will have the night off. I want to be alone when I talk to Frankie. No outside interruptions. I'll talk with Reggie about all that's been going on later and why the fuck he didn't clue my ass in.

We talked briefly earlier and my blood ran cold when he said that he'd intercepted another letter, this one saying that next time "We won't miss." Assuming they're talking about their attempt on Drew's life. And that if he doesn't cooperate soon she'll be next. My fucking ass she will. As well as a picture of Frankie in one of her classes, that sent my blood from cold to boiling. Reggie said he was pretty sure it was taken from outside of the studio though. Had he told me any of this, I would have come the fuck home immediately. Reggie assured me that if he felt that it was out of his control, he would have had my ass on the next plane to Chicago. It's just hard to trust someone else with her safety. Now that I'm not so pissed anymore, I can see how stupid it was leaving her here to begin with.

The smell of garlic and tomatoes cooking greets me the moment I walk in. Music floating softly around the room. Frankie is standing at the stove stirring a big pot. Hearing me enter, she turns and smiles tentatively. I'm not sure what that's all about.

"Hey, I made chicken cacciatore and pasta; it has a few minutes yet though," she tells me in that sweet voice of hers. Nodding, I lean over her shoulder to look into the pot, breathing deeply. She thinks I'm trying to catch the scent of the sauce simmering, but really it's her that I want filling my lungs.

"Perfect, I'm starving, and I can use the carbs right about now. Sonny is working my ass hard."

Frankie just chuckles. "It's the belt, Deac. You're gonna be pushed to all of your limits and then he's gonna push you farther still. That's why you chose him to train you. He'll never let you give up." I nod in agreement. She's right. I wouldn't be where I am in my career without Sonny.

"Yeah, well, with the way we're training now, I'll be in top form come fight night."

"I'm sure you'll be all that and more, so that's good. If you want, I can work up a couple routines for you. You'll need strong foot work to stay off the mat with this guy." She turns and rests against the counter, watching me. Then she totally flips the script on me, talk about needing quick feet. "Why didn't you call?" Frankie asks quietly. Looking down at her bare toes for a second before bringing her eyes back up to mine.

Sighing deeply, I glance away to collect my thoughts, searching for the words to explain how I feel without hurting her. Meeting her steady gaze, I say gruffly, "I was mad. I was mad as fuck, Princess. I'm still a little pissed to be honest." I shake my head in disgust. "Not one ounce of me understands your need to see him. It fucked with my head until all I saw was you lying in that hospital bed. All those fucking machines. God, I was so scared." I press my thumb and index finger into my closed eyes, trying to rid myself of the image. Dragging my hand down my face, I rub my lips roughly before continuing, "I've been to war zones that didn't scare me as much as the

possibility of living a life without you in it did. I've seen horrible shit, but none of it compared to you lying there lifeless, a machine breathing for you." I laugh humorlessly, "You wanting to see him for even a moment just did my ass in. It was too much for me. I've never been that angry with you, and I didn't know how to deal . . . so I left." I cross my arms across my chest, part of me wanting to shake her just recalling the conversation we had, and the other part wanting to draw her into me and claim her until there's no room left in her mind to even think about going to see him. I'm lost in my own turbulent thoughts when she jars me with her raspy voice.

"Dance with me, Deac. Please? Dance with me?" There's a soft plea behind her words that undoes me. I let my arms fall and reach for her, pulling her in close and molding our bodies together. The music plays as we sway back and forth, just barely. There's no finesse or even skill to what we're doing, but I don't care as long as I can hold my girl. I smile thinking about her news today, my little family. The words of the song wash over me. My girl, speaking music. It's no accident "Say You Love Me" is playing. She's telling me what my leaving did to her faith in us, in my feelings. I run my hand up the center of her back, fingers splayed wide as they make their way over her nape to tangle in her hair. I pull gently, forcing her head back so that I can see her. "I love you, Princess. Always have. Always will. I'm not going anywhere, you feel me?" Tears fill her eyes as Jessie Ware sings on in the background. Frankie closes her eyes, the tears escaping from behind her lids. Wiping them away, I touch my thumb to her bottom lip, pulling down on it, before covering it with my own. As she exhales, I swallow the relief that breath holds. Deepening the kiss, I pull her tighter against me, my tongue tracing the seam of her mouth as my fingers trip over the bumps of her spine.

Frankie arches into me, pressing every inch of her softness into the hard planes of my body. She keeps that shit up and she knows what's gonna happen. Open palm sliding over her ass, I pull back, placing one more kiss to her swollen lips. "Why don't you tell me a little more about this baby thing?" my smile instantaneous. "Why didn't you call me to tell me, and how did you find out?" I ask as I lead her over to the island and lift her onto a stool, taking the one next to her.

"I did call and text. You barely answered any of them and it's not something I thought I should tell you over the phone." She puffs out a breath. "I was planning to leave with Cristiano as soon as you got back. I just wasn't sure when that would be." Hopping down from the stool, she goes over to the stove and gives the sauce a stir. I ignore the "leaving with Cristiano" shit for now because I can see the wheels turning as she stares into the pot like it holds all the damn answers of the world.

"What is it? Just go ahead and ask, Frankie." I have a feeling I know what she's thinking about, but I want her to say it. My reasons are more than selfish. One, I don't want to bring it up if I'm wrong, and two, I like it when she's jealous. It's hot as fuck. I don't want her to ever be insecure or not trust me because I meant what I told my brothers: I'll never cheat on her. Clearly, I'm a fuck up when it comes to breaks, but I don't plan on any more of those, so I'm golden.

"I want you to ask me, Frankie." I watch her profile, the way she has her lips pursed, chewing on the inside corner as she thinks about what she wants to say.

Finally she speaks up. "Did you see Jodi while you were in Cali?" She's trying to be nonchalant about it. I grin smugly. "I always see Jodi when I go," I answer being obtuse on purpose. I really should put her out of her misery; she's been through enough. But for the first time in what feels like forever, I don't have to worry about my answer. And fuck me if that doesn't feel good. "Are you asking if I fucked her while I was there or just if I saw her? The answers are different so I want to be clear." My elbows resting on the granite countertop, I watch as she wars with herself. She wants to ask but is afraid of the answer and that hurts my fucking heart. I want her to be sure of the answer. To have no doubt that she can ask and not be hurt by what I tell her. That's on me though, not Frankie. "I want to hear you say it, Princess. Don't pretend you're not over there dying to ask. So ask."

"We're not together, Deac, so it doesn't really matter, does it?" she asks as she places the spoon down.

"Who's not together?" I snort out a laugh. "You pregnant with my baby?" Not waiting for her to answer, I go on, "Trust me, Princess, we're together as fuck. You tell yourself whatever it is you need to, but your ass is mine. Now ask me," I demand.

Eyes narrowed, she watches me a second. "Did you sleep with Jodi while you were there?" she asks in a rush.

Without hesitation, I answer, "No. Not her or anyone else while I was there. Now will you kindly feed me and then let me *eat?*" I flash her a wicked grin and let my gaze travel down her body and then back up, my smile growing with every inch of her skin that flushes under my perusal. "I've worked up quite an appetite over the last twelve days, Princess." I watch as her breathing deepens. "And you're the one that I want." As I'm about to get up and carry her ass off to the bedroom—dinner can wait—I hear the front door open and then slam closed. The fuck?

"Hey, Deacon?" I hear Sonny call out before he is standing in the kitchen with us. "Oh, good, you're home. Hey, Frankie. That smells incredible," he says as he places a kiss on her head. "You have enough for one more? I'm starving." We both answer at once, my emphatic "no" ignored as my pain in the ass brother takes a seat next to me at the island.

"He can take his shit to go, Princess," I tell her, glaring at Sonny's profile. He's always been a cock-blocker.

My shitty tone does nothing to deter my brother, never has, probably why he and I have thrown down on more than one occasion. Seems like the only way to get him to take my mood seriously. Maybe I should dot his eye now, then he might get the hint that he should take his ass home. My girl clearly doesn't think I'm intimidating either.

"What do you want to drink, Sonny?" Frankie asks as she places a pasta bowl in front of him.

"I'll take a beer if you have it." Fucker. He's well aware that I can't drink right now. "Mmmmmm, did someone tell you I was coming over? Your chicken cacciatore is my favorite." The Princess smiles at his praise.

"No, as a matter of fact, they did not. Wanna know how I know? Because she was just about to let me take her upstairs and fu—"

Smile now gone, Frankie interrupts me by shoving a piece of hot Italian bread into my mouth. "Shut up and eat, Deac," she demands. Shooting daggers at me as she sets my food down.

Jameson shakes his head at me in mock disappointment, clucking his tongue like a ninety-year-old prude. "Is that any way to speak about the mother of your child?" he deadpans, fighting to keep a straight face. Turning to Frankie, he sets his smile on her. "Speaking of which, I never got a chance to properly congratulate you before Tarzan here kicked us out. I never thought I'd see the day that Deacon would become a dad. I damn sure didn't think that he would be the first," my brother says chuckling, although I detect a hint of sadness behind his words.

Frankie walks around the counter and into his embrace, murmuring to him low enough that I can't hear them, so I just look on and watch my oldest brother, coach, and best friend interact with my girl while I dunk my bread in the sauce pooling around the chicken on my plate. They're obviously having a moment. "If you two are finished hugging all up on each other, why don't you tell me why you're here, bro?" I go back to my food and wait for him to answer. Finally, he sets Frankie aside.

"We need to go over your schedule for the next week. I have them putting the Cage up in the basement. They took it down to paint, but I want you in it every day, getting a feel for it. You train better when you're surrounded by chain link for some reason," he says grinning. "I also have a wrestler coming in to help us figure out how to beat Rude Awakening on the mats. I had Mav call Crew to recommend someone for us to reach out to." Sonny pauses to take a bite, I watch him, trying to figure out what his deal is.

"And why did this have to go down tonight? Wasn't I just in the gym with you for the last ten fucking hours?" What the hell is going on? "Do I not have a seven A.M. gym time tomorrow as well? Why the house call, Jameson?"

Sighing, he shrugs, "I just wanted to come check on the Princess." He jerks his head in her direction. "That was quite the bombshell that you dropped on us earlier." Sonny chuckles and then sobers, turning to face Frankie fully. "Are you feeling okay?" I can hear the tinge of worry in his voice. He's concerned about her, I get it, but he's acting strangely.

Frankie slides onto the stool next to him and rests her head on his shoulder. "I'm fine. Just normal pregnancy stuff that finally makes sense to me. I couldn't figure out why I was so tired all the time, or nauseous, why my boobs got so damn big."

Pointing my fork at her, I interrupt. "My brother does not need to know a thing about your tits. At all. Ever." Eyebrows raised in a "you feel me" manner I nod and go back to my food.

"You're impossible, you see that, right?" she asks as she tries to smother the threatening grin.

"Impossible or not, no tit talk." I wink, taking a bite of chicken.

Jameson laughs from his spot in between us. "I'm siding with Deac on this one, Princess." To soften the blow, he places a quick kiss to the side of her head and goes back to his food.

About an hour later, I finally get Jameson to leave, locking up behind him. Alarm set, I head back to the kitchen and watch as Frankie flits about, cleaning up our dinner mess.

"Can I help with that?"

She jumps, startled. "Oh my God, Deacon. You scared the shit out of me." Hand to her chest she laughs nervously. "No, I'm all finished," Frankie tells me right as she lets out a huge yawn. "I'm sorry, I am so exhausted. This is later than I've been up in a couple of weeks," she admits.

I can see just how tired she is. Apparently she hadn't slept well while I was away either. Slowly I raise my arm and hold out my hand for her to take. When she places her tiny, soft hand in my rough, calloused one, I'm home. She's all I'll ever need and now she's so much more. Frankie is not only my best friend, the love of my fucking life . . . she's the mother of my child. The only one who will ever own that title. The only one I want to. I'm going to wife the fuck out of her. She just doesn't know it yet.

CHAPTER
Thirteen

I'VE BEEN BACK for a week now and although Frankie warned me that she would be way busier with Flashdance gone, I didn't realize *how* busy. Between my killer hours I've had to put in at the gym to be ready for a fight I'm not sure will happen and her schedule, I haven't seen her for shit. I'm worried that she's doing too much, but you can't tell her stubborn ass anything. My brothers are keeping a close eye on her, especially Sonny, so that makes me feel better.

She's asleep when I leave in the morning and sleeping long before I get home, and not always in my room. She's still trying to make sure we take it slow, and I'm still all, "Get in my fucking bed." If she happens to be in hers, I just pick her up and carry her to mine. She can try to be cautious all she wants, as long as she does it from the king size in my room.

On my way to the weight room to meet up with my brothers, I slow down to glance into Frankie's studio when I hear Rihanna singing some dirty shit. I know what that means and I know that if I watch too long, I'll be bench pressing with a massive hard on. I can't not watch for at least a minute though. Grabbing the frame above my head, I press my forehead to the cool glass of the picture window. A window that obviously is a glimpse into heaven or as close as I'll ever get. Shaking my head, I tear my eyes away from my girl twerking like she's starring in a rap video and reluctantly leave. Fuck me, she is hotter than any woman should be. Adjusting myself, I try to get into the mental space to throw some weights.

A couple hours later, I'm in the basement, finally finished for the day, just lying on the floor of the Cage going over the techniques we worked on that I would need to beat Rude Awakening. My brother was right as usual—I do train better in the Cage. Popping up, I walk over to my gear and pull out my phone and shoot Frankie a message.

Me: You still here or home?

I'm running a towel over my sweat dampened skin when I get an incoming text.

Frankie: Still here, just finished my last class. What's up?

Perfect.

Me: Come to the basement.

Frankie: Be right down

Dropping my phone and towel in the corner with the rest of my stuff, I go over to the gate of the Cage and wait for my girl. It doesn't take long before the door opens and she's standing there, fuck-me heels and all.

"Lock the door, Princess," I call out. She shoots me a puzzled look but does it any way. As she makes her way toward me, I take in the soft swell of her belly. Now that she's told me that she's pregnant, it seems so obvious.

"What are we doing here?" Frankie asks as she makes her way up the two steps that will bring her to me.

"It's quiet down here and I can have you all to myself for a little bit," I tell her, snaking an arm around her waist and

pulling her in so that all of her is pressed up against all of me. My hand is splayed wide on the small of her back, holding her there. I dip my head to place a kiss to my spot. "Just wanted to get hands on you before we both have to get back to work."

Her hands flutter over my abs, then around to run up my back, effectively making me shudder. "So you brought me down here to the basement to have your wicked way with me? Is that right? Up against the Cage?" She follows her line of questioning up with light kisses against my chest, my bicep, wherever she can reach as I tower over her.

I wish I could say that she was wrong, that I called her down her for something other than to dirty her up, but I didn't. I had every intention of fucking her in this Cage, just like I said I would and never had the chance to. "Remember that bet? It was months ago, and it's time to pay up, Princess," I tell her. She looks up at me through heavy lids.

"I thought that you forgot all about that. It's not like you to wait so long to call in a bet."

"Oh, trust I didn't forget. Just waiting for the perfect time to collect," I say as I lower my head to nip at her lip. Frankie opens her mouth to allow me access. I don't take it. Instead I pull her farther into the Cage, dancing us backwards until the gate slams shut with a soft clang. "You're in my house now, baby. It's all about my rules here." Winking, I settle both my hands on her ass, squeezing and kneading through the puffy material of her skirt as I watch her thoughts play across her face. First the want, then the worry, then the want again. "I'm not sure what you're worried about, but you can lock that shit up, Princess. It's just you and me here, and I want you wrapped around me, sooner rather than later. So no worrying, you feel me?"

She looks at me a little surprised that I could read her so well though I don't understand why. I've always been able to. She's like an open book to me most days.

Frankie smiles that smile at me, the one that pulls me in,

consumes me, gives and takes, and it's all the invitation I need. My hand tangles in her long hair. I yank gently, pulling her head back so that she's arched, her tits pushed forward and her neck exposed. The pulse fluttering against smooth skin as inviting as her smile. My mouth makes its way to that spot, gliding over the elegant lines of her throat, my tongue tasting the salt on her skin. Lips pressed to her neck, I make it to where it meets her shoulder and bite, eliciting a low moan from Frankie. It always gets a reaction. My favorite kind of reaction.

I find my way to the plunging vee of her top and place an open-mouthed kiss to the tops of each rounded globe. Running my nose along the edges, I nudge the material out of the way until one of her creamy tits is free. My mouth closes around the dark pink nipple. Releasing it slowly, I turn my face and do the same with the other side. Now that both of her tits are uncovered, I take my time laving over each, sucking as much into my mouth as I can. Her hands are resting on my forearms, fingernails biting into the skin. The pain fueling my need to be inside her. I drag callused fingertips over her exposed back, under the skirt she's trying to kill me with, until I hit the crease of her ass tracing the line under the cheek at the top of her thigh before lifting her. My mouth never once leaves her flushed skin. Dipping inward, I rub against her pussy as she wraps her legs around me, locking her ankles at the small of my back, pressing us tighter together. My shorts are no match for my cock, straining against the thin nylon material. Her head thrown back, she moans softly.

"God, I've missed you so much, missed your hands and mouth on me. The way you make me feel," she says, hips rolling in a sensual pattern, my cock jerking against her ass as she does. "I want you to fuck me. Fuck me against the Cage, Deac. Show me how much you missed me."

Growling around the nipple in my mouth, I release it with a pop, "I'll fuck you, Frankie. I'll show you everything, baby, but

it won't be against the Cage." My gaze touches on every bit of her exposed to me. "Nah, there's no way I'll let the Cage leave its mark on you," I tell her as I stalk to the coated chain link and lean so that it's my back against it, my skin that will be left wearing the indentations our fucking will definitely make.

"Wrap your arms around me and hold on, Princess." Once she does, I let go of her and yank down my shorts and boxer briefs, my cock surging forward like it's searching for her. She has a tie at her hip that she tugs on, her skirt falling open completely before it drifts to the mat, leaving her in nothing but the tiniest scrap of lace and the little black top that might as well be on the floor too since it's doing nothing to cover her. "You're fucking beautiful, you know that? Abso-fucking-lutely perfect." With her hands wrapped around my shoulders and her legs around my waist, I'm able to let go. I settle her a little lower on my hips so that I can easily slip a hand in between us. Palm flat, I push back on her chest gently, forcing her to lean back just a little. Dragging one finger up and down the seam of her panties, over her clit and back down, I can feel how wet she is. Pushing the lace into her wetness, I allow one more pass over her clit before snagging my finger in the lace keeping me out of the pussy I want into so badly. With a yank, my finger rips through the fragile material. I work my fingers inside the tear and widen them until I've created crotchless panties. "There it is. There's that sweet pussy I love so much," I tell her with a wicked grin. Frankie doesn't wait for direction from me as she lifts herself so that my cock is between us. Rubbing against it, her head falls forward, resting against mine as she teases us both.

"*You're* so fucking wet, my *cock* is so fucking wet . . . from you," I tell her just before I catch her hips and thrust into her hard and high, her breath catching. "You wanna keep teasing me, Princess, or you wanna fuck me?" I growl as I work myself inside of her even further, the head of my cock bumping against the walls of her pussy. Her hands shoot up to grab onto the chain link over my shoulders, giving her a better hold. Using her legs and her grip, she raises herself up almost completely and then slams back down. Both of us moaning in unison.

"I heard about pregnant pussy being the best pussy and didn't believe it, but they were right. Jesus fuck, they were right. Put it on me, Frankie," I murmur through gritted teeth as she pulses around me in waves. She uses the Cage as leverage as she bounces on my cock, each time taking me deeper than the last. I bury my face in her tits. Nipping and licking, sucking and biting in a state of desperation. It's almost too much, what I feel. What she's doing to me and where we are all adding to my heightened senses.

Sliding my hands under her ass, I hold her suspended away from me, just the tip of my cock being squeezed as I pull out, waiting until her blues land on me. Once she's looking into my eyes, I slide back in to the base, over and over, fucking her as she clings to me, completely trusting, completely open. I feel her tightening around me, tensing in my arms, telling me that she's close. Frankie's head lolls back on her shoulders, her long hair swaying against her back. Feathering over my hands gripping her ass. Her mouth falls open, my name leaving it on a breathless whimper that grows in volume as she falls apart, her pussy like a vise around my cock, the pulsating grip almost painful.

"That's it, baby, you know what I want," I grunt as I fight off my own orgasm. Moving her slowly now, I allow her to ride it out and give myself a chance to regain some control. I wasn't lying—pregnant pussy is a beautiful fucking thing. She's tighter, if that's even possible. I thought so before, but figured it was because we hadn't been together in awhile. She's more responsive to the slightest movement it seems. It's making it nearly impossible to keep from losing my shit right now. Frankie leans back in my arms, her hands at my nape, tangling in my hair, and looks to where we're joined. She wants a show, I'll give her one. With a tight hold on her hips, I pull out, the shaft of my cock glistening with her come. "Mmmmmm, you see that, Princess?" I ask, my voice pitched low.

"Tell me, Deac," Frankie whispers and I know what she needs. Slamming her down to meet my thrust, I pull back again, her eyes still locked on our bodies.

"Look at us," I tell her as I glide in and then back out. "That's *you* all over *me*. Only you, baby. Only me. Only us." Crashing her onto me again, I feel my release start at the base of my spine as it grabs a hold of my balls. My hands tighten on her hips as I push her away again. "No one else, ever again. That's a fucking promise." My words turn into a long drawn out groan as I pump into her faster, harder, chasing after my orgasm. Frankie's grip on my hair tightens as she meets my every demand on her body. With one final thrust I let go, shuddering with the intensity behind it.

After a minute of just circling my hips, pressing her down on me, she breaks the silence, "Oh my God, you can put me down now. I have to be getting heavy."

Scoffing, I smirk at her, eyebrow raised in amusement. "Why do you think I'm in the gym throwing weights around all the time?"

"Hmmm, because it's your job!" she rasps out on a throaty laugh.

"Well, there's that, but I do it mostly so that I can fuck you standing up," I tease. "Gotta stay strong for my girl and her voracious sexual appetite and her wall, or in this case, Cage, fetish." Biting back a laugh, I slap her ass.

"Ha! *My* wall fetish? You're the one who has never passed a wall you didn't want me pinned against," she huffs.

"Can't argue with that, Princess." I shoot her a wink and run my hands from her waist to her ankles. Unlocking them from behind my back so that I can put her down. Frankie makes sure to slide down so that every inch of her rubs up against me. It's the sweetest fucking torture. "You're evil, you know that, right? How can something so small and angelic be so damn mean?" I duck my head and smother my smile in her neck, raining kisses on her.

"Come on, mean girl, let me get you dressed so that we can get you home and clean you up." Bending, I pull my shorts and boxer briefs up with a tug before bending to snag her gray ballerina skirt off the mat. "No bra?" I ask. Watching as she tucks her tits back into her top.

"This is a bra. A sports bra. You texted me just as I was getting in the shower so I just threw my skirt back on and came down here."

"Yeah, you did." I smirk, nodding my head in agreement.

Frankie lets loose a laugh and smacks me on the chest. "You're impossible. Take me home and bathe me, you animal," she says, still laughing.

"What's gonna happen if I get you in the shower?"

Walking to the door of the Cage, she looks back at me over her shoulder, her skin still flushed, her hair a wild, just-fucked mess. "I'm gonna get fucked," Frankie says throatily.

"Yes. You. Are."

CHAPTER
Fourteen

"DEACON, WHERE THE fuck are you? Why does one person need a house this fucking big?" Indie yells, her voice echoing around the front entryway.

"Who the hell let your loud ass in?" I ask, coming up behind her.

"I don't need to be let in; Frankie gave me the code." The smug smile stretching across her face leads me to believe she's telling the truth.

"Good to know; I'll change it tomorrow." Turning, I head back up the stairs to finish getting ready. We're doing our birthday dinner tonight even though our birthdays aren't until next week. This was the only time that the whole family is in town.

"Go ahead, she'll just give it to me again. Maybe we'll change it so *you* can't get in!"

I spin on the stair, almost knocking her down since she's following so close behind me. "You wouldn't fucking dare." She just looks at me and does that slow blink shit without saying anything. "Yeah, you totally would." Shaking my head in mock disgust, I turn and continue to my room, Indie still on my ass. "Why are you here? Frankie is with Sonny. Isn't there someone else for you to aggravate?"

"Oh, fuck off, cranky pants. I was just stopping by to make sure you picked up her gift and that you knew where you were going." Indie flops on the bed as I walk over to my dresser.

Watch in hand, I look at her in the mirror, fastening the clasp. "Of course I got her gift. I've had it for days." I can tell that isn't all she wants. What is it with people popping up here uninvited and being all cagey and shit? "What's up, Jones? Everything okay? You're not being followed or threatened, right?" It's easy for me to forget that she could be in danger too.

"No. God, no. Nothing like that. I would tell you guys. I'm not about to fuck around and get killed over Drew's dumb ass," she tells me with utter certainty. "So a baby, huh?"

"Anyone ever tell you that you're subtle as fuck?" I ask, chuckling.

Indie shrugs her shoulders, making the ink there dance. "Yeah, subtlety not one of my strong suits. So, a baby. I'm not gonna lie, I'm not surprised. You are a total Neanderthal and even more so when it comes to Frankie. You, like, ooze testosterone. You probably knocked her up just by looking at her." My eyebrows kick up with the dubious look I throw her way. "Whatever. You know what I mean," she huffs out. "Anyway, I'm glad that you didn't let her run away with Cristiano to Spain." Indie raises a hand to stop me from speaking. Probably a good thing because I was about to unleash on her ass. "I like him, don't get me wrong. He loves her, and although he comes off as a self-centered, somewhat skeevy douche, he's really not bad, and like I said, he loves her. He just can't love her like you do, and she for damn sure doesn't feel the same about him."

She takes a breath and I cut in, "Why the fuck are you rambling? You don't ramble. Just go ahead and hand me my balls so that we can go, yeah?" Turning away from the mirror to face her, I roll the sleeves of my white dress shirt up my forearms and wait her out.

"I just—I'm happy that she didn't go, and that if she's having a baby, she's having it with you. All the way. And not with Flashdance pulling her in the other direction."

I can in no way hide the smile fighting to break through. "I'm sorry, Jones. Are you trying to say that you like me? Maybe even love me? Or am I being Punk'd?" Smothering my laugh with a cough, "Is Ashton gonna pop out at me any minute?" I pull open the closet door and pretend to look for the show host.

"Oh, go fuck yourself, Deacon. I just came by here to congratulate you and ask you to not be an ass for once in your life and take care of my friend, and you have to be a total dick about it," Indie says, completely disgusted with me now. She hops off the bed and shoves me out of her way as she goes to leave.

"Awwwww, Jones don't be like that. I'm just not used to you saying nice things to me and it threw me." Before I follow after her sourpuss ass, I snatch my keys, wallet, and gift bag from the dresser. Indie is just making her way out the front door when I catch up to her. "Can I ride with you or am I not allowed in your car?" I joke.

"You're not allowed in my car. I'd rather stab myself in the face than ride with you." I would say that she's joking, only she's in her car already backing down the drive, her arm thrust out the window flipping me the bird.

"You said you love me! I won't forget that shit!" I yell out as I watch her whip her little Mini Cooper out of sight. "Crazy bitch. Why does my girl have to find the craziest chick in Chicago to be friends with?" I mumble as I make my way to the garage.

FINALLY MAKING IT to RPM, Frankie's favorite restaurant in the city, I hand the Rover over to the valet and make my way in, stopping at the hostess stand to let her take me to our table. The Princess wanted to do something with just the family, totally fine by me. It feels odd not throwing her a big party though.

Frankie and I got with Indie and planned this dinner a week before either of our birthdays, since it's playoff hockey season and there's a home game on both of our birthdays. Not even a birthday party for Frankie can interrupt playoff hockey, and the beauty behind that is she totally agrees. Gotta love a woman who understands what the priorities of life are, and that hockey is right at the top.

When I reach our table, I see that I'm the last one to arrive. My eyes lock on Frankie immediately, sitting next to Sonny, talking animatedly while everyone laughs around her. She has her hair down tonight in soft waves that flow over her shoulders. I love her hair. I love wrapping my fist in it and pulling. I love the way it drapes over me when she lies across my chest in bed. I love the way it tickles my thighs when she has her lips wrapped around my cock.

"Ahemmmm!" I turn away from the sight that is my girl, and my filthy thoughts, when Indie clears her throat. "You want to sit down or are you gonna just stand there and be all stalker-ish?" she asks, still clearly pissed at me. Instead of going straight to the empty chair next to Frankie, *my seat*, I head for Indie, slapping the backs of my brother, Reggie, and Pop as I make my way. When I finally reach her, she looks up at me through squinty, I-wanna-junk-punch-you eyes. Bending, I whisper in her ear so that only she can hear me, ignoring the questioning stares from everyone at the table. "I'm sorry I poked fun at you earlier. Thank you for caring and thank you for looking out for my girl. I promise to not be an ass and to always, always take care of her. If not, I give you permission to kick my ass. You can even get Mav to help." I press a kiss to her head because I really am grateful, and straighten, ending the debacle we've made by being pleasant to one another for a change.

Halfway to my seat, Indie stops me by saying—loudly—"I'm

sorry for being cunty." I throw her a smile as Guy mutters under his breath in Italian, Mav, with eyes squeezed tight just shakes his head, and the Princess lets out a giggle. That's the most sincere apology I'll ever get from Jones and we all know it.

Sliding in next to the Princess, she raises her eyebrows in question, and shrugging my shoulders, I grab up her hand and place a kiss to my spot. "You look gorgeous," I tell her, placing her hand on my thigh and lacing our fingers. I pick up the menu briefly before putting it back down. I always order the same thing when we come here—the Porterhouse that's supposed to serve up to like four people or some shit, and then I finish whatever pasta Frankie gets.

All throughout dinner, the talk at the table alternates between hockey, the fight, and of course, the baby. It's been made clear that Guy wants to have a talk with me about the whole thing. He may love me like a son, but this is his daughter. His *only* daughter, and he's old school Italian. You don't just go around living in sin in his world. I'm hoping that I can put him at ease a little with her gift tonight though.

As the table is cleared of our dinner plates and the desert being set down, Frankie leans into my side and places her head on my shoulder. Turning my face, I kiss the top of her head and squeeze the hand still on my thigh. It's all so natural that I can't imagine not being with her like this. I don't want to. I love that she feels comfortable enough in front of our family, or dads especially since they were the last to be told, to openly show affection. To allow me to love on her and not hide. This is the way it should have been from the start. I regret letting her keep it from anyone. I've said it before—she's mine. I want the world to know and it starts here. This is our world. Nobody really matters outside of these people.

"You ready for your present?" I ask, bringing the hand on my thigh up to my mouth for a quick kiss to the inside of her wrist.

She looks stunned for a moment. "Deac, I didn't bring yours. I thought we would wait until our actual birthdays."

"I didn't want to wait. You can just give me my present in bed tonight," I whisper in her ear, smiling at the pink that creeps across her cheeks.

"I think that can be arranged. Your present is more for both of us anyway," she says with a saucy grin filled with promise that has me adjusting myself under the table.

"You keep it up and you know what's gonna happen, Princess," I tell her gruffly.

"Yes. Yes, I do," Frankie answers before kissing me softly, turning her attention to Indie who is standing at the head of the table now.

"Just wanted to thank you all for coming. I realize it's not the norm for the Princess, but it's nice to have it only be us here to celebrate. Hope you all enjoyed your meal; it's on Deac, so I loved the shit out of mine," Jones says cheekily as she raises her gin and tonic. "Happy birthday to my very best friend and to the biggest pain in my ass. I love you both. Mostly." Laughing we all respond with a collective "cheers" and clink glasses around the table.

Chatter picks up around us again, but quiets as I pull the gift bag from under my chair. Moving her plate out of the way, I place the present in front of her. "Happy birthday, baby," I say, trying to hide my nerves. This can go one of two ways, and right now I'm hoping that it goes my way. Her smile beaming, she reaches into the bag and pulls out the small, white, wrapped package with the red wax seal. Glancing at me in startled recognition, eyes wide, she fingers the seal tentatively like she's afraid to ruin the wrapping.

I hear Indie breath out, "Holy shit," from her seat at the head of the table and grin.

"Go ahead, open it," I encourage Frankie, nudging her leg with mine. She nods and slips a fingernail under the seal,

breaking it to reveal a red ring box. Her eyes dart to mine and back down as she flips the top to reveal a gold ring set in black velvet. A tiara with diamonds dotting the ends of each peak catching the light from the candles on the table.

It's almost an exact replica of the one my brothers and I gave her when we were kids for her sixteenth birthday, except this one is from Cartier and not the stand in the mall. Frankie looks up at me with tears in her eyes, slipping to roll down her cheeks. "You remembered. I was so sad when the other one broke." Her smile is soft, her voice full of emotion as her gaze flicks between me and the little box clutched in her hand.

Reaching over, I pluck it gently from her fingers. Aware that we have an audience, I slip it on her ring finger and watch as her eyes widen a bit. I drop a gentle kiss over the ring. "I remembered how much you loved the original. I hope you'll love this one as much." Lips kicked up in a grin, I continue, "It's a promise ring. A promise that I'll always be faithful. A promise that I'll always love you more than anyone else can, and a promise that one day *our Princess* will be *my Queen.*" Placing another kiss to the tiara encircling her finger, I lock into her blues and press a kiss to each corner of her mouth before resting over her parted lips. "I promise." Kissing her deeply, I let her feel the truth in my words. I don't care that everyone at the table is watching us. All of them a little stunned over what just transpired. They'd better get used to it. This is only the beginning. I plan on keeping every one of these promises and making more along the way.

My girl, my baby, and my belt. None of it will be easy, but it will all be worth it. Stick and move. Stick and motherfucking move.

CHAPTER
Fifteen

"IS THIS WHAT all the hot pregnant chicks are wearing now?" I ask as we make our way to the door of Frankie's baby doctor. I give her a once over, a wolfish smile spreading across my face. She has on her favorite—and mine—"Hitman" shirt, hanging off one shoulder leaving it bare, jean shorts with pockets longer than the hem, flashing me her ink, and these tiny ass, black, fuck-me heels with the thinnest straps I've ever seen. I keep expecting one to snap. My favorite part of this whole outfit though is the fact that her shirt stops above her belly button, exposing her stomach and the obvious bump. *That's my kid in there.* Just the thought makes my heart swell with too many feelings to name. Frankie glances down at herself worrying her bottom lip.

"Do I look okay? I mean, I'm showing now. Should I not wear stuff like this? Does it weird you out that everyone can see?" she asks, indicating her stomach and the Love, not so hidden inside.

"Baby, first, you look hot as hell. I'm trying to decide the quickest way into those fuck-hot, little shorts as soon as we get out of here." I throw her a wink and watch as she tries to fight back her smile. "And two, hell no, it doesn't weird me out. Show em' all! Fuck, I wish you'd let me take out a damn billboard! 'Deacon "The Hitman" Love, knocks up smokin' hot girlfriend.' I'd put it all over the damn city," I joke, pulling her to me and running my hands over that cute as fuck little bump and around, settling them on her lower back, fingers skimming over her ass.

"Girlfriend, huh?" she questions playfully, her hands resting against me. Neck craned, she looks up at me, the sun glinting off the silver band she has holding her hair back.

"Yeah, well, 'Almost, kinda, one day wifey-girlfriend, even though she loves the cock,' wouldn't really fit, Princess." My teeth sinking into my bottom lip, fighting to keep the laugh I can feel from creeping up.

Laughing, she smacks me in the chest, "You're such a dick."

"Did I lie? Tell me you don't love it," I challenge her in a low voice. Hips thrust forward in a gentle little nudge, she gasps at the hardness that presses into her. Innocently, I grin, "He loves you too." A deep belly laugh makes its way past my lips at her expression.

"Oh my God, you're impossible." Frankie can't hold back her laughter any more than I can as we make it to the door. Just as I go to open it, my phone starts with Mav's ringtone.

"I gotta take this, baby. He's been in meetings all day with the EWF." With a small nod, she follows me over to a tree off to the side, offering a little privacy.

"What's up, brother?"

"Yo. I need you at the EWF offices downtown in an hour," Mav says.

"No can do. I'm at the doctor with Frankie. We're just walking in now, not sure how long we'll be." I'm not missing this visit. I'm in the gym constantly getting ready for Rude Awakening; who knows when I'd make it back here with her?

"Is she okay?" Worry evident in his voice.

"Yeah, man, she's fine. Just a regular checkup."

"Right on. Here's the thing, little brother. You can't blow this off. They want to do a shoot with you, try to drum up some good promo since you have all this bad press shit following you everywhere." He pauses. "Just a quick thing, take some pictures, answer a few questions, and you're outta there."

"I'll be there when I'm done here. She comes first, Mav. Ain't nothing gonna make me put her on hold while I play nice for the Federation. I didn't do anything I regret and I wasn't wrong. It's all a shitstorm, but if they don't need me in the Cage in the next hour, they can wait. Tell them you couldn't get a hold of me, that I'm most likely in the gym training. I'll be there as soon as I can."

I'm met with an exasperated sigh. "Yeah, all right. Just get here right after, Deac. They need this, brother. *You* need this."

"I feel you. We'll be there," I say to him as I guide Frankie out from under the tree and to the door, again.

"See you then. Give the Princess a kiss for me."

"Oh, I'll kiss her for you all right. While she's in those stir-rup things, right on her pretty little p——" I chuckle as the line goes dead.

"He hung up on you, didn't he? At least he's a gentleman," she says in mock disappointment.

"What? I'm not a gentleman?" I ask holding the door open for her. She nods in thanks, her lips split in a radiant smile. And then I smack her ass as she passes, earning me a yelp and every set of eyes in the place on us. She shoots me what's supposed to be a murderous look, but fails miserably, before straightening her shoulders and walking past all of the onlookers. More than one guy in the room checks out my girl while sitting next to their own. Now I'm the one with the murderous look, and mine is right on fucking point. I nail every motherfucker in there with it as I follow behind Frankie. Making them shift uneasily in their seats, dropping their gazes. I see what Frankie looks like—I don't blame them—but I won't stand for it either. Especially now when she's pregnant and when they're sitting with their women.

At the desk, she is giving the bored, bubble gum popping

girl her information. Once she's all checked in, the girl hands her a little cup and points to the bathroom, giving instructions on what to do when she's finished.

"You need some help, Princess?" I ask, winking when she shakes her head and points at the room behind us. "I think I can handle this, Deac. Go find us a seat and try not to hurt anybody." On tiptoes, she lands a kiss on my jaw and sashays away to do her thing.

Clearing her throat, the bubble gum chewer extends a clipboard for me to take. Flipping her hair over her shoulder, she gives me a flirtatious smile, her eyes taking me in from head to toe.

"You ever got your ass beat by a pregnant chick?" I ask, glancing down at the papers she's handing me. That gets her attention. Eyes wide as saucers now, she shakes her head no. "Keep that shit up," I twirl my finger at her in a little circle, "Today will be the day. I'll have my girl fill these out." I turn from the window, dismissing her and her advances, and make my way to an empty loveseat in the corner. Nodding at women in all phases of pregnancy as I pass. Too many of them staring back at me with dreamy expressions. Holy fuck, this place is insane. Staring down, I concentrate on not making eye contact with any of these hormone-crazed women until I feel the cushion next to me dip with Frankie's presence.

"You okay, baby?" Concern creasing her brow, she brushes a strand of hair that escaped my bun behind my ear.

"Yeah, Princess Just don't leave me alone in here again," only half kidding, I plead. Confused, she looks at me questioningly. "Here just fill these out." I push the clipboard at her, ignoring her curious glances. "When you bring that back up there, don't be too nice," I whisper as she moves to return the paperwork.

"She hit on you?" she hisses incredulously. I just give her the big-eyed stare, the one with the slow blink that her and Indie always give me. "I may have told her you would beat her ass if she kept it up. So yeah, don't be all nice and shit."

Her eyelids flutter shut. "Can I take you anywhere?" She surprises me by laughing. Shrugging, I reach for her, my hand on her nape, dragging her closer so that I can put my lips on her and taste that smile. "I am fucking you so dirty when we get out of here. You know that, right?" The words fall from my mouth into hers as I nip at her bottom lip, slowly drawing it into my mouth and sucking. My other hand comes up to cradle the side of her face, the calloused thumb playing at the corner of her mouth. Just as I'm about to deepen the kiss, I hear her name being called. Pulling away, I smile at the glazed over look in her eyes.

"That's us, baby." With the clipboard tucked under my arm I stand, reaching a hand out to help Frankie up. As we walk by the receptionist, I hand her the forms, her eyes shifting to Frankie a little nervously. Chuckling, I walk with Frankie into the back where they weigh her, take her vitals and shit, before ushering us into an exam room and leave us alone. Helping her up onto the tall table, I snatch up her hand and place a kiss to my spot. "Have you not seen this doctor yet?" I question.

"No, I saw the one out of Rush at first and called my usual doctor for a referral because he doesn't deliver babies anymore," the crinkly paper under her loud in the otherwise quiet room. "A dude? Your crotch doctor is a guy?" I ask, appalled, and I'm not gonna lie, a little jealous.

Frankie snorts out a laugh. "He's called a gynecologist, ass. And yes, he's a 'dude.' I prefer them; I think they're gentler," she says, like it's no big deal that once a year she has some guy, who isn't me, poking around in her lady biz.

"This is a woman though, right?" It's not really a question and now she's the one who is giving me the big-eyed look with the slow blink. "Are you fucking kidding me, Princess?" My voice is raised a little, the thought of what this dude is gonna see, all while I stand in the room, making me feel a little crazed.

"Oh, calm down, Deac. He's a doctor, and just think, you can ask him all the ridiculous questions I'm sure you have without being embarrassed." Smiling at me like she's just given me a prize.

"Have you ever in the history of knowing me, ever seen me be embarrassed by anything? And I don't have questions. My 'Who's Your Daddy' app tells me all I need to know," I inform her, rather proud of myself.

"Did you just say the 'who's your daddy app,' really?" Her eyebrows shoot straight up into her hair, her mouth dropped open.

"You better close that pretty mouth, before I put something in it." Hand going to my cock, I throw her a wicked grin. Before she can answer, there's a soft knock at the door and in walks the doctor. Oh hell motherfucking no. My head swivels to Frankie, her eyes avoiding mine. You bet your ass they're avoiding mine. The man that just walked in the door is in his mid-thirties, built like a fucking brick shit house, and looks like a goddamn movie star. And she knows it.

"Miss De Rosa, how are you?" Doc Hollywood extends his hand, prompting me to take a step closer to her. "My name is Dr. Dean," he says, sandwiching her hand between the two of his. Frankie still hasn't looked at me and I still haven't taken my eyes off her. She feels my gaze burning into the side of her face, I'm sure of it.

"Hi," she replies, in a breathless tone. No fucking way.

Clearing my throat, I hold out my hand. "Deacon Love. I did that," I say, jutting my chin in Frankie's direction. Not missing the strangled sound that leaves her mouth. Doc Hollywood chuckles.

"Yes, I can see that." Taking my hand in a firm grip, I have to fight myself not to squeeze until I feel bones crack. "I'm a huge fan, Mr. Love. I messed around with a little boxing in high school and college. Chicks dig scars, right?" he asks, smiling at me and pointing to the scar cutting through his bottom lip.

"Not my chick." Arms crossed over my chest, I glance over at Frankie when she punches me on the arm.

"Good thing my wife does then." He makes his way over to the sink and washes up, glancing over his shoulder. "She works here in the office, you'll meet her I'm sure. She's a fan as well. Though I think she likes your ink and hair more than your Muay Thai." Laughing again, he plops down on a wheeled stool rolling closer to us. "Okay, so we know that you did this, do we have an idea of when?" Frankie is bright red and I'm sure ready to kill me.

"The doctor that I saw at Rush last month said she thought I was around ten to twelve weeks. Hard to tell exactly since I'd had an IUD implanted, or so I thought. She couldn't find it, so assumed that it wasn't placed correctly and fell out. She did a sonogram and verified that it wasn't there.

"Regardless, it had been about eight weeks since the last time I'd had sex, so going off that and the measurements, that's what she came up with." As she talks, he takes notes, listening intently. When she finishes, he looks at me. "No sex between fights? My trainer had the same rule. I hated it."

I glance at Frankie. "Nah, my brothers don't bother with that. I fucked up and the Princess showed me the door." My voice is casual, my feelings aren't though. "She's fierce, my girl." Winking at her I turn back to Hollywood.

"Guess she'd have to be," the doc says as he stands and moves to Frankie's side. Again, making me step closer to her as well. I can't help it. The thought of him putting his hands on her is driving me mad. "Is it okay if I call you Francesca or do you prefer Miss De Rosa?" he asks as he rubs his hands together, like he's about to start a fire. He can fuck off with that shit. No fires will be started in here.

"Frankie is fine," the Princess says, smiling prettily at him.

"All right then, Frankie, can you lie back for me so I can take a look at what I'm working with." His tone is gentle as he helps her lie back. Once she's lying down, he places his hands on her belly, pushing and prodding, feeling for what, I'm not sure. I get why he was warming his hands now though. From a drawer on the table, he pulls out a measuring tape and a little machine that looks like a microphone and old ass tape deck. Eyes on Frankie, I watch as he measures her belly and writes her numbers in the chart. "Hmm, judging by your measurements, I would say that you're a little further along than that. We'll make an appointment for an ultrasound to get a firm due date, okay? It's not unusual to measure bigger or smaller, so nothing to worry about." Frankie nods. "You should be far enough along now to hear the baby's heartbeat with this," Doc Hollywood tells us as he presses the wand to her stomach, moving around until a rapid thumping amidst a ton of white noise fills the room. "That, you guys, is your baby's heartbeat. It sounds great, very strong."

Frankie squeezes my hand and smiles up at me, tears making her blues glisten brightly. "I did that," I say reverently.

On a chuckle, he states matter-of-factly, "You did that."

Bending, I place a kiss to Frankie's upturned lips. "We did that," I murmur against them.

WE WALK OUT of the doctor's office with all of Frankie's vitamins, appointment cards, and extra swag that pregnant chicks apparently get at their first visit. "Do you mind coming with me to the EWF?" I ask as I open the door and help her into the Rover.

"No, that's fine. Will you feed me after though?" she asks me, buckling in.

"Oh, I'll feed you all right, Princess," I tease, smiling as she laughs.

Hopping in, I maneuver us out of Lincoln Pak and head toward Michigan Avenue where the offices are located. I'm not sure exactly what they have in mind, but I hope they have clothes there for me. My cargo shorts and Hawks shirt probably not what they're looking for if they want to do a photo shoot. I guess we'll find out. As we pull into the underground garage, I look over at Frankie who has fallen asleep, her head resting against the glass. "Baby, time to get up, we're here." I run the back of my fingers across her face, then pick up her hand and place a kiss to her wrist.

Eyes fluttering open, she pins me with those blues and I can't help but smile. We may not be all the way yet, but we're close, and close is good. I do my best not to push her. A lot of shit has happened between us, and right now I'm just taking it day by day, bit by bit, at the pace that Frankie has set. Today has been an especially good day though. A glimpse at what our life together will be like once we get rid of all this bullshit, fear, criminals, and whatever else. We'll get there though. There's no other option for me.

Placing a quick kiss to her lips, "Come on, my gorgeous, knocked up girl. Let's see what the fuck they want so that we can go get you some eats."

Frankie nods, flipping down the mirror on the visor to mess with her face and hair as I make my way over to her door. She pops a piece of gum, offering me one as we head into the building. "Did Mav say what they wanted you here for?"

The elevator doors slide closed behind us. "He said something about promo stuff, a shoot maybe. I don't know."

Once we arrive on the right floor, we make our way to the receptionist, who I'm thrilled as fuck to see isn't the same one who propositioned me the last time I was here. I don't even have to give her my name. "Mr. Love, Miss De Rosa, you can go on back to the studio, your brother is waiting. Can I bring you anything?" she asks, her gaze flicking between the two of us.

"Just some water would be great, thank you," I tell her, my hand on the small of Frankie's back, guiding her down the wicked long hallway to the last door. I don't bother knocking, just walk in, and immediately start looking for Maverick. Frankie spots him over by the window, talking with Caz, a producer and photographer that we've worked with on a few different campaigns for the EWF.

Mav looks up just as we start his way. "Little brother, Princess, glad you guys made it. We were just talking about the spread and what we need to get done."

I shake Caz's hand, as Mav pulls Frankie in for a hug, kisses her forehead, and pokes at her belly. "Go ahead in the dressing room, Deac. I ran home and got your shorts. They still have to do makeup and all that shit though. Then we can get started."

There's no use bitching about the makeup, so I just nod and lay a quick kiss on Frankie and head off to get ready. The quicker we get this shit finished, the quicker we can get out of here and I can work Frankie out of her clothes.

An hour later and we're still here, taking picture after picture. I'm not sure how many fucking pictures they need of me, and I'm just about to ask when I hear a bunch of giggling and high-pitched voices. Glancing toward the door, I see a group of Cage girls, hovering in their tiny ass bikinis, hair and makeup done like they're on their way to fucking prom. The fuck? I don't need to see who they are to know that I've fucked them all. This is the last thing I need right now. I turn away from them to find Frankie watching me, an unreadable expression on her face. Mav standing next to her looking apprehensive. My gaze trained on the Princess, I call out, "Caz, what are they doing here?"

He pokes his head from behind his camera. "Oh, they're here for either your billboard or the cover. Not sure yet. We're still waiting on one mor—"

"I'm here," interrupts a whiny, shrill voice. Veronica.

Still locked on Frankie, her face is no longer unreadable. She's furious and I can't blame her. Never paying a second of attention to Veronica who is now stopped in front of me reaching her hand out to touch the Mizpah charm hanging from the chain around my neck, I snatch her wrist before she can touch it. "No," I say loudly. It's meant for her. It's meant for Caz. There is no way in fuck this is gonna go down. I let go of Veronica, and take a step back out of her reach.

Alarmed, Caz puts his camera down. "No what?"

"No, I'm not posing with her. I don't want to pose with any of them, but I definitely won't be posing with her." I still have yet to look away from my girl. I need her to see that I choose her. Even for something as simple as this. It's Frankie.

"D, it's just a few pictures," Caz says.

"Don't care what it is; not doing it, my man. If you have to call Derek and tell him, that's cool. I really don't give a shit. There's nothing and no one who is gonna change my mind." Maverick hasn't uttered a single word. He doesn't even bother.

"Oh my God. Baby much?" Veronica hisses as she stomps over toward Caz, ready to light into him, I'm sure, when she comes to an abrupt halt and does a double take in Frankie's direction. "You're fucking pregnant?" she all but screeches. Whipping around to face me, her eyes filled with hatred, though I'm not sure if it's for me or the Princess. "What a fucking joke. It's probably not even your kid, Deacon. Everyone knows that you guys have been broken up. It's all over the circuit; the girls were all really happy about it," she says snidely, making it seem like they were benefiting from my single status. They were not. Turning her snake eyes back on Frankie, Mav steps between them.

"Caz, you need to get her the fuck out of here before shit gets ugly, you feel me?" My voice is tight, my resolve about to

snap.

"That's enough, Veronica. You can go now. Caz will make sure that you get paid for your time," Mav tells her firmly, still shielding Frankie.

"This is almost comical. All of you are so pussy-whipped." Tapping her chin, she faces me again, a sick look of merriment mixed in with all that venom. "You all bang her, don't you? She has the Love brothers jumping at her every word. You're. All. Fucking. The. Princess." She snorts and turns to Frankie who has come out from behind Mav's protection. "There's no way that's his baby. He always wraps it. Always. No matter how many of us he had in his bed. He never forgot," Veronica says smugly.

I'm just about to hit a woman for the first time in my life when Frankie takes a step closer to Veronica. "See, that's where you and I are different, doll. For one, he's never wrapped it with me. Never. There was no forgetting. And it's only ever been him and I in his bed." Frankie shrugs her shoulders nonchalantly. "He doesn't have to compensate by bringing other girls into our bedroom because I'm enough for him. I fuck him so good, it's only ever gonna be me in his bed. Oh, and that's another thing. You've never even been in *his* bed."

I watch in awe as my girl smiles coyly at Veronica. It shouldn't turn me on to watch her put this bitch in her place, but fuck me if it doesn't. A quick glance at Mav and I see that while he may not be turned on—fucker better not be—he's still impressed with the way the Princess just handled Veronica. Caz's fidgeting catches my attention—homeboy just looks nervous. Bet he won't make this mistake again.

My lips kicked up in a smile, focus back on Frankie, when Veronica says, "You're nothing but a whore and he'll get tired of you and that fucking kid. You should do yourself a favor and go have an abortion n—" She's stopped mid-word by a smack across the face. And then before she can react, another one cracks through the room, echoing in the sudden silence before the melee erupts. Charging forward, I push past the half-naked women standing there gawking and gasping and rushing to Veronica's aid as she stands with a hand to her flaming cheek to usher Frankie away from the chaos, Mav right beside us.

I make it about three steps before Frankie ducks under my arm. "You never, ever speak of my child again. There's only one whore in this room and it's you. Be pissed off all you want that you were just another of 'Deacon's girls,' and that I'm *the* girl, but I swear on everything that is holy if you ever even *think* about my baby again I will snatch those extensions out of your head so quick you'll be bald before you know what the hell happened." Frankie spins on her heel and strides into the dressing room slamming the door. My brother and I look at each other too shocked to completely understand how shit went south so quickly.

"I'm going to check on the Princess; you handle Caz and this whole clusterfuck." Mav nods in agreement and I take off after my girl. As hot as that was, she scared the shit out of me. I'm pretty sure pregnant chicks shouldn't be slapping people around. No matter how much they deserve it. Pushing open the door, I step into the small room they use for wardrobe, closing it behind me. "You okay, baby?" I ask gently.

She nods from her spot on the couch, her head resting on the back. "I'm fine. Now." Her voice is barely above a whisper, but I hear the tremble in it.

Three long strides and I'm kneeling in front of her. "You sure you're okay? The baby?"

Slowly raising her head to look at me, she nods again. "I'm sorry, I shouldn't have hit her. I just . . . she just . . . I'm sorry."

"Frankie, you have nothing to be sorry for. I'm not mad at you for hitting her. I think I was just about to. I'm just worried about you and the baby. You can't be going around beating chicks up. " Brushing back the hair that's hiding her blues from me, I tuck it behind her ear and smile. "You know you're a total badass though, right?" A small snort leads to a laugh and just like that, everything is right in my world. "Listen here, little mama, no more fights for you, my tiny scrapper." Chuckling, I raise her wrist to my lips and lay a kiss on her, standing as I do.

There's a knock at the door and Mav pokes his head in. "Both my fighters okay in here?" he jokes, trying to keep shit light.

"Yeah, we're good, brother."

"Good. Caz just needs a few more shots and he said he'll have enough for what Derek wants."

"We're done for the day, Mav. I want to get her home and fed. It's been a long day." Making eye contact with him, I see that there's no room for argument here. I have to jump through the Federation's hoops until they decide whether they're going to let me fight, and Frankie still has no clue about any of it. She'd feel immense guilt and I won't have her feeling anything over that fucker, Andrew, ever again.

Groaning, I turn back to Frankie. "You wanna stay in here?" I ask, giving her an out. I just want to get this over with.

Eyes narrowed, she addresses Mav. "Is *she* still here?"

"No! Hell no! I had no clue she was coming. If I'd had any idea that she's who Caz called, I would have told him it wasn't gonna happen."

"But he still has to pose with the other girls?" the Princess asks him.

Scrunching up his face as if it pains him to say it, he answers her in an apologetic tone. "Yes. I promise it will be quick though."

"I'll stay here, Deac. Come get me when it's done. I'm emotionally drained and seeing them hang all over you might be enough to put me over the edge. Or at the very least have me smacking bitches again," she jokes.

The Princess may be joking around, but she's not feeling

it. She's still on edge. Watching my girl, "Mav, tell Caz I'll only pose with one girl. If he doesn't like it I can pose by myself."

"Okay, bro. I'll tell him to pick one and then we'll get the fuck out of here. I'm about done with this place for the day too." He goes to close the door but I yell for him.

"No, Mav. Tell him to send them all home. I'll pose with Frankie if he wants a chick in the mix." Both of them stare at me open-mouthed.

"Uh, Deac? She's pregnant."

"What the fuck does that matter?" I ask him.

"Deacon, I look like hell and he's right—I'm pregnant, nobody wants to see all this," she says, waving a hand in front of her body.

"I want to. Don't really care about what anyone else wants." Shrugging, I look at my brother, "Make it happen, mighty Mav." With a smart ass salute, he leaves us alone to tell Caz about the change of plans. My attention back on Frankie, I tell her, "I'm gonna send the makeup chick in here, I'll wait with the guys." Before she has a chance to argue, I get the hell out of there. As I see it, this is a perfect solution to the day's problem.

CHAPTER
Sixteen

TWENTY MINUTES LATER and Frankie finally makes it out of the dressing room wearing a hot pink sports bra and tiny ass black shorts, the "Hitman" shirt dangling from her fingers. "Hey, Nadalynn, where the hell are her clothes?" I ask the stylist. "I thought we sent her back there to get dressed; you sent her out with less clothing than she went in with."

"Well, the other girls all had their bikinis on. I didn't have an extra one lying around, and since she's not a ring girl anyway, I didn't want to make her look like one. It was either this or naked. Your choice," she says smugly.

I don't really care about what she's wearing—I know where she belongs and to whom, I just like to blow her shit. Its payback for making me wear makeup for these shoots. I shake my head in mock disapproval and hold out my hand for Frankie. "Come on, Princess. Let's get this over with so that you can put some clothes on." My teasing makes her laugh and Nadalynn shoots me the bird.

Still laughing, I lead Frankie over to where Caz and Mav are waiting. "Okay, I'm going to pose you a few different ways because I'm still not sure what their plans are. Do you want me to try and shoot around . . ." he asks as he indicates Frankie's bump. We both answer at once—"Yes." "No." Caz's head swivels from me to her and back, looking ready to bolt.

"No," I say again emphatically.

Huffing, she gives in. "Do whatever he wants, I just want to go and get some food," Frankie tells Caz, who now looks relieved.

For the next little while, Caz poses us and takes what feels like a million pictures. We're just about to wrap up when Derek Eliott, President of the EWF and my boss, bursts into the room.

"What the hell is this bullshit that your little girlfriend smacked up one of my Cage girls? I won't have one of your flavors coming into my building and causing trouble," he booms angrily.

Stepping forward, I put myself in front of Frankie before he makes it over to us. "She had it coming, Derek. And watch what you say when you're speaking about my girl," I warn, my voice low. There's a stunned silence that takes hold of the studio and everyone in it. I don't really care. He won't talk about Frankie like that. "Speaking of ring girls, I don't want Veronica working my fights any more. She's fucking crazy and she crossed a line tonight, a few of them actually."

Derek scoffs and points a ringed finger at me. "D, I hate to break it to you, but you're in no goddamn position to be making demands."

Brushing aside his comment because I don't want to get into a conversation about where I stand with the EWF in front of Frankie, I interrupt him before he can say more. "I'm not making demands, Derek. I'm simply stating that if she's working the Cage, I will not be in it. Simple as that. Chicks like her are a dime a dozen. Find someone else."

"See, this is why fighters need to keep their dicks in their pants. I don't need this shit right now and I for damn sure don't need your girlfriend busting up my girls' faces, D! It's unacceptable," he bellows. I'm about to answer him when Frankie steps out from behind me.

"I apologize for hitting someone under your employment,

Derek, but Deacon is right, she had it coming," she tells a stunned Derek.

Once he's able to close his mouth and collect himself he stammers out, "F—Frankie? You're the girlfriend?" he asks. This is not a stuttering man. He is all business, all the time. I'm not sure why he's so surprised. Or maybe it's the fact that he was trash talking one of the most respected men in MMA's daughter. "I'm sorry, I guess I nev—" he stops mid-sentence and focuses on me. "Is she pregnant? Are you pregnant?" His attention on Frankie again before bouncing back to me. "Deacon?" Derek looks a little frazzled and a whole lot confused. "Not to be insensitive or anything, but now is not the time to be losing focus. We're talking about the belt here."

"Yes, Frankie is having my baby. And no, you don't have to worry about me losing focus. I know what I have to do."

He looks like he wants to argue but instead nods his head in agreement. "Okay then. Caz find a way to spin this. His female fans will be pissed, but the guys will appreciate Frankie. Use it to our advantage. Make it sexy, but not too sexy or else I'll have Guy all over my ass." Leaving as abruptly as he came, he stops at the door. "I'll make sure that Veronica isn't on your circuit. Just do me a favor and stay out of goddamn trouble, D. I can only do so much." The door slams loudly behind him.

I grin down at Frankie. "That went well, yeah?"

MY BIRTHDAY, AND I can't even catch a break. Sonny has had me in the gym since five this fucking morning and it's now nearly nine. Walking into the house, I toss my keys and the rest of my shit in the bowl on the counter. The house is quiet aside from the music that Frankie always has playing. Walking into the media room, I see Reggie and Trent picking up cups and bowls. "Hey, brother, happy birthday," Reggie greets. Trent raises a fist for me to tap.

"Thanks. Where's the Princess?" I ask as I move aside so that they can get through the door.

"Upstairs lying down. She went up as soon as we got home. Said that we could go as soon as you got here."

"Yeah. Get out of here. Just set the alarm on the way out, bro," I instruct as I turn for the stairs. I showered at the gym, so my plan is to just crawl into bed with Frankie and crash.

I'm just about to call her name when I see her. I stop in the doorway and lean against the jamb as I watch her move around the room in nothing but a t-shirt that barely hits her thighs. Those legs of hers—toned and the color of honey—call to me. They turn me on as much as the rest of her. Without a doubt, my favorite place to be is in between them. To have them wrapped around me. My waist, my head . . . doesn't matter.

My hand has found its way into my sweats as I stand there admiring her. Releasing the hold I have on my cock, I slip my hand out and push away from the door. Frankie still hasn't seen or heard me. Coming up behind where she stands lighting a candle, I place a kiss to the side of her neck causing her to jump.

"Deacon, you scared me . . . mmmm." Whatever she was about to say is forgotten. She tilts her head to the side, allowing me better access. Softly, I trail my fingers up the backs of her bare thighs, up and over her waist, taking the shirt with me so that it's bunched at her hips.

"No panties . . . were you waiting for me, baby?" I ask in a voice gritty with need. Grasping her hips, I pull so she's flush against me and thrust against her ass. She stiffens, just enough for me to notice.

"You okay, Princess?" Turning her so she's facing me, I palm her ass, giving it a little squeeze. I freeze when I bump against something hard and cool. Eyes wide, they land on Frankie who is flushed with more than just want. "Is that what I think it is?"

My tone is incredulous, hopeful. She watches me a little warily as she chews at the inside of her lip.

"It's a plug. I've been wearing it all week. Indie said it would help," she says breathily.

"Wait. What? You mean to tell me that you've been walking around rocking a butt plug all week and I didn't know? How in the fuck is that even possible?" My mind is racing. I'm not sure if I love that she's been wearing it and I didn't know or if I hate it. And where the fuck did Indie come into all this?

"I wore it mostly when you weren't home," Frankie admits shyly.

"Jesus fuck, I'm glad you didn't tell me. You wouldn't have made it out of the bedroom." I bend to kiss her slowly and then spin her in my arms again, her back to my front. Kissing a path down her neck, I gather the soft cotton material of her shirt and deftly lift it up and over her head, tossing it to the ground before resuming my path straight down her spine. Squatting now, I place a kiss on each of the twin dimples hovering over her ass at the small of her back and then down and underneath each taut ass cheek. As I spread her gently, I get my first view of the sparkly little gem she has nestled there. Groaning low in my throat, I open her just a little wider to get a better look. "Tell me again why you've been wearing this and what Indie has to do with it," I say right before I go to placing kisses all over her perfectly rounded ass.

"I wan—ted to do something special for you." Her voice hitches as I run my tongue along the crease where cheek meets thigh. "I was going to give you a private show, a little late night dancing at home, but that's kind of hard to do when you're seventeen weeks pregnant and still try to look sexy, yo—" her words are swallowed by the gasp that leaves her mouth when I take a bite of her ass for saying shit like that.

"I don't want to hear that shit from you. You're sexy *because* you're pregnant. Beautiful and full of my Love. Perfect," I insist and then resume my light kisses.

"I wanted to give you something, to show you what you mean to me. How much I trust you. Something only for you." Frankie sighs and relaxes into my hands, resting her head on the tall dresser in front of her, hands gripping the edge. "I have nothing to give you, Deacon. No rings or custom jewelry, no flashy parties, or anything like that. All I have is me and I want you to have that. All of me. Always."

This woman. This woman is everything. "That's all I want, Princess. All I need. Always." Rising I wrap my arms around her from behind, swallowing her up, palming her swollen belly. "You don't have to do this though, not unless you want to. I don't need this to know how you love me, baby." I press a reassuring kiss into her hair.

"I want to. I want to be with you like this." I meet her gaze in the mirror hanging in front of us. "Fuck me in the ass, Deac. Take me. Make all of me yours," Frankie tells me in a husky rasp.

"Jesus fuck," I hiss between my teeth as I sweep her up and stalk over to the bed. Gently, I place her on top of the cool silky sheets and crawl over her, nudging her legs open as I do. Careful not to put any weight on her stomach, I settle in the vee she's made for me. My rigidness against the softest part of her. "Tell me again that you want me to fuck your ass, Frankie." Dragging my nose across her cheek, I place my ear closer to her mouth. The mouth I plan on taking along with the rest of her, if I can control myself long enough.

"I want you to be my first, my only. I want you to take my ass, Deacon. Please?" she breathes her words onto my skin, sending an electrifying shiver up my spine. My whole body is rigid, trembling with the urgency to do what she asks. I have to go slow, be gentle.

I kiss a path to her mouth, swiping my tongue across her lips, "*Just the tip*, right?" I tease. Her smile is instantaneous.

"Maybe."

"Maybe not," I retort, making her giggle.

All my attention is focused on her, on the way the flush covering her chest has crept into her cheeks. The way her eyes smile even though her lips are screwed into a nervous little purse. How through my trembling I can feel hers. This right here is what it's all about. This is passion and love and every other fucking thing I never wanted with anyone but her. I have it all, right here in my arms.

Sitting up, I straddle her thighs, looking my fill at the vision in front of me. She's pure sex. And she's mine. "Touch them, Frankie. I want to see your hands on your tits," I command her hoarsely. I smile when she does as I say without hesitation. Her tiny, pink- and black-tipped fingers pluck at her beaded nipples, her eyes fluttering closed as she scrapes a nail over one, then the other. Her eyes pop open as I rise off of her, pushing my pants and boxer briefs down and kicking them to the floor before I position myself between her knees that are now bent. Kneeling there, I watch as she goes on to knead and pinch, palm and squeeze. One tit and then the next.

My hand skates up through her bared pussy, collecting the wetness there before smoothing it over the head of my cock. I do it once more and she jerks upward, chasing my retreating hand. Teeth sunk into my bottom lip, I watch her as she watches me. Cock in hand, I squeeze the base and then slide my hand up to the tip, rubbing the underside with my thumb before making my way back down, spreading Frankie all over the sensitized skin. Her eyes now locked on my hand as I pump my cock, I rub the tip against her clit, eliciting a low moan from her. My control slipping with every sound, every movement, every breath. This was supposed to be for her. To get her ready, wanting and needing so badly to make it easier for her. I never want to hurt her. It will, but I want to make the pleasure consume her, make her forget about everything else and for her to just feel.

On the nightstand, I see a bottle of lube she must've put there. I reach past her and grab it, placing it on the bed next to us. "Roll over, Frankie," my tone soft, yet firm. Moving out of the way so she can do as I ask, I place a pillow beneath her to keep her from being flat on her stomach. "We'll go slow, I promise," I reassure her, my lips once again landing on the dimples at the small of her back. Moving in closer, I position myself directly behind her so that I'm kneeling between her spread legs and her ass is resting across my thighs, covering me in her wetness. Growling, I reach between us and slide my hand down and cup her pussy, pressing against her clit while with the other I tug gently at the plug nestled into her tight ass. Frankie tenses when I give it a twist.

"Shhhh, easy baby. I need you to relax all of your muscles and just let me make you feel good. I promise you it won't hurt for long and I will stop whenever you want." Soothing her with my words, I feel her body melt, her muscles stop fighting the invasion. "That's it, Princess, I'll fuck you nice and easy with this and then we'll try my cock." Fingers sliding through her slick heat, I dip first one inside of her before pulling out and pushing back in with two, my thumb circling around her clit while still gently twisting the plug with the other. I can feel when she's close, her pussy clamping down on my hooked fingers. "You want to come, Frankie? You want to come all over my fingers while I fuck your ass with this plug?" I ask, my movements a little faster now.

"Please. Please let me come, Deacon," she whimpers into the pillow. I start to work the jewel-tipped metal in and out of her ass in rhythm with the fingers I have buried inside of her. When she's close, her body rocking into my hand, I pull the plug from her completely and reach for the lube. Squeezing a generous amount in the crack of her ass, I rub my fingers around the rim, testing her tightness with the pad of my thumb. When she doesn't pull away, I know that she's ready. Never allowing the

fingers playing her pussy to slow, I apply some of the slippery oil over the head of my cock, massaging it in. Straightening, I slip my fingers from her and move them to her clit at the same time I glide my cock to her ass. Pressing the head into her slowly, gently. "Jesus fuck, your ass is so tight, Frankie. So fucking tight. I'm going to make you feel so good," I vow as I inch forward just a little bit more, stopping when she resists. "Don't fight me, Frankie. Let me in, baby. Let me fuck you dirty." The words come out as a rumbling growl low in my throat.

Just as Frankie relaxes, her body tenses again as I hook one finger in her pussy. "Oh God, Deac. Oh, God."

As the tremors from her first orgasm start to take over, I push until I'm a little farther in her ass. She's so goddamn tight, it's nearly painful. I need her to take all of me, but I won't rush it. She groans through it, hissing out a breath when I inch my way deeper still. "Ahhh, that's my girl. Take all of it, baby." I feel her relax more and more as I make my way past every tight ring. As easy as I can, I thrust, putting her ass right to my stomach and holding her there.

The sweat pooling at the base of my spine right now is the only thing keeping me focused. She feels so fucking good. Allowing her to become accustomed to the feel of me, I fight the urge to thrust. Bit by bit, I feel some of that tension lessen. As it does, I begin to rock slowly into her. "This ass was made for me to fuck, Frankie. It fits me like a fucking glove." Slowly I pull out, stopping when she whimpers. "Shhh, I got you, baby," I soothe as I again slide two fingers into her pussy. As I work her over, bringing her closer to another orgasm, she starts pushing back onto my cock. "That's it, Frankie. Fuck me. Make us both feel good." At my words, she begins a steady pace, my finger moving in time with her. I can feel the rippling of her walls as her movements become more frantic. It's more than I can take when she cries out, her legs trembling almost violently. "Please, let me fuck you, baby? I don't want to hurt you, but I need to fuck this perfect little ass," I plead.

Frankie throws her head back and lets out a low sexy moan. "Yes, now. Please, please, please," she chants, giving me the permission I need. I pull my fingers from her and tangle my hand in her hair, pushing her head down against the pillow, forcing her ass higher into the air. My left hand on her hip, I pull her back onto my cock until I'm completely seated, then pull all the way out to the tip and do it again, every time making it a little easier to get all the way back in. "I've wanted in this ass for so fucking long," I grunt, thrusting at a slow pace, building her back up. "So tight, so damn tight." I lose all finesse when she spreads her legs even wider and starts rubbing her clit, the spasms in her legs more noticeable. "Princess, this ass is mine, that pussy is mine. *You're* fucking mine," I growl right before my own orgasm takes hold of me. It has me babbling incoherent shit as I ride out wave after wave of intense pleasure right along with the moans and cries of my girl.

I would live in this ass if I could, but I want her off her stomach, so I gently pull back. With no shame, I spread her cheeks and watch my come trickle out of her ass and into her pussy. "Jesus fuck," I hiss out.

Rolling her over onto her side, I get up and snag a towel from the chair in the corner and bring it back over to the bed. Carefully, in case she's sore, I give her a quick wipe before lying down behind her, tucking Frankie tightly against my sweaty body. "Thank you," I whisper hoarsely into her hair. "Thank you for trusting me to take care of you. There's nothing in this world I love more than you. Not a single thing, Princess," I tell an already sleeping Frankie. I place a kiss to her shoulder, chuckling softly to myself. I keep fucking her to sleep like this and my ego is gonna be out of control.

CHAPTER
Seventeen

FRANKIE'S BIRTHDAY COMES and goes with a bang. We got to watch our boys bring home the Stanley Cup on home ice with my brothers. Reggie and Trent sitting in the bar across from the United Center because although we're keeping every letter that comes to the house from her and have changed her cell number, she's still on edge. She won't admit it to any of us, but I see it.

Her nightmares have been more frequent as well. I'm not sure if it's that she's not the only one in danger but also our baby that has all of a sudden caused a spike in her fear or the fact that she now knows it wasn't Andrew who attacked her. That whole "evil you know" way of thinking. Whatever it is, she was at least able to sit back and enjoy one hell of a hockey game on her birthday. Best present ever. Well, aside from the gift she gave me for my birthday. It was also the perfect excuse to buy her a double hockey stick charm for her bracelet.

"Yo, Deac! You with us, brother?" Sonny asks, exasperated. I have the title fight coming up. The. Title. Fight. And here I am daydreaming about the Princess. Typical.

I toss the jump rope I've been torturing myself with and head over to the mats where Mav has some guy, who I'm assuming is Scott the wrestling guru, waiting. Rude Awakening is a strong wrestler, which is my weakest area, so this dude is supposed to be some kind of fucking wrestling genius sent by my good friend, Crew Gentry, who knows his wrestling. We'll see. I shake his hand and listen as Sonny goes over my strengths, like the armbar. Not strong like Ronda Rousey strong, but it's not bad. And my weaknesses. Fuck him. I don't have any weaknesses. Well, I have *one* weakness, but he's not talking about that.

"Yeah, I'm here, bro. Calm your shit. I was just waiting for you to finish telling him how to beat me." Smirking, I take a swig of my coconut water and pay attention to what they're saying now. Sonny wraps it up and tells me to lie flat on my back so that this guy can pin me. The fuck?

My face must convey what I think about this plan because he shakes his head at me. "Stop being a fucking pussy and get your ass on the ground. I need to see how fast you can get out of this hold since its fast becoming Rude's signature move," my brother informs me.

We work shit out like this all the time, not sure why I'm giving him so much hell. I think it's all this gym time and the uncertainty if they'll even be letting me fight still hanging over my head. That shit with Andrew is kicking me in the ass about as bad as I kicked his. I still haven't even told Frankie that there's going to be a hearing at the EWF in the next week or two to determine if I'll be contending for the title or not. I'm more worried than I'm letting on right now; this being in limbo bullshit is really starting to fuck with my head.

Flat on my back, I wait for Scott to put his balls in my face or whatever fucked up position I'm about to find myself in. He hovers over me as Sonny explains what he wants. Just as Scott starts to work his wrestling magic, I hear Frankie's raspy voice talking to my brother.

"Yeah, Princess. Just give us a minute and we'll break for lunch and he's all yours for about twenty, okay?" Sonny tells her in his gentle "Princess" voice.

"Thanks, Sonny. I'll wait over in th—"

"What's up, baby?" I ask hoisting myself off the mats and brushing past Scott. As I near her, I see that she's upset and been crying. I can't have that shit; it never ends well for me. Scooping up her hand, I flip it and place a kiss on my spot and notice the rapidness of her pulse. What the fuck is going on now?

As I'm about to ask her what happened, Sonny chimes in, "Deac, we ha—"

"To take a break so that I can talk to Frankie," I interrupt and finish for him. He sighs loudly but knows there's no fucking point in arguing.

"Yeah, might as well. We'll meet back here in twenty, no fucking longer, Deac." I get the "don't fuck with me" voice, definitely not the "Princess" one she got. Waving them off, I turn back to Frankie and see tears glistening in her blues, her throat working to swallow and I'm scared. We're finally in a good place. This—whatever *this* is—better not set us back.

"Princess, what's wrong? Why the tears and shit?" Her hand still in mine, I tug her a little closer, fuck it that I'm covered in sweat. She looks away, shaking her head no, her lower lip quivering. That's all it takes for my stomach to bottom out.

"No what? You're starting to fucking worry me, what's going on?" I demand.

"I-I can't, Deacon. I have to go," she stammers and I have no clue what the hell she's talking about.

"Go where, baby? What the fuck are you talking about, Frankie? What are you running from? Why are you always fucking running from me?" I ask exasperated with her.

"I'm not running *from* you; I'm running *for* you. I have to leave to protect you. You're too much of a big deal right now with the championship and if they hurt you to get to me, I'll never forgive myself. If anything were to happen to yo—" Her voice breaks on a sob. It's gotta be these fucking pregnancy hormones I've been reading about making her talk crazy like this out of nowhere. Either that or she's not telling me something.

"Princess?" I ask, warning lacing my tone.

"He's dead, Deac. Andrew is dead," she says on a hiccupping sob. Stunned, I look up to see Reggie standing off to the side in the corner of the weight room. He nods his head in affirmation.

"What do you mean? How do you know, Frankie?"

"Agent Ri-Riley contacted me. Andrew and Agent Baird were ambushed. Both of them were killed. Sh-shot," she stammers. "He wants me to go into protection," Frankie informs me quietly.

"Yeah, because that shit kept Drew real fucking safe," I spit out. She stands there, her forehead resting on my chest as she cries.

"I told them I wouldn't go, that it didn't save Andrew. But Deac, I have to go. I can't stay here and risk something happening to you or my dad, any of my Loves or Joe. You're all in danger because of me. You'll do everything to keep me safe, but who's going to keep all of you safe?" As she takes a deep breath and straightens her spine, her eyes find me again. "My dad is making the arrangements now. I'm going to Italy until this trial blows over. You have to be here training and don't need to be worrying about me. You're stressed and it's because of me and all the extra time you're putting in to make sure I'm okay. If I go stay with my uncle, my cousins can all keep an eye on me. I'll be far enough away that you won't have to worry and they won't find me," she says it all so quickly, like she has to hurry to get it out because it's bullshit and it's not gonna fly with me.

"Baby, look at me." I wait patiently although I feel anything but. Taking a hold of her chin, I bend at the knees so that I'm peering right into the blue flames I love so much. "Look at me. Hear me, Princess. You leaving isn't protecting me. If you go, I go. Simple as that," I tell her matter-of-factly, raising my shoulders nonchalantly.

"Deac, the fight. You can't. I won't let you," she says

forcefully, like she believes she has a choice. Slowly I brush away the tears that have slipped past her lashes. Laughing softly, I just shake my head and place another soft kiss to her wrist. "Nothing matters to me more than you. You and the baby. Never doubt that." My tone is fierce—I need her to understand what I'm saying is fact. Nothing else matters, not the belt, not the trial, not these fucks trying to stay out of prison, nothing. They may have been able to get to Drew, but I'll kill them before they get close to her. I'll die first.

Shaking off the darkness those thoughts take me to, I bring my focus back to my girl. Her hand in mine is so small, I marvel at all I hold, all she means to me. This tiny, strong, warrior of a woman, carrying my baby, our *Love*. Her running ends now. It's not her style. Never has been until me, and I don't fucking like it.

"I won't let you sacrifice *us* to save me or you anymore. I see what it's doing to the both of us and it fucking stops, here and now, Frankie. I don't need you to protect me from shit else but you, baby." Leaning down I kiss the left corner of her mouth, brushing my lips softly against hers before doing the same to the right and then finally covering her mouth fully with my own. With a low groan, I break away. I can't allow myself to get swept up in her right now. Not with Sonny and the wrestler waiting on me, not with everything we just discussed, although every part of me wants to sweep her up and love her into seeing that I would always keep her safe.

Her eyes are still closed when I pull away and smile. "No more running, Princess. If you don't trust me to keep you safe, then *we'll* go to Italy. You aren't going anywhere by yourself, you feel me?" She nods in agreement though I can tell she isn't thrilled about this turn of events. Oh well. She thinks I'm un-reasonable, I know it. She hasn't seen shit yet. My girl. My baby. My way.

CHAPTER
Eighteen

AS BO PULLS up in front of the EWF headquarters, I slap him on the shoulder and follow my brothers out of the Rover. My pop and Guy are already up there, hopefully sweet-talking the bigwigs into letting me fight. This meeting is a huge fucking deal. It could be the end of my career depending on what they decide. I pull my suit jacket closed, buttoning it as I walk beside Mav and Sonny, straightening the pink tie around my neck that they've been blowing me shit for.

Mav looks over at me and shakes his head. "I've never met another man alive who wears as much pink as your ass does." Straightening his own more conservative blue tie, he shoots me a pointed look, gesturing toward it. "You should've worn something a little more manly. They're gonna see that tie and ask themselves, 'Is this guy badass enough to be the EWF champion?'" Clucking his tongue at me like a disapproving little old lady, "Just saying, you've got your work cut out for you as it is, you might have made it a little easier is all."

"You about done, Maverick?" Sonny bites out. "The color of his tie is the least of his fucking worries." Mid-step he turns to me, making both Mav and I come to an abrupt stop. "For once in your life, Deac, I need you to keep your cool. I'm sure Pop already lectured you, but listen to me, okay, little brother?" He pauses and peers into my eyes, willing me to hear what he's

saying. "These men don't give a fuck about anything but winning, keeping fans interested, and their noses clean. We can't tell them shit as it is, so you let Pop and Guy do most of the talking. They're a bunch of suits who have little to no respect for some young punk fighter who can't keep his temper in check and that's exactly how they see you. These guys aren't Derek—they don't have a passion for the sport, they just see the dollar signs. Show them your worth, Deac." Not expecting a response he nods and turns back to the doors. "Let's go finish this shit so we can put it behind us and really start training."

The fuck did he say? *Start* training? My feelings must be written across my face because Mav laughs and elbows me in the ribs.

"Yeah, pussy. *Start* training," he mocks as he follows Sonny into the cool interior of the building.

Sometimes I hate these fuckers.

AFTER THREE GRUELING hours of trying not to lose my shit and allowing men who have no clue what the sport of MMA is really about pick me apart, we're heading back out to the car. Pink tie hanging untied around my neck, I can feel the tension leave my body. This huge goddamn weight has been lifted from my shoulders.

Sonny claps me on the back. "I'm proud of you, Deacon. There just might be hope for my hot-headed baby brother yet," he chides as he takes his sports coat off and hops into the front seat.

Maverick snorts. "Yeah, right!"

"Nah, probably not, but I appreciate the vote of confidence." I slap Mav on the back of the head as I slide in behind him.

As we pull away from the curb, I pull out my phone to text Frankie. She knows I had another meeting today, but I still haven't told her the extent of the trouble I had been in with the Federation. She would feel guilty and I didn't want that. Bringing up her name, I shoot her a text.

Me: All is good, baby. See you when I get home.

My arm on the back of the seat, I listen to my brothers go over schedules and promo shit. I don't even bother trying to get involved in that whole conversation. Sonny shoots Mav down when he starts talking about bringing Leo in to help with some of the training. It's a sore spot for Sonny. I think he felt that Leo had taken his place the years that I trained with him. Leo couldn't though. Nobody could. Yes, their styles were similar, which is why I didn't mind training with Leo when I couldn't train with my brother, but there's no one in the world I'd rather win fights with. I hope he realizes that. I'm just about to tell him when my phone chirps.

Frankie: I'll be waiting. Don't take the suit off. Make sure you bring the tie.

Jesus fuck. I think my girl just told me to tie her up.

CHAPTER
Nineteen

IN FRANKIE'S NEW meeting room at the back of the gym, I sit on the fancy ass loveseat with her tucked into my side listening to Indie lose her fucking mind. "No, I don't think you fucking understand. People are crazy. They want me to plan these weird ass fetish parties for them, and when I tell them I do weddings, showers, bar mitzvahs and shit, not fuckfests, they get all uppity! Like I'm the asshole." She huffs in disgust. "This is why I need to write full-time. Because then I won't have to deal with the crazies of the world, only the ones in my head!"

It's obvious that me being cleared to fight is a huge weight lifted off all of our shoulders. My brothers, Reggie, and Frankie are all laughing their asses off while I just look at Indie in absolute amazement. Where does she find these fucking people? Before I can open my mouth, there's a light knock on the wall.

I glance up to see Cristiano standing in the opening, tapping an envelope against his hand. Smirking at his murderous glare, I greet him, "Flashdance." I was told that he hadn't left yet, I just haven't seen him. Reggie and my brothers are watching him and I can see Indie's head ping-ponging between him and I. I think she's spoiling for a fight after all of her ranting.

His gaze turns more hateful than it was, if even possible. Ignoring me completely, he approaches, "Francesca, this is for you." His tone is soft when he speaks to her. I fucking hate it.

"I just wanted to drop by to see if I can help with anything." He points to her bump, "You're getting bigger, must be hard to dance like that. You look beautiful though; pregnancy agrees with you."

"Thank you, Cristiano," she says as she reaches for the manila square he holds out to her, careful to not give him any encouragement, lest she get him killed. A little fucked up that she even has to worry about that, but at least I'm consistent and she's smart.

He has to step closer to me to hand it over and I refuse to make myself smaller for him. I don't know what the fuck he's doing here or what he thinks he's going to help with, but it's not gonna happen. She already told him to leave once. I'm worried that the chance of her doing it again isn't in my favor.

"Aren't you supposed to be in Spain by now?" My shoulders lift in question, face twisted in disdain. Flashdance opens his mouth to answer, but he's cut off by the frightened gasp that comes from Frankie.

"Princess, what is it?" The hand covering her mouth is trembling as well as the one holding whatever has her upset. Taking the piece of paper from her, I see that it's actually a photo.

"Motherfucker!" I roar, surging to my feet. I have Cristiano against the wall before anyone has a chance to react. His head hitting the wall with a satisfying thunk, little pieces of plaster floating down around him. My arm banded across his throat, I shove the picture in his face. "Did you take this picture? Huh?" I demand, spittle flying from my lips as a haze of red-hot rage makes my vision start to fade around the edges. My blood is screaming through my veins, my muscles tensed and ready to rip his ass apart. His eyes widen in fear when I put more pressure against his throat. "You better fucking answer me. Did you take this?" Arms pulling me back, I release him enough to let him talk, but not completely.

I can hear Frankie crying softly, Indie consoling her. Sonny and Mav on either side of me, closing in around him. Reggie is still holding on to me, preventing me from crushing his trachea, which I was most likely on the verge of doing.

Mav reaches for the picture in my hand. I bring my arm up out of reach shaking my head no. There is no way anyone else is gonna see this. Eyebrows raised in question, he jerks his chin at me asking me what the fuck. Gaze boring into Cristiano's, I tell him. "This bold motherfucker just walked in here and handed my girl a picture. A picture of the two of us *together* in bed. My fucking bed," I seethe. "Now you want to tell me how the fuck you got a picture of us in my house?" When he still doesn't answer, I use my arm to push him harder into the wall, making his head thump against it again.

"Deac, ease up. He can't tell you anything if you knock him out," Sonny scolds.

"I'm not easing up shit. He has a fucking picture of Frankie. Naked. In my home. I want to how the fuck that happened." Never mind that I'm in the picture too. That I don't care about. What I care about is that some sick fuck took a picture of us. With my girl spread out on the bed for me. Only for me. The atmosphere changes a bit once my brothers and Reggie learn exactly what Cristiano gave her. Their anger mixes with mine and the air crackles with it.

"Indie, take the Princess and go give Detective Adams a call for me," Sonny orders calmly.

"Okay, Jameson. Let's go, Frankie. They can handle this," Indie coaxes.

"D-Deacon?" Frankie stammers out tearfully.

"Go ahead, baby. Listen to Sonny. Stay with Indie though and then go find Pop. Don't come back in here; I'll come get you." I try to keep my tone as neutral as I can even though on the inside I already have this motherfucker dead, I'm so livid.

"Let him go. He's not going anywhere," Maverick assures

me, placing himself in front of the entrance. There isn't a door on the room, so we aren't able to just lock him in. Not that he has a chance in hell of getting away from us anyway. When I don't release my hold on him right away, Reggie tugs on my arm.

"It's okay, bro. He's gonna answer all of our questions. Ain't that right, Flashdance?" Reggie prompts.

He tries to nod his head but can't, instead managing a strangled sounding, "Yes."

Reluctantly, I drop my arms and pace away from them to stop myself from going at him again.

Sonny doesn't waste a single moment. "How did you get the picture, Cristiano?"

"I had no idea what it was. I swear," he replies in a rushed panic. "I was walking into the gym when a man stopped me. He said he recognized me from dancing with Francesca." My back is turned as he speaks, gazing down at the picture. My vision blurs with rage all over again at what whoever took this picture saw. "He—he seemed like he knew her. The man just asked if I could please give that to her. I didn't think anything of it. I swear I had no idea what it was. I would never hurt her." Cristiano is desperate for us to believe him. It's evident in his words. I just don't give a fuck.

Picture clutched in my fist, I whirl around and stalk over to him, Reggie stopping me before I can put hands on him. Leaning into his arm, I struggle to get closer to Flashdance. "You expect me to believe that you had nothing to fucking do with this? Why the fuck aren't you gone, huh? You sticking around here to make sure that she doesn't talk?" My voice is raised, people in the gym looking our way in concern.

"Deac, lock it up. We don't need an audience, brother," Mav warns.

"Why the fuck aren't you gone?" I repeat, my voice lowered, the heat behind my words cranked way the hell up.

"I—I love her. I would never hurt Francesca. I'm prepared to leave my whole life in Spain for her." Cristiano stuns me with his admission. Not because I'm surprised by the words but that he had the balls to say them. "You don't deserve her. You, you'll just break her in the end. Look at all the pain you've already caused. You don't deserve her," he states firmly.

In a lightning quick move, I'm able to get a hold of his shirt, dragging him forward even as Reggie and Sonny try holding me back. Almost nose-to-nose, I snarl in a lethal tone, "She's mine, you fuck. Don't you dare fucking tell me who or what she deserves. You don't know shit. You have no idea about what we have." Scoffing, I toss him away from me. "Flashdance, you think you love her. Maybe you do. I can fucking promise you that you feel nothing compared to what I feel for that woman. My whole goddamn life, she's been the center of my world." I brush Reggie's arm away; I'm finished with this asshole. "I told you that I would go to war for her. You though? You left her when she wouldn't conform to your perfect little vision of life as a dancing team. So you can fuck off back to Spain. She made her choice. It's not you. I fought for her. I'll never stop. She's mine," I reiterate heatedly.

The tension in the room is palpable, the energy electric. Cristiano turns to leave and Mav steps in his path. "Oh, I don't think so, amigo. If you think you're leaving before you talk to the cops, you're even crazier than I thought a minute ago when you tried my brother," Maverick scoffs. "If what you're saying is true about this random guy, then he's still out there, watching the Princess. That's not okay. I would try to keep my fucking mouth shut until they get here though so that you're still breathing when they show," he warns. "You're one word away from getting your ass handed to you by my little brother, and to be honest, I'm not feeling much friendlier toward your dumb ass."

My phone pings alerting me that I have a text.

Indie: Cops are here, headed your way. We're with Trent and your dad in his office.

Me: Is she okay?

Indie: Yeah. She's fine now. Worried about you killing the asshole I think.

Me: Tell her I love her.

Pocketing my phone, I cross my arms over my chest. "Adams is here; Indie sent her back. Pretty soon you'll be their fucking problem, not mine anymore."

"I haven't done anything wrong. I just wanted to see her and you never allow it," Flashdance says petulantly.

"I never let you? You shouldn't even fucking be here! She told you a long time ago to go back to Spain, yet here the hell you are. Why is that? Did you honestly think that she would come back to you?" I laugh humorlessly. "You had your chance, you blew it. Didn't really matter though; she was never yours to begin with. Frankie was always gonna be mine." My smile mirrors the confidence in my words.

"Gentlemen, is there a problem?" Detective Adams asks from behind Maverick. He steps aside so that she can enter. "Mr. Love." She meets all of our eyes briefly, encompassing us all in her greeting.

Sonny moves forward, arm outstretched. "Detective. Thank you for coming out." Nodding she shakes his hand.

"My partner is upstairs with Ms. De Rosa. Do you boys want to tell me what's going on in here?" Her eyes go to the indentation in the drywall left by Cristiano's head, then to me. Obviously she's come to know me pretty well.

"Have you met Cristiano Palomo yet?" I question. "He just

hand-delivered a picture to Frankie that he insists was given to him by some guy outside the gym."

I hand her the picture, now tucked inside the envelope it came in. I loathe that anyone will see that picture of her, but I have to give it to them. I know I do. There's no part of me that will be happy about it though. She handles it gently, with a tissue, sliding the photo out and then quickly back in, her expression never changing. She's a professional through and through. She just saw not only my girl but also me, in all of my naked glory, cock in hand, and she never even flinched.

Adams looks over at Flashdance. "Mr. Palomo, is that true?" Taking her little notepad out of her back pocket, she looks to him expectantly.

"Yes. It's correct. As I told them, I was on my way in and he stopped me. Acted like he knew Francesca, and about us even."

"There's nothing to know about, dick," I interrupt.

"That's enough, Deacon," Sonny warns. "Let Detective Adams ask her questions so we can be finished with all of this. I'm sure Frankie is not handling it all that well. The quicker we finish the sooner you can go check on her." That is enough to shut me up.

"Mr. Palomo, had you ever seen this man before?" When he shakes his head that he hasn't, she continues, "Can you describe him? What he was wearing?" I listen as Flashdance recounts his story, going into detail about the man's clothes and facial features. Glancing over at Reggie, he nods, letting me know that he's paying attention and committing it all to memory. "Did you see what he was driving?"

"I think it was a BMW but can't be sure. The guy who handed it to me got into the backseat, but I wasn't able to see who was driving."

"Do you think you could pick him out of a lineup, or take a look at some pictures back at the station, talk with our sketch artist?"

"Yes, of course. Anything to help Francesca. I only want to keep her safe," Cristiano speaks solely to Adams, turning his back on all of us.

I've stayed quiet long enough. "I want you gone," I say forcefully, my voice filling the room. Waiting until he turns to look at me, I continue, "Frankie told you and now I'm fucking telling you. I see your ass here again and shit's gonna get ugly. I can promise you that." There's truth in my words, and I know he hears it.

"Are you threatening me in front of an officer of the law, Deacon? Did you hear that, Detective? He threatened me." Cristiano smiles at me smugly. I delight when it slips quickly from his face with Adams' answer.

"I didn't hear anything." It surprises the hell out of me and clearly surprises Flashdance. "Come on, let's get down to the station. We can file your report and get to work on the other stuff. Your Visa is in order, right, Mr. Palomo?" she asks as she ushers him out of the room.

"It'd be a real shame if it wasn't, Flashdance. A real fucking shame," Mav calls after them, stopping Cristiano in his tracks. He turns and is faced with a smiling Maverick.

Eyes narrowed, I will him to feel my heated glare, what I have to say won't be repeated again. When finally he glances my way, I intone in a deadly calm voice, "Don't test me. I'm done with your bullshit. I've knocked your ass around once. I won't hesitate to do it again." Stabbing my finger in his direction, "Don't come back. There's nothing here for you. That's *my* girl. *My* baby. They're mine. Not yours. Mine."

Adams puts a hand to his back, urging him to go ahead of her. Hopefully that's the last time I have to see his ass.

CHAPTER
Twenty

Francesca

I MAKE MY way up to the bedroom calling for Deacon. My Loves are here to take us to lunch before we head to the gym for the rest of the day and then to the doctor. They've all been doing their best to keep me busy, keep my mind off the Cristiano and picture debacle. And I love them for it. He and his expired work Visa are back in Spain where he belongs.

At the top of the stairs, I call out for Deacon again, stopping right outside of his slightly ajar office door when I hear that he's on the phone. I'm just about to go to the other room and freshen up when I hear him say, "Carter, I don't care what the fuck you have to do, you bury that shit. Frankie doesn't need to see it. I can't deal with anymore bad publicity right now. I just got the okay I need to fight." He goes quiet, clearly listening while Carter talks. I slowly push open the door, and lean against it. He's shirtless, facing the fireplace, his back turned to me. I let my eyes roam over the tattoo of his family crest on his flank that I can just make out from this angle. The hearts and dagger-covered shield that all of the Loves have. Then to his back and the tattoo that covers the whole left side. Running along his spine, bleeding into his shoulder and arm, linking all of the artwork. My attention is drawn back to his conversation. "No, I haven't told her about all of them." He pauses. "I really don't fucking care what you think, Carter. Everything is finally good with us. I'm not fucking that up with all of this bullshit. I'll tell her what she needs to know and nothing more." He tosses the phone to the side in disgust and runs his hands roughly through his hair.

My blood is boiling. When will this infuriating man realize that keeping things from me is not the way to go? The last time he pulled this shit, it exploded in both of our faces and we both got burnt. By the sound of it, this time might be worse. I know that I don't have any room to talk, clearly our communication skills suck, but it doesn't make it right.

"What is it that you don't think I need to know, Deacon?" I ask, straight to the point, no bullshitting. He whips around and his face tells me everything. This isn't going to be good.

"Baby, I didn't even hear you come in."

Taking a step toward me, I raise a hand to stop him. "I heard you talking to Carter. I suggest you tell me what the fuck is going on, and you can start at the beginning." My arms crossed over my growing-by-the-minute chest, I stare him down, waiting. He obviously sees that I'm not letting him off the hook, that I won't be coddled and kept in the dark. Not anymore. How can we ever be a team, move forward, if he's constantly picking and choosing what I need to know and what he thinks he can keep from me?

Deacon looks pained as he drags his hands down his face, tugging on his bottom lip before expelling a deep breath. "Why don't we sit down?" He's just trying to buy some time and I'm not having it. When I make no move to sit, he sighs. "That picture from Flashdance wasn't the first picture of you or the last." Shrugging, he says, "That's it. That's all there is to tell you." He's full of shit and we both know it.

"Why wouldn't you tell me that? I thought that everything

just stopped. I felt safer! Have there been more letters too?" When he doesn't answer, I throw my hands up in exasperation. "Jesus, Deacon! Did you know that Andrew was in witness protection as well?" My voice is dangerously low, and I *feel* just as dangerous. I cannot believe that he kept this from me. If he knew about that . . . I don't know if I can forgive him. Knowing how I struggled to remember that night, my attacker.

"I had no clue that they had him, Frankie. All I know is that there are bad fucking men out there who want to get to you because of him. We don't know who they are or where they came from. I don't know how deeply he may have involved you, or what they want with you." He's getting pissed, and I really don't care. I'm pissed too. "Be mad all the fuck you want, Princess. I was protecting you and I didn't tell you because I figured the less you knew, the less trouble you could be pulled into, and I don't want you to be scared any more than you already are." Looking at me in that defiant way he has, I want to hit him. Deacon knows damn well that he's wrong, but there's no making him see reason when he's like this.

"And now? Why were you still keeping it from me?"

His shoulders hitch up in a small, nonchalant shrug. "Because I still don't know the depth of the shit he's involved you in. I'm not okay with you being put in danger for his ass any more than you already are, Frankie. The letters are all pretty vague. None of the pictures are like the one Flashdance brought us though." He doesn't have to say it, I know what he means. That picture was invasive and demeaning. It tainted something beautiful that Deacon and I had shared in the privacy of our home. Listening to him huff out deep breaths in frustration, I get pissed all over again. Why the hell is he upset?

"Isn't that my decision though, Deac?" My voice is raised, my temper a second away from detonation. "You can't just keep shit from me because you think it's what's best for me! Regardless of what you think, I am a grown ass woman. A competent woman. A smart woman, Deacon. You don't get to make my decisions for me." I'm flushed with anger; I can feel the color creeping over my skin with every word I speak. Then he goes and blows me away.

"I can and I will, Frankie. You're mine to protect, you and my baby. Be pissed all you want, but I would do it again in a heartbeat if it meant keeping you safe." Mouth set in an I-don't-give-a-fuck-smirk, he watches me, daring me to argue, and I'm about to.

"Let me see them."

"Not gonna happen, Princess. There's nothing good that can come of that." His bottom lip caught between his teeth, he shrugs his shoulders yet again. It makes me want to physically harm him.

"Deacon, let me see the damn letters. I know you have them!" I demand. My voice rising in tone and volume.

"You're right, I do have them. I'm waiting for Detective Adams to come and get them, just like she did last time." He says it so nonchalantly, so matter of fact is his demeanor.

"I want to see them—right now!" I shout.

"You want to see them? Fine, you can fucking see them. It's not gonna do shit but upset you though, and that's what I've been trying to prevent." He stomps over to his filing cabinet and yanks it open. Pulling a large manila envelope out, he tosses it on the desk. I watch as it slides across the smooth surface, right off the edge, the contents littering the floor as they spill out. Gingerly I walk over to the mess and stoop to pick up one letter, "We know you have it," and another, "He's next—won't be so brave without your man," and another, "Don't think because you're knocked up you're safe." One by one I flip through the garbage, feeling my anger and fear rise with every one I set eyes on. I don't realize that he's come from around the desk until he reaches out to take them from me.

"You shouldn't be touching these," Deacon says softly.

"Frankie, I'm sorry. I just—I just didn't want you to worry. Wanted to try to make it all go away for you." Lifting my hand, he places a kiss on my wrist.

Pulling it from his grasp, "This is my life too. I'm a part of this. You just choose for me. I'm not a child." Hands a trembling mess, I stalk away from him, putting some much needed distance between us. "What are we doing? We don't talk. We're always so concerned with protecting the other one that we're getting it all wrong." I shake my head and am just about to continue when his phone dings with a text message and then immediately starts ringing. Deac ignores it, still watching me. The phone stops and then starts instantly all over again. Throwing my hands in the air in exasperation once more, I stomp over to the couch and scoop up the annoying noise maker. The song stops just as I reach it, the missed call log and message filling the screen.

My gasp fills the now silent room when I see the text he received. My heart feels like it literally starts to shatter as I stare into the sleeping face of my fighter with not one but two naked women draped over him. Touching his bare skin, his ink, *my* ink. Smiling coyly as they snap a selfie. His voice breaks through the deafening sound of my heart pounding in my ears.

"Princess, what's wrong? Who called?" He sounds cautious, like he thinks he knows but hopes like hell he's wrong. Gathering all the strength I have left in me, I meet his gaze with tear-filled eyes.

"Is there something else you want to tell me, Deac? Something else you've been *protecting* me from?" I practically snarl.

Eyes wide, he shakes his head no until I flash him the phone with the offensive picture on display. "Fuck. Fucking, fuck. Frankie, I—"

"You what? Do you know what that says? It's on her Twitter account, in Portuguese. Would you like for me to translate?" I ask him, my voice breaking in pain and rising in anger all at once. Not waiting for an answer, I read the caption to him, "*Nós trepamos com o campeão*—We fucked the champ." Looking at him, his guilty expression is enough to set the pieces of my shattered heart on fire. Here I had been dying inside because of the hurt I'd caused us both by staying away from him. All the while just doing my best to keep him safe from whatever danger was lurking. And he was out having orgies with hot Brazilian chicks. How do I compete with that? Do I even want to? Is this what my life with him will always be?

My head is swimming with too many questions that I don't have answers to. "I guess this doesn't matter, just like Veronica didn't matter because we weren't together, right?" Sniffling, I laugh softly at my own stupidity. "It shouldn't hurt this much, Deac. Love. It isn't supposed to feel like this." I flick the tears from my cheeks. "Every time I forgive you, every time I get my heart pieced back together, you break it all over again. I know that we weren't together, but how can you replace me so easily?" My voice is low, but I know he hears me. He's watching me, a look of defeat on his beautiful face. "How can you tell me that you want to fight for us, for me, and then turn around and fuck random women? I just don't get it."

The phone in my hand feels like it weighs a hundred damn pounds, like it holds the weight of all of my problems, all my heartache and despair. Slowly I look up at him, my eyes resting on the grim set of his mouth, "Do you know how many people I've slept with since my birthday last year?" When he stays silent I let my gaze meet his. He's confused, and if the tick in his jaw is anything to go by, pissed. I go on to answer my own question, "One. Just one."

"You mean two. Me and Andre—"

Cutting him off, "One. After you told me how you felt that night, there was no way that I could let him touch me, let him inside me, because you were already there and a part of me knew it."

He groans like he's in pain. "Princess, we didn't talk for months."

My lips kick up in a small, sad smile, "Sixty-three days. For sixty-three days, I agonized over you and my feelings and what to do about them. For over two months, I made excuse after excuse to my fiancé about why I couldn't—wouldn't—sleep with him. Do you remember how many women there have been since that night?" There is no way I want him to answer, I just want him to see that this isn't the way it should be.

As I watch him, he goes from upset and a little bit sad to angry. I can tell by the subtle shift of his stance, the way his eyes go from that mossy green to a murky color I can't pinpoint. Like a mood ring. I watch in fascination and wait him out. It doesn't take long, "Yeah, well, that's great, Princess. What about Flashdance? You flaunted his ass in front of me at every turn. You might as well have been fucking him, you were with him so much," he seethes.

I deserve that, I know I do. I hurt him unnecessarily because I was too lost in my own spiraling out-of-control fears and need to stay away from Deacon. "You're right, Deacon, and I'm sorry." Not what he was expecting. "I wasn't doing it intentionally though. He was never a threat to you or us, and that made me get a little too comfortable, and for that I'm sorry." Getting this off my chest is actually a relief. I didn't like who I was when Deacon and I were apart, I wasn't myself. I was a coward, weak, and I wasn't raised to be either of those things. I'm a fighter too. I just lost my way. "I was lonely and scared and hurt and I reacted badly, but I never took it farther than anything you had to witness." My voice hitches on a little sob as I swallow past the tears clogging my throat. "I guess that's where we're different. You say I belong to you, that I'm yours, and I believe it." In a voice thick with emotion and raspy to the point of being hoarse, I ask him a question that a week ago, hell, ten minutes ago, would never have crossed my mind. "This ring, this promise, was it a lie? Something you gave me out of obligation because I'm having your baby?" I look down at my finger twirling the ring around over and over. The thought of that being true obliterating my very being. "No. Love shouldn't be like this. It shouldn't *hurt* so much, *burn* your soul. That's not the kind of love I want."

He wants a fight to make himself feel better about what he did, but I don't have it in me to give it to him. Placing the phone down, I quietly walk out of his office and out of his house with Reggie and Trent scrambling up off the couch to catch up with me.

CHAPTER
Twenty-One

DEACON

MY HEAD HUNG down in shame, I don't even bother calling after her or try to stop her. We both need a minute, and honestly, I have nothing. No excuses, no defense, no sweet words to soften the blow. How much can we possibly put each other through before it's enough? Not for me—there's no limit for me—but for her. She's cautious about a relationship with me, and she has every right to be. Picking up the phone in disgust, I pocket it and stride into my room just as Mav walks in.

"Yo, what the fuck? Why was the Princess crying? You better not be stressing her out, little brother. It's not good for her and the baby, especially after Drew knocked her around and all that shit she went through." His eyebrows are raised in warning.

Fuck! What else can I possibly fuck up today? "Is she downstairs?" I ask as I head that way to check on her.

"Nah, man. She left. Didn't say a word to any of us, just walked out the front door crying." His accusing glare isn't lost on me, but that's the least of my worries right now.

"Alone?" He better pray that he isn't up here blowing me shit if Frankie just left the house by herself.

Maverick snorts out a mocking laugh, "Yeah, right! Like

Reggie and Trent are going to give you a fucking chance to kill them. I've never seen two big fuckers move that quickly in my life. Reggie's black ass vaulted over the coffee table and the back of the couch after her." The thought of that almost gets a smile out of me. "Then Sonny said he was going to talk to her. So what'd you do now?" Sad that he's sure it was my fault. Even more so that he's fucking right.

"She overheard me talking to Carter about the Feds being at her place when Reg went to get her stuff." I turn my back like that's all there is to tell.

"What else? Frankie didn't walk out of here crying because of that. 'Fess up." My brother knows me better than that, knows Frankie better too.

My phone starts ringing. Pulling it out of my pocket, I see that it's Reggie and immediately answer it. "Is she okay?" I ask, worried that he's calling.

"Calm down, D, she's fine. She and Trent are in the gas station right now getting something to drink. I'm taking her to the studio; she said she wants to work on some stuff there. Indie is on her way, I think. I just wanted to give you a heads up. She didn't want me to call you. Said you were probably busy with damage control." I can hear the question in Reggie's voice and it goes unanswered.

"Thanks, bro. We'll be there in a little while," I tell him before disconnecting the call.

Before I put it away, I open my texts to shoot Frankie a message and that's when I see what she saw. "Dumb mother-fucker," I mutter under my breath.

"Yes, you are, but why this time?" Mav asks.

Flipping him my phone, I head into my closet to get dressed. I have to go talk with her. I hear Mav let out a low whistle, "Wow, you let them get a picture? You really fucked up with this one, huh? Is that Twitter? Do you know what it says?" Hitting me with rapid fire questions, he looks back down at it.

"Oh, yeah, I know. Frankie was kind enough to translate for me because of course it's in a fucking language she speaks," I call from the bathroom. I yank my hair back and secure it with a pink fucking hair band. "It says, 'We fucked the champ,' and yes, that's the chick's Twitter page," I say bitterly. "Where the fuck were you when this was going down? You and Sonny are supposed to keep me from doing dumb shit like that. You know how drunk I was the whole time we were there." He's not to blame—I am—but that's not gonna stop me from giving him hell. "I don't even remember what fucking night that is or who they are, I was so hammered."

"Where was I? I had PR shit to handle for '*The Champ*'!" he says using air quotes. "Sonny was in charge of your dumb ass. Where in the fuck was he?" Maverick demands.

"I don't know, brother. I don't know. Come on, let's go to the gym so I can check on my girl and try to explain."

"Explain what? Explain how? Dude, there are two chicks in bed with you. Naked. Taking selfies and posting them on social media." He snorts. "I hate to break it to you, little bro, but you ain't explaining shit." Mav laughs sardonically as he pushes his shaggy air out of his eyes, settling the ball cap back over his head.

My chin hits my chest. "God, I fucking know. Why couldn't that shit be in German? I don't think she speaks German."

"Nothing lost in translation there, my friend. Tits and ass are tits and ass in any language. When they belong to another woman or in your case, women, the only language you need to speak is the one with a whole fuck ton of I'm sorry's and expensive jewelry."

"Fuck me, I know that's right."

STALKING INTO THE gym with Mav, I don't bother slowing for the people calling my name. My hand raised in greeting
as I make my way through to the studio, I don't even see Sonny
until he's right in my face, his finger in my chest. "Make this shit
right, Deacon. Fix it now. She doesn't deserve this and if you
were anyone else, I'd kick your ass."

I knock his hand away, snorting at him in disgust. "You
could try, old man." I push past him, but before I can open the
door, he puts a hand on it. Turning, ready to give him hell or
start swinging, I'm brought up short by the grieved look on his
face.

"Deacon, listen to me. That woman loves you so much
that she'll walk away to keep you guys from destroying each
other. She'll walk away with your baby and you'll be forced to
just accept it. She doesn't need you, little brother—she wants
you. There's a difference. Be the man she wants, Deac. She deserves that." He pauses looking past me into the studio where I
can hear Frankie's music. "People are always saying stupid shit
like, 'There are other fish in the sea,' 'If you love someone let
them go' . . . all bullshit. When you find your person, that's it.
End game, brother. No matter where you look or for how long,
you're still not going to find what you have with her because it
only exists once."

Swinging his gaze back to me, he cups the back of my neck.
"I love you, little brother, and I know we've had this talk before,
but for her, for you, make this the last time we do. I know who
you are, Deacon, and so does she. Frankie loves you because of,
not in spite of it. Be her man, because she's your woman. She's
your woman, Deacon," he says emphatically, squeezing my neck
affectionately before he walks away. I'm not sure what's up with
my brother lately, and I don't have time to figure it out now, but
Frankie being pregnant has stirred something up in him.

Quietly, I enter the studio and pause. Frankie has her eyes
closed as she dances to the song streaming from every corner,

blanketing us both. The words are hauntingly appropriate for the turmoil that is *us* at the moment. Sliding down the wall, I sit on the hardwood floor. She's beautiful. Everything about her. Every movement, every inch of her is just . . . beautiful. It takes my breath away. *She* fucking takes my breath away. I've never understood what the fuck people meant when they said that, but sitting here and watching my girl with one hand curled possessively around her stomach while she sways and dips to the words, "If We Don't Move Together, Just Come Closer" . . . watching her dance with my baby, I know what they mean.

She may be a ballroom dancer, but when she dances like this, it brings out the ballerina in her. She's all elegant lines, extended arms, and passion. So much passion. The song ends, and I watch with a heavy heart as she wipes tears from her cheeks. "Don't cry, Princess," I say to her softly, startling her in the now quiet room. I push up from the floor. "Please don't, it kills me."

She dashes away more of her tears and turns from me. "What are you doing here?"

"Where else would I be? We need to talk. I told you, no more running. Either of us."

"I wasn't running, Deacon. I needed time away from you to think." Frankie flits around the room picking things up and putting them back down, her agitation obvious in her movements. Finally, she turns to me. "What are we doing, Deac? I don't want to feel like this. It hurts, *you* hurt. I just want to love you and I feel like you won't let me." My heart aches looking at her, tears streaming down her face. "I want to be enough for you. But I won't compete with anyone. Ever."

"You got it all wrong, Princess. You're not in competition with anyone. They're all in competition with you. Won't matter though. Nobody can even come close, baby." My mouth kicks up in a small, reassuring smile. "And you're more than enough. You're more than I deserve, and I know that. I told you that I'd always be faithful, I meant it. Brazil was a mistake that won't happen again because we'll never be apart again." Moving closer to her I stop just short of touching. "I want to deserve you. Teach me, Frankie. There's never been anyone who had the power to hurt me but you. You hurt me and I do stupid shit. Fall back on my old ways. I don't want to do that. I don't want to be that guy. So, stop. Stop hurting me," I suggest like that's the answer. It's as simple as that, isn't it?

She blinks slowly. "Are you kidding me? Are you honestly blaming me for acting out? For you sleeping with other women?" She's pissed and when she says it out loud like that, I can't blame her.

"No—"

She lifts a hand to stop me from speaking. "That's exactly what you're doing, Deacon. It doesn't work that way, dammit!" Her voice is raised in anger. "Sometimes you get hurt. Sometimes you get mad. That's what being in a relationship is, Deac. You don't get to do whatever the hell you want when you're pissed or your feelings are hurt though." She huffs out an exasperated breath and pushes against my chest, trying to make me step back. I don't. "You don't 'fall back on your old ways.' We fight. We fight with each other if we have to, but we always fight *for* each other. I thought that's what you wanted." She looks up at me, her blue eyes shimmering with fresh tears. "Do you even know what you want?"

I take a step forward, closing the last little bit of distance between us and take her hand, brushing my thumb over the ring I put on her finger. The first, but not the last. I raise her hand to my mouth and lay a kiss to my spot. "I know what I want," I tell her softly, firmly. "I want you. I want this baby. You, my baby, and the strap. That's all I need."

"Then show me. Be the man we both know you are. I can forgive hiding the letters and pictures from me, because you're right, I was doing the same thing. It all stops here though. We need to protect each other together by talking things out. No more secrets, big or small." With her hand over my heart, she takes a deep breath. "What do the Brazilians want?"

The muscle in my jaw takes off at a rapid beat as I clench my teeth together. She isn't going to drop this, but I don't want to fucking talk about it. "Money."

"Or what? For what?" The exasperation and trepidation in her voice give me pause.

I lift my shoulders, I have no clue what they're hoping to accomplish. Carter handles this shit, not me. "I'm not sure exactly. Carter spoke to them and he said they want cash, a hundred grand and they'll take the picture down."

Frankie paces away from me, swearing under her breath in Italian. When she makes her way back to me, her eyes are blazing with anger. "Can any of them claim that they're pregnant?"

I know what she's asking without actually having to say the words. These aren't things you want to talk to your girlfriend about. I answer instantly. "No." I don't bother telling her that I don't remember the night in question, but I do remember waking up still wearing a rubber. Some shit you just keep to yourself.

Frankie nods but won't meet my gaze. "You don't give them a dime. Not a single penny. You have never paid off any of your other skanks; this time won't be any different," she says bitterly. "The damage is already done anyway. They posted the picture, it's over. I won't have this discussion with you again though. Not about them or anyone else. This 'we weren't together' bullshit . . . I don't care anymore. There are only so many times that I can be hurt by you until I just go numb toward you. I don't want that. I want to feel, Deac. I want to feel what it's like to love you and for you to love me. Don't ruin that. Please. And I promise you the same."

Her words resonate throughout my entire being. I know she means them. I know that what Sonny said was right. Frankie doesn't need me, but she wants me, and she is it for me. No one else will ever hold a candle to her. No one else ever has.

With a gentle tug, I pull her into my arms and cup her face in my calloused hands. "Only us, Princess. From now 'til forever. Only you." Placing a kiss on her red tinted lips, I whisper against them, "Me and you, we're the real deal. It's our time, baby."

With a soft smile playing over her lips, she leans into me, "Stick and move, right?"

On a relieved laugh, I counter, "Stick and motherfucking move."

CHAPTER
Twenty-Two

I PRESS THE button on the steering wheel and tell my truck to call the Princess. She picks up on the third ring. "Hey," voice groggy like she's been sleeping or about to be.

"Hey, baby. I'll be at the house in a few minutes, be dressed, and tell Reg and Trent they can stay home. We're going out."

"Deac, I'm taking a nap. Can't we stay home and cuddle?" she tempts.

For a second I almost give in, but I'm trying to do shit different with her, romance her and shit, like I said I would, whatever the fuck that means. "Nope, we're going on a date and I want you dressed. For the first part of it at least," I can't help but tease her.

The rustle of sheets in the background tells me I've got her. "A date, huh? Okay, let me go change. I'll see you soon."

Before she can hang up, I cut in, "Don't get all dressed up and shit, Frankie. Simple, no heels or anything. Comfortable and easily accessible is what I'm looking for." The silence on the line makes it impossible not to laugh. "Calm down, baby, I'm kidding. Kind of." Swallowing back my laughter, "I'll be there, be ready. Love you, Princess." Before she can argue with me, I disconnect the call and crank the radio, "The Kill" filling the cab of my Rover.

"Frankie, let's go!" I yell up the stairs then head into the media room where I hear the guys talking over the TV.

"Hey, D, how long you guys gonna be gone? Frankie said that you didn't want us coming with you. You know the trial's like soon, right? So is the fight, which with everything going on is getting even more coverage than it would have," Reggie says.

"Yeah, I know. We won't be gone for more than a couple hours. I can take care of my girl, fucker." Punching him in the arm not giving him a chance to say anything else, I walk back to the door and glance toward the stairs, "Princess, move your fine ass! I don't want it to get dark on us."

There's a clamor and a whole lot of cussing in a sexy voice announcing her presence at the top of the landing. "I'm coming. Give me a damn minute; nothing fits me," she huffs, making her way down to where I stand waiting. At twenty-two weeks, according to my baby daddy app, she has gotten a lot bigger, though from the back you would never even know she's pregnant. Then she turns around and you're all "Heyyyy now! Where did that come from?" It's quite possibly the sexiest thing I've ever seen. Not sure if it's because I'm the one who made her that way and I know how, or if it's just flat out the sexiest thing I've ever seen.

My lips kicked up in a smile, when she reaches me, I take her face in my hands and bend so that I can see into her eyes. "You're beautiful." Sweeping the hair off her face and tucking it behind her ear. I kiss her lightly on the lips and then say to her with a wicked grin, "And I want to do filthy fucking things to you, so stop. I love this body and all that's inside it, you feel me?"

Going up on tiptoes, she kisses me softly. "I love the way you love me, Deac."

"Thank fuck for that; it's the only way I know how," I tell her and wink. "Come on."

Hand in mine, we walk to the door of the media room. "Shit, I forgot my phone. It's in the kitchen; I'll be right back,"

Frankie says as she saunters off.

I reach out and slap her ass, eliciting a little yelp, and then turn to the guys, "We're outta here. I'll see you at the gym in a few hours."

Reggie speaks up, "Where you headed?"

"It's a surprise, why?" I ask, eyes narrowed.

"Just text me with where you're going and when you get there, okay?"

"Reg, what's your deal, man? You can't be all ass hurt because I'm leaving you home. Take a few hours off, get your dick sucked—you need it, you fucking nag." Trent and Bo are snickering over on the couch; they love when I blow him shit.

Reggie just stares me down, eyes wide, and that's when I get it. Another letter must have come today. They've been easier to intercept now that Frankie is staying here. But they've been coming regularly, and I've promised not to keep them from her anymore. We'll talk about it after our date though.

"Okay, Deac. I'm ready," the Princess says, coming up beside me.

I look down and smile before turning back to Reggie, "I'll text you." That's all I need to say to let him know I'm picking up what he's throwing down. My hand on the small of her back, I usher Frankie out the front door and into the Rover.

"Where we going?" she asks once we pull into traffic heading out of the city. Her shoes kicked off, painted toes planted on my dash, she looks about thirty seconds away from falling asleep.

"It's a surprise."

"I don't want to be surprised, just tell me now," she pouts.

"No can do, baby. It's a surprise." Sticking to my guns, I just smile at her.

"You know, I shouldn't get overly excited—I could go into early labor." I glance over at her and laugh when she bats her eyelashes at me. My girl is too damn much.

"You weren't complaining about being 'overly excited' last night," feigning pain when she punches me in the arm.

"Cute, Deac. Now tell me."

Sighing deeply, "Out to the Forest Preserves where our dads like to pretend they can fish." Aviators cover her eyes when she looks my way.

"The place with the swans?"

"Yup." Smile on my face, I relax into the leather seat. Taking her hand, I kiss my spot and place it over my thigh. "Why don't you take a nap? I'll wake you when we get there. Now that you've ruined the surprise."

She nods and reaches for her phone. When the song she chooses comes on, she snuggles down into her seat, head turned toward me.

"Why do you make me listen to this girly shit all the time?" I groan.

"Because I love to torture you. Now shut up and listen. It's two girls singing 'Boom, Clap,' how can you not love that?" She's gotta be fucking with me, right?

"You know, for someone so small and innocent looking, you're mean as fuck."

Flashing me a saucy grin, "So you always say. I learned from the best though." She effectively shuts me up by raising the volume. She's a pain in my ass. And I love it.

CHAPTER
Twenty-Three

THE ROVER COMES to a stop beside a lake, the pebbles crunching under the tires. This place is secluded. Nobody ever comes out here because it's off the beaten path from the actual preserve. It's the reason my pop says he prefers to fish here—nobody to bother him. More like nobody to laugh at his ass and his lack of fishing skills.

Glancing over at a sleeping Frankie, I take a second to just look at her. She's been so tired lately, but thankfully not sick anymore. Her blonde hair is pulled back in some kind of braided thing on the sides and back, leaving her neck bare. Quietly, I place a kiss to that spot, inhaling her scent. I swear that it's changing the more pregnant she gets. It's sweeter. Pulling away, I take one last look at her and slip out of the Rover. In the back, I have a radio, blanket, and a picnic that I ordered from the Italian place by the gym. I made sure they added all of her favorites and that fancy ass water she likes. I let her sleep as I take everything to a spot under a tree right near the water.

Once I have everything set up, I carefully open her door so that she doesn't topple out. "Frankie, we're here. Come on, baby, time to get up." I stroke a finger down her bare leg eliciting a little shiver. Smiling, I do it again. Slowly she turns to face me, pushing her sunglasses to the top of her head.

"Mmmmm, we there?" Stretching awake she straightens

and takes the hand I offer to help her down.

"Yeah, we're here, little mama," I chuckle, leading her over to our picnic.

"Oh wow! You did all this?" she asks in awe.

"Don't sound so surprised; I have *some* moves," I say, affronted.

"Oh, I know you do. But you usually save them for the bedroom."

"My girl, always got jokes, huh? Fine, no food for you then. I'll just have to eat the cannoli all by myself." My teasing voice earns me a scowl.

"I will kill a man for cannoli and you know it, Love." It's true, she would.

"Come on then, I've got a cannoli for you," I tell her suggestively, helping her to settle on the blanket.

She sighs. "This is so perfect. Thank you for bringing me here and for doing all of this." I sit next to her and she lays her head on my shoulder. "I miss you, Deac." I know exactly what she means. With the fight coming up, I practically live in the gym, and when she's not in the studio, she's sleeping.

"Miss you too, Princess." Kissing the top of her head, we just sit in comfortable silence and watch the swans and ducks swim lazily across the lake. When I hear her stomach growl, I know it's time to feed her. She laughs and looks up at me sheepishly.

I chuckle as I move away from her and start setting up our food. "Okay, we have a salad, some capellini, a stuffed artichoke, and your cannoli."

"Mmmmmm, all of my favorites. You really have thought of everything," she says in appreciation.

"Yeah, well. You're kinda scary when you're hungry now, so. . . ." Ducking out of the way when she goes to slap me, I toss her a smile and start dishing up the food.

We eat in comfortable silence, the music playing in the

background. Once we've eaten all the food—well, once *I've* eaten all the food—I pack away our mess and sprawl out on the blanket, my head in Frankie's lap. She smiles down at me and pulls the hair tie from my hair and gently runs her fingers through the long strands, massaging my scalp as she does.

"You keep that up and I'm gonna pass the fuck out." No joke, I'm ready for a nap and her touch is hypnotic. "She is Love" comes on and I smile. It reminds me of the Princess so much. I take her hand from my hair and press a kiss to my spot before releasing her to continue with her soothing rubdown.

"Do you think we're having a boy or a girl?" Frankie asks absently.

"With my luck, it'll be a fucking girl."

Laughing, "Why 'with your luck?' Why do you make it sound like a bad thing?"

"Have you seen you? I have. Our daughter will be just like you, gorgeous and a giant pain in my ass. You think we were protective of *you* growing up?" I scoff. "Imagine me and my brothers with a little you. Their niece. My daughter."

"Yeah, that is kinda scary," she says and pretends to shiver in fear. "Well, I think it's a boy. A rotten little Love, just like his daddy and uncles."

They always say that pregnant women glow and it always sounded so ridiculous to me. Until I watch Frankie talk about our unborn child. She literally glows. *Love* shining from the inside out. It is so fucking beautiful.

"So what should we name this rotten little Love? Deacon?"

Her hand stills. "Ummmm, no," Frankie tells me, rolling her eyes.

"What's wrong with Deacon?" Totally affronted now.

"Oh, shut up, I'm playing with you. But still, no." She tugs my hair and giggles. "I was thinking something more Italian, like Rocco, Ignazio, or Giovanni."

"Are we having a baby or starting our own mob?" I laugh,

peering up at her. My smile fades when I see that she's serious. "Princess, Rocco?" My tone is teasing.

"Yes, Rocco. And, no, we aren't starting our own mob. Those are all family names, Deac," she informs sternly.

"Yeah, the Godfather's family. Is he gonna call me Don Love instead of Daddy and come out with pinky rings for the family to kiss and shit?"

She punches me in the chest. "Oh my God. I'm telling my dad you're making fun of us dagos. He's gonna whip your ass. Ignazio was his dad's name."

Rolling over, I push her to her back and pin her down with her hands over her head. "Yeah? Is he gonna make me sleep with the fishes, Francesca Victoria Teodora De Rosa?" I goad, using *all* of her wicked Italian names. I'm careful to keep my weight off of her so I don't squish her and my kid. I dip my head down and place a kiss on her lips, swallowing her sigh when she opens for me. Our tongues brush together in a languid rhythm. Releasing my hold on her wrists, I lace our fingers together and deepen the kiss. Every part of me wants to devour her. Here, outside in the sunshine, next to the lake, and I'm about to when I feel something against my stomach. Frankie lets out a gasp and pushes at my shoulders.

"Did you feel that?" Excited she looks at me in absolute awe.

"I did, what was it?" I ask in confusion.

"It was the baby, Deac! I feel *him* from time to time, but never that hard, and never when I can share it with you." She's beaming with tears in her eyes as she moves to a sitting position, forcing me back onto my haunches. Frankie scoots closer to me. Settling onto the blanket, I sit and pull her so that she's sitting in front of me, her legs tucked under my bent knees. Taking my hands, she places them on her belly, pressing lightly. We sit in quiet anticipation, both of us looking down at our joined hands, willing the baby to move again. When *she* does, our gazes lock and the smile that spreads across Frankie's face is one that will forever be etched onto my heart.

"Holy shit. Does it hurt? It feels like *she's* giving it hell in there."

"No, it doesn't hurt, but *he* is giving it hell. It just feels like little pushes right now." After a few minutes and a couple more kicks, her voice is soft, reverent, as she asks, "Isn't it the most amazing thing, Deac? We didn't mean to, but we made a life, out of love." Looking at me with a watery smile that I return, I can only nod as I take a moment to swallow past the lump in my throat.

"Our Love, Princess." This moment is so un-fucking-believable I can't even feel like a pussy for tearing up over it. I raise her hand to my lips and kiss her wrist. I stand and tug, helping her to her feet. Once she's standing, I crouch down and put my lips to her growing belly and whisper, "Don't hurt your mommy; she might take it out on me, little Love." Straightening I smile down at my girl and wipe the tears from her cheeks. "No crying, yeah? Dance with me instead. That ginger dude is on again and I kind of dig him." Lips kicked up, I close the distance between us and mold her to me just how I like, *cuts to curves.*

As I sway us back and forth to the sound of Ed Sheeran, I think about everything I can do in my down time from the gym to spend more of it like this with Frankie. I know that she comes first, but the title fight is a big deal, and she won't stand for me fucking off with my training, even if it is for her. I have to stick to the original plan: fight and then the girl. Stick and move. Stick and motherfucking move.

The sun is starting to go down and I'm lazing with a sleepy Frankie when I see a black SUV barreling toward us with two more close behind. Quickly I stand, yanking the Princess to her feet as gingerly as I can in a rush.

"Baby, get up and get in the truck, now," I demand firmly.

"What? Why? What's going on?" she asks, her eyes darting

past me. I know the moment she sees them. Stumbling forward, I catch her from falling but it's too late for anything else—they're already too close.

I watch the three vehicles split up and surround us, blocking any escape route we may have. Tucking Frankie behind me, I widen my stance, protecting her as best I can with my body. She clings to my back, her body pressed into mine, the swell of her baby bump reminding me of all I have to lose if shit goes wrong here. I'm not sure who has just crashed our picnic, but I have a pretty good idea.

I do my best to regulate my breathing and remain calm. "Princess, no matter what, you listen to me, you got it? I don't care what happens, if I tell you to do or say something, you do it, you feel me?" Her face buried in my shirt, she nods and lets loose a quiet sob. "Baby, I need you to get your shit together. I need my fierce girl right now."

With idling engines, doors swing open, almost in synch, and men of various shapes and sizes step out. Jesus fuck, no good can come of this. Six men move toward us while three drivers stay behind the wheels of their Audis. One man stands out, leading the other men, knowing they'll follow. He stops directly in front of us, the others fanning out and surrounding Frankie and I on all sides. I can feel her trembling against me and my blood starts to boil, rage sending my body into "fighter" mode. Fucking Andrew still putting her and now my baby in danger.

"Mr. Love, we have not had the pleasure of meeting. My name is Kiernan," he says in a thick accent that sounds like it might be Irish. He extends his hand for me to shake. Ignoring it, I never take my eyes off of his soulless gaze. His eyes are black, his coppery hair slicked back and tamed as if it didn't dare disobey him. "Is that any way to greet a new acquaintance, Mr. Love, or have all of yer manners been beaten outta ya, hmm?" He lets out a low laugh. "I don't want to make this difficult . . . well, any more difficult than you've been making

things." His cool and controlled tone slipping a little as he says that.

My arms crossed across my chest, I stand as tall as I can. I'm sure they're packing heat, but I have to seem as intimidating as possible if I have any hope at all of getting us out of this.

"I'm not looking to make any friends. What the fuck do you want? I would think by now you would get the message that we can't help you." With narrowed eyes, I look down my nose at him, pinning him with an animosity-filled glare.

"Yeah, pity that." Shifty eyes going to where Frankie is trying to remain as small as possible behind me, he says as if he's talking to a child, "Miss De Rosa, you can step out from behind him now. We can do this the easy way or the hard way." I can feel Frankie start to move to my side and I wrap my arm around her, keeping her where she is. This defiant move causes him to sigh dramatically, "I was afraid of this. The hard way it is then," Kiernan says in fake resignation.

I catch movement to my left as a man of average height with brown hair comes closer to us, pure malevolence shining from his brown eyes trained on Frankie. Just as he takes the final step, putting us within a couple feet of him, he draws his gun and points it right at Frankie who sucks in a loud lungful of air. I twist her as far from him as I can and push his outstretched arm away forcefully, but it snaps back quickly.

"Don't you fucking point that gun at her, you moth—" Before I can finish, we have six guns trained on us and Frankie is snatched from behind me. I whirl around and see yet another man with an arm banded across her chest and a Glock to her temple. Frankie's eyes go wide in fear and a flash of something I can't name.

"Cherries," falls from her lips and I know. The man with the gun to her head is the same man who beat her within an inch of her life and left her for dead. That was the one constant in all of her incomplete memories. The scent of cherries and tobacco. Looking at him now, I can understand how she could mistake him for Andrew. The all consuming rage I feel is blinding. I quake with the ferocity of it. I know in my soul that they will not hesitate to kill her. They've already killed Drew; what's one more? I need to keep my head because there's no way that I can fight us out of this. Muscle ticking rapidly in my jaw, I try to focus on taming my anger for once in my fucking life.

"O'Reilly has already met our darlin' Francesca here, haven't you, bud?" He nods in agreement and I'm forced to watch in horror as he palms one of her breasts and squeezes. The growl that escapes me, alarms him, giving him pause, but the weight of the gun in his hand must remind him of the position we're in. He smiles evilly.

"Yeah, we've met, though we never got to finish what we started. Did we, darlin'?" When I see his tongue snake out to lick down the side of her face, I surge forward, but am stopped by the butt of a gun being struck against the base of my skull. Grunting in pain, I drop to one knee. Slowly getting to my feet, I turn toward the asshole who struck me. "That's the last one you'll get for free, the next one will cost you," I sneer.

"Enough for fuck's sake," Kiernan booms. He takes a calming breath. "Now, darlin', me bud here asked ya for somethin' when he visited yer gaff. Ya didn't deliver, so now we're here to collect."

You would think that he's asking for a cup of sugar with how cool and collected he is, whereas my insides are a tsunami of hatred, rage, and malice. This motherfucker is talking like we're all going to have dinner after this.

Frankie shakes her head, the gun held there pressing into her tender flesh, making her wince. "I have no idea what you're talking about. I don't have anything. I never have!" she shouts, close to hysterics. As soon as I find a way to get her out of here safely, I'm killing all of these fuckers. I don't care if I spend the

rest of my life in prison for doing it either.

Glancing at Kiernan, I see him watching Frankie, eyes boring into her, like he's trying to determine if she's telling the truth. I'm not sure what he sees, but whatever it is has him in front of me in two long strides and a nine-millimeter dug into my forehead. Frankie screams out in terror but it's quickly muffled when O'Reilly covers her mouth. Tears streaming down her face and over his hands, she looks at me with wide, panicked eyes. I don't look away from her, willing her to stay calm. I can't take Kiernan out without risking her. I need to wait him out and hope to fuck he doesn't shoot me. "Since yer not makin' this easy, bud, shit's gonna hit the fan." His face morphs from bored, almost docile, businessman to crazy as fuck killer in three seconds flat. "Ya got two seconds to tell me where the fuck it is or I'll blow her bleedin' brains all over this fuckin' lake. Hand it the fuck over. Now!" he roars, cocking the gun. My eyes close for a beat before opening again and bringing them to Frankie's blues. O'Reilly's hand falls away from her mouth and she starts babbling incoherently, the sobs sticking in her throat. When he snatches her hair and wrenches her back, giving her a little shake, I see red, blood red. Not thinking about the gun pressed to my head or the madman holding it, I knock him to the side and charge forward. I make it exactly three steps before I hear the crack and feel the fire burn as fast as the bullet that tears through me. Stopping, I glance down and see the red blossoming, staining my shirt.

CHAPTER
Twenty-Four

MY ATTENTION IS drawn from the spreading warmth of the blood when Frankie screams my name and clutches at her stomach. It's in that moment I realize how precarious of a situation we really are in.

"For Jaysus sake, shut her the fuck up, already," Kiernan demands.

O'Reilly prods her in the shoulder with the gun he just had to her temple moments ago. She is folded in on herself, her shoulders hunched in pain, her arms wrapped around her swollen belly. Ignoring everything, including the pain, I speak calmly but loudly to be heard over my girl's cries. "Princess, baby. Shhhhhh, please. If he puts his hands on you again, I'm going to get us both killed. Please, for me, stop crying. Okay? I need you to stay calm for the baby," I plead with her gently. My words must penetrate—she stops crying, her breathing coming out in short, little gasps. "That's my girl." Doing my best, I smile reassuringly through the pain. Somehow, someway, I will get her out of this safely.

Never taking my eyes off of her, I ask Kiernan. "What exactly are you looking for and what in the fuck makes you think that she has it?"

"Her fella was either very clever or a complete fuckin' tool—"

"Ex—they haven't been together for the last year," I interject. I need to remind him of that for my benefit and also to clue him in on just how long it's been since Andrew has had any influence on her.

"Yeah, well, her bleedin' *fiancé* has spent the last couple of years building a case against us and expects us to believe that he doesn't have a fuckin' clue where the evidence is. What a load of ol' bollix," he spits, his gun now pressed into the tender flesh behind my ear. Frankie shivers, but I give her a stern look, willing her to lock it up. "We know it's not at his gaff and that he doesn't have it, Lord rest his filthy soul, so that leaves us with this little fine thing standing right here." His voice has an air of merriment to it. This fucker is so unstable.

"I have no idea what you think I have, but I assure you that I don't. He never even spoke about his cases with me," she says earnestly.

"If that's the truth, then we'll have to take you, darlin', as a pawn until we get what we want," Kiernan says, with a flick of his wrist, putting his men into motion. O'Reilly tugs on her arm and starts to drag her in the direction of the vehicles.

"No. Take me." I step in their path. My voice is steady, my heart is not. It's beating so frantically at the thought of them trying to take Frankie, it makes even my skin pulse. My blood bubbling past the hand I have clamped over the wound on my shoulder with every beat. If they attempt to leave with her, I will get us killed, but not before I take down each and every one of them.

"Why the fuck would we take you?" he sneers.

"Do you know who I am? If I go missing, it will be all over every news channel in the state, hell, the country. They'll be scrambling to get you what you want in order to look good for the media." I have no fucking clue if that's true; in fact, taking a pregnant woman is probably a better bargaining chip, but it's all I have, and as long as she's not the one they're holding,

I don't care. "If Frankie has what you think she does, she can convince them to tell her what to look for. They aren't gonna give me shit if you take her. They're just going to come at you guns blazing, and I have no idea where Andrew would hide anything anywhere. She does."

Holding my breath, I wait and hope like hell he believes my bullshit theories. O'Reilly looks ready to argue, so I hurry to ask, "Frankie, you can do this, right? You can make them tell you what he hid?" I try to keep my tone encouraging, nodding at her to agree. When she does nothing but stare at me blankly, I go on. "As soon as they catch wind that I'm gone, the Federation is going to put out a press release and contact every media source they can. You need that kind of circus to get them to act. Once they do, you can take your evidence and slink off to the hole you crawled out of and nobody will know shit."

I can't see if what I'm saying is sinking in since he's standing behind me, but I know the moment he decides that what I'm saying might work by the look on Frankie's face as she watches him over my shoulder. O'Reilly holsters his gun and gives her a shake, "Give me your phone." He begins to drag her over to the blanket when I call out, "She didn't bring hers, but mine is hooked up to the radio in my truck." Frankie's eyes widen at the lie. Hers is the one in the Rover, mine is tucked away in the picnic basket. If they're going to leave her stranded out here, I don't want them to know that Reggie knows where to find her, and since I texted him from my phone when we arrived, they might see that message. Plus, I have her cell phone finder on. All Reggie has to do is track her phone and he'll know where these fuckers are.

"Get her phone and keys. She can figure out how to make it out of here on her bleedin' own. She won't be taggin' along to fuck this up more than she already has," Kiernan commands.

I stand, stoic and unmoving, trying to convey whatever strength and confidence inside of me to Frankie. She looks like

she's going to faint from all that has happened, and I need her to be strong. O'Reilly comes back with the phone and keys, a smug smile across his bastard face.

"Have fun walking, darlin'," he sing-songs as he walks to stand beside Kiernan and I.

"We'll be in touch in twenty-four hours. Don't be stupid, and fuck this up. No coppers. I'll flat line him if you betray us," Kiernan warns a trembling Frankie.

Suddenly, I'm surrounded by his men as they move me toward one of the idling vehicles. I call out to her, "You can do this, Princess. Fuck keeping anyone but you and the baby safe. You hear me? You do what Sonny and Mav tell you to. They'll know what to do!" I yell over her cries as they push me into the back of the SUV. It's all too reminiscent of the night I was arrested for beating Andrew's ass.

"I love you, Deacon!" she calls out to me on a sob that echoes off the lake.

They box me in on both sides so that I have no way of escaping before I get a chance to reply. Kiernan settles in the front seat, and as we drive away, I duck my head to look at Frankie standing next to our picnic. I reach past the sweaty fucker to my left and place my palm against the glass. I do it to reassure her. To tell her that I love her. To express that I have faith in her. I'm not sure if it does all of that, but knowing that she's safe as long as I'm with them soothes me enough to make a promise to myself that if they harm her in any way, they all fucking die.

CHAPTER
Twenty-Five

Francesca

RED.

Red.

All I see is red.

Blood.

So much bright, red blood.

It's like déjà vu. I stand alone and watch the man that I love, my world, my everything, be driven away in the backseat of a car. Bleeding out from a gunshot wound, and I am absolutely powerless to stop them. This time though, it's not the cops, the good guys, that have him. It's the Irish Mafia. The bad guys, the *Mob*. The. *Mob*. How do we fight them and win? How can we not? They have Deacon—there's no other option.

My breath is coming in short hiccupping puffs as I try to calm myself. I have to think. Deac said to be his fierce girl. It's up to me to save him. Oh God. It's up to me to save him. As the enormity of that sinks in, I stumble to the blanket and the picnic basket where Deacon's phone is. I don't know why he told them I didn't bring mine. At the moment I don't care. As long as I have some way to call for help. Upending the basket,

I riffle through our leftovers until I locate the phone. My hands are shaking so badly, it takes me three tries to get to the contacts. Who do I call first? Sonny, Mav, or Reggie? I can feel the panic rising and the pangs in my belly have started again.

I kneel down and rub a hand over my baby. "Please, little Love, please be okay in there. I can't handle anymore. I can't stay strong for daddy without you," I tell *him*, my voice cracking as I swallow past the tears that haven't stopped raining down my face since they wrenched me out of Deacon's arms.

With a deep breath I decide to call Reggie first. He has more connections and would know what to do. I rock back and forth on my knees as I wait for him to answer, my breathing becoming more and more labored with each second that ticks by. When I finally hear the deep rumble of his voice, I completely break.

"Yo, brotha. What's up, you done playing hide and seek in the forest now?"

"Re-eggie," I stutter between gasping, soul-shaking sobs.

"Frankie? What's happened?" When I can't get anything out beyond my nearly silent breath-stealing crying, "I need you to breathe, girl. Just breathe," he demands gently.

"They-they t-took h-him. They took Deacon. They sh-shot him and then they m-made him go with them," I wail.

"Motherfucker. Motherfucker!" he roars. Then there's a lot of commotion on the other end of the line. The rest of my Loves must be there. I can faintly hear Sonny in the background. "Where are you, Princess? We're coming for you now," Reggie tells me in a more gentle voice.

"At th-the lake. They took the k-keys and my phone."

"Okay, okay. We're driving now. Get in the truck if you can and lock the doors for me, okay?" His voice is commanding and soft all at once. It helps to calm me. Makes me feel less alone in this moment where I am so very much alone. My world crumbling around me with every tear that falls.

IT TAKES THEM thirty-five minutes to get to me. Thirty-five minutes that felt like hours upon hours. Thirty-five minutes where I had nothing to think about other than the fact that the Irish Mafia had the father of my unborn child, my soul mate, my best friend, and I have no clue where they have taken him. Deacon was shot trying to protect me. SHOT. I try not to dwell on that and just pray that he's okay. Pray that these men of deplorable dishonor so desperate to get the evidence that they need that they will keep him alive and unharmed. I know who and what Deacon is, and I know that he can take whatever beating they deliver. I just wish for him to not have to endure any of that pain. Not over me. Certainly not over Andrew. The fact that they shot him troubles me more and more as the minutes tick on.

By the time they arrive, I am a tear-stained, weeping mess. I jump from the Rover and lunge at Sonny, babbling incoherently, just trying to explain to them what happened, but I can't. I cannot get a single coherent syllable out, and then I hear Deac's voice in my mind, *I need my fierce girl right now.* He does need her. He deserves her. My body won't stop trembling and the fine sheen of sweat brought on by anxiety makes my skin sticky, but I straighten my spine in determination and pull on all of my resolve and strength. Resolutely, I wipe the tears tracking down my face and blow out a breath and explain to them in as steady a voice as I can muster exactly what went down.

When I finish, I look at them one by one expectantly. "What do we do now? Do we call Adams and Flores, the marshals, who?" I implore anxiously.

The fear is written all over each of them in varying degrees, and I just want to shut my eyes and ignore it because it terrifies me even more that they're scared.

"First, let's get the fuck out of here. Once we're back at the house we can figure out how to move forward," Reggie insists.

Mav touches my temple gently. "You have a bruise here. Did they hurt you? Should we take you to the hospital?" The concern in his voice is evident. I haven't felt any more pain in my abdomen and that's my only concern for myself at the moment.

"No, I'm fine. Deacon didn't give them the chance to hurt me too badly."

He nods and wraps an arm around my shoulder, ushering me to the truck and helping me in. I watch as Trent cleans up our picnic and stows everything in the back of Deac's Rover. Reg tosses him the key. "You drive D's truck, we'll meet you at the house."

Once Reggie and the Loves are all in the vehicles, we take off in a silence crackling with tension. Nobody speaks because we're all lost in our own debilitating thoughts. Reg breaks the silence. "Frankie, you sure they were Irish?" he asks, meeting my eyes in the rearview mirror.

I nod solemnly. "Positive. I could tell by their names and accents, but they also used the word 'gaff' instead of house, so I'm pretty certain." His mouth set in a grim line, I can almost see his thoughts as they flicker across his face. "Tell me right now that we can get him back, Reggie. Tell me that we will," I plead.

Blasting me with his ebony gaze, he utters with utmost certainty, "We will get him back, Frankie. No matter what we have to do. What laws we have to break. You understand me?" he asks sternly.

Sonny turns in his seat toward me and Mav tucks me more firmly into his side and squeezes my shoulder. "My little brother will come home safe and in one piece, Princess. There's nothing that will keep him from coming back to you. Not even the

Mob," Sonny assures me. "We just have to do all that we can on this end to make it happen," he states before turning around in his seat again.

Once back at the house, they bombard me with more questions. "Where was he shot? How bad was he bleeding? Why did they take him and what in the hell do they think you have that can put them away?" I answer each one in a detached, monotone voice. The longer he's gone, the more distraught I become.

"They said twenty-four hours is when they'll call. They have my phone; couldn't we just call them?" I ask. All I want is to hear his voice, have him tell me that he's okay.

Reggie's head pops up. "They have your cell, Princess?"

"Yes, for some reason Deac lied to them and had them take my phone instead of his. I'm not sure why," I say, confused.

"That brilliant motherfucker. Looks like our time in the sandbox stuck with him. OORAH, brother!" We all stare at him, baffled by his outburst. Pulling his phone out of his pocket, he starts explaining. "While you were in the hospital that time, he downloaded one of those phone finder app things. As long as it's not shut off, we will at least be able to track the phone from my phone and his," Reg says, smiling for the first time since they came to my rescue.

Sonny chimes in, "So we'll know where he is? Then what?"

"We won't necessarily know where *he* is, but we'll have a location on the phone, so we can at least go to it and force whoever has it to bring us to Deac. It's definitely not our first course of action, but it's a solid Plan B."

"Okay, what about Plan A, bro?" Mav asks him, pacing the room.

"I think that we should have Frankie call the marshals and ask, again, why these guys think that she has anything. They gave her their card, let's use it. Feel them out a bit and go from there. One of those guys is still alive, right?" He takes a deep breath and his eyes dart to mine. "Not to be dramatic or anything, but we call the cops, they're not gonna want to negotiate shit and the Irish will feel betrayed and . . ." His voice trails off.

"They'll kill him," I finish for him. "Won't they? They'll kill him because . . . just because." My voice is tinged with a low-lying panic, bordering on hysteria, hovering right at the precipice and dying to bubble over. None of them answer me. They don't need to. "I'll go find my purse and the card," I tell them absently as I head for the hall table where I left it.

Making my way back to them, I doubt our ability to bring him home and I immediately feel guilty. They love him as much as I do and they won't give up on Deacon. I can't either. Reggie hands me Deac's phone. "Just tell him that the letters are coming more frequently and becoming more aggressive, Frankie." I look up at him startled—I had no clue. "Don't give them more than you have to just yet." I nod and take the phone from him, dialing in Deputy Riley's number and listening to it ring over and over before I get his voice mail.

Hanging up, I try the other number on the card for his partner, Deputy Baird, and get the same thing. Frustrated, I thumb the end button. "Nothing. Neither of them are answering."

Sonny is pacing along with Mav now, stabbing his fingers over and over through his short dark hair, his usually clean-shaven face sporting a five o'clock shadow. "Why don't we go to the house and look around. Frankie might be able to find something that they couldn't or at least maybe something that would point us in the right direction."

Reggie stands. "That's actually a good idea. You still have your keys, right?"

"Yeah, I have them. I don't know if I'll find anything that they couldn't, but I need to do something."

We all move as one toward the door when Mav stops abruptly. "We need to call Pop. He's on his way here to talk about the fight and the new promo. He needs to know. Oh fuck. How are we gonna tell him, Sonny?" Just then the door opens and Joe and my dad both walk through it, smiling when they see us and then just as quickly their smiles slip when they notice our solemn expressions.

"Che cosa, bella?" my dad asks worriedly. We all look from one to the other. I can feel the tears starting to prick at the backs of my eyes. The thought of having to tell them, having to relive it all again, is almost unbearable. My father must be able to see the pain written across my face because he starts speaking to me in Italian, not giving me a second to answer him. Immediately he thinks it must be something with the baby.

"No, Dad. The baby is fine," I tell him in English so that the Loves know what we're talking about. When my dad gets overly emotional, whether it be mad, sad, excited, whatever, he reverts to Italian.

Joe looks to Sonny, his eldest son. "What's going on, Jameson? Where's Deacon?" he asks warily. A tiny sob escapes me, causing them all to turn in my direction.

"Pop, Guy, let's go sit down for a second and talk," Sonny says. Then turning to us, "You guys go ahead, Trent and I will catch up."

"Are you sure, Sonny? We can wait," Mav assures him.

"No, you go." They're using words to speak, but they're communicating more through looks and some silent understanding that I can't figure out.

"All right, brother."

That said, they lead me out the door and to the house I haven't been back to in all this time.

WHEN WE PULL up into the driveway, Reggie turns in his seat as much as his large frame will allow. "Now, I don't know how much they've cleaned up since that night. When Trent and

I were here, it was a mess and I doubt it'll be much better now. I just want you to be prepared. Okay?" I look out the window and stare at the house I called home and shiver as I remember the last time I was inside. Reaching for the door handle, I nod in agreement and step out of the truck. The three of us meet at the front of the vehicle and slowly make our way to the front door. Me fumbling with the keys and them close behind me, looking over their shoulders for what, I don't know, while I unlock the door. I stop and face them. "Are we even allowed in here?" The thought never even occurred to me until now.

"Do you care?" Reggie deadpans. An answer isn't necessary. I don't give a single fuck if we are allowed or not. If it means getting Deac back, I will break every goddamn rule known to man.

Stepping in the front door, I'm taken back to that night. I was happy here for a very short time, but the memories of my attack wipe every happy moment I ever had in this place. I flip the switch for the hall light not expecting anything. I'm surprised when it actually goes on. "So where do you want to start?" I begin and then stop abruptly when we turn the corner and I see the dining table and two of the chairs overturned, russet stains smeared on the material and the oak floors.

Mav places himself between me and the mess in front of me. "Princess, I know this is hard being back here. I know it is. But, Frankie, we have to try to find whatever it is that they're looking for if we want to save Deac, okay? If there was any other way, we wouldn't be here." I swallow past the lump of fear, aggravation, and just plain damn hurt and head for Andrew's office. "I'll look in here first then."

"There's our girl," Mav says encouragingly.

Slowly, I push open the door that leads into the office and gasp at the mess I find. Drawers are dumped and tossed aside, picture frames smashed and broken, leather chair and love seat slashed, stuffing spewing from the cushions. It's like every damn cop movie I've ever seen. Careful not to touch anything I don't have to, I make my way to the desk and see that even the locked drawer has been somehow opened. I pick my way through the chaos and over to the floor to ceiling bookshelves, none of which hold any books since they've all been torn from the shelves, and reach behind it to pull the lock. I then slide the entire shelf to the side revealing Andrew's safe. He was so excited when they installed these cases and the carpenter gave him the idea to have them lock and roll together or apart.

Face to face with the safe, I try to remember what book he had the combination written in. He never told me, but I had seen him in and out of it enough. It was a poetry book, collections by Christopher Poindexter. The only reason I remember is because he's one of my favorites too and I recognized it. I survey the mess I'm standing in. How will I ever find the book I need amongst all of them scattered around the room? Crying out in frustration, I whip a book at the wall safe, dropping to my knees, and let the feelings of desperation and desolation overcome me.

Great big wracking sobs drown out the muffled sounds coming from the other rooms, leaving me alone yet again with my pain. I place my forehead to the carpet, my arms wrapped around my belly, my baby. Trying to hold on to the one thing of Deacon's that I can. The one thing that I know will keep me fighting when all I want to do is lie here and give up. The tears fall, faster and faster, but I do my best to regulate my breathing so that I'm able to think.

My mind racing, I let my thoughts take me to Deac. I've spent my life being protected by him, loved by him in every capacity. But he also taught me to always fight for myself. Now, I have to fight for both of us. It's my past that's threatening to destroy all that I am, all that we are. I have to prove I'm fierce enough. I'd die for him. He went to war for me. Now it's my turn. He's my man and I love him. I'm ready to fight. He's mine and they can't have him. None of them can. He. Is. Mine.

My resolve firmly in place, I pick myself up off the floor both figuratively and literally and walk over to the safe again. I pick my way through the debris, keeping watch for the book that will give me the code. Toeing books aside and flipping them over. Frustrated when I've been through nearly all of them and still haven't found it. My fingers thrust in my hair, I spin in a circle, not knowing what to do, when I catch sight of a familiar book underneath the desk. Rushing over, I crawl under as quickly as I can and snatch the book up, crying out in relief when I see that it's indeed the one I am looking for. Carefully backing out and standing, I start flipping through the book slowly until I find the page I'm looking for. I shuffle forward and stop in front of the safe saying a little Hail Mary that it holds the answers.

My hands are shaking as I key in the code. When the lock tumbles and the safe beeps, I close my eyes as I swing open the heavy door. Almost afraid of what I might find. After a second, I open my eyes and am instantly deflated. There's nothing inside other than two stacks of money that I couldn't give a shit about. I slam the door closed. "Fuck. Where the hell is it, you asshole?" I ask the room, not caring about speaking ill of the dead. If anything happens to Deac . . .

Going into the bathroom connected to his office, I go under the sink and pull out the yellow gloves that Andrew's maid always used to clean and put them on. I want to be able to comb through this whole damn house and not have to worry about what the hell I touch. I stalk back into the room and start flipping through every book I see, putting them in a pile when I'm finished. When I still find nothing, I turn with determination to the paperwork scattered all over. There must be something here that they missed.

Sitting on the floor with utter destruction surrounding me, I blow out a frustrated breath. My back aches from being hunched over, reading over every scrap of paper I come across.

Legs asleep from the awkward way I've been sitting, I stretch them in front of me to try to relieve the numbness. Reggie fills the doorway, making me jump. "You scared the shit out of me, Reg," I breathe, holding a hand to my chest, trying to calm my racing heart.

"Sorry, Frankie. You find anything?"

"No, nothing," I answer in a deflated voice. "You?"

"Nope. We've been through the whole fucking house. There's nothing here," Reggie tells me, his disappointment obvious. He kicks shit out of his way and holds out a hand to me. "Come on, we should get out of here."

My gaze shoots to him. "We can't give up. *I* won't give up," I insist, batting his hand away.

"I don't expect you to, Frankie. We just have to regroup. We don't have time to waste time here." His eyes bore into me and I know he's right. Reggie would never quit Deac—none of us would.

"Okay," I reply quietly, taking the hand he's once again offered. "Did Sonny and Trent ever make it back here?"

"Yeah. A couple hours ago," he answers.

I gasp in shock. "We've been here that long?" He nods that we have.

I feel the panic welling up when Mav says from the door, "You okay, Princess?" Shaking my head no, he reaches for me and envelopes me in a hug.

A noise from the living room has us all turning. Before I have a chance to say anything, Mav is pushing me behind him, back through the doorway. Reggie has a gun in his hand heading toward the sound, motioning for us to stay put. My heart is lodged in my throat at the thought of any more violence, which is ironic considering what the man I love does for a living and where I grew up.

"Mav, Frankie? Where are you?" Sonny calls out, allowing me to let go of the breath I'd been holding.

"Motherfucker," Reggie grumbles. "You about got your ass shot up, Jameson!" he bellows down the hall. Trent and Sonny follow the sound of our voices and fill the doorway.

"Sorry, brother. You guys find anything?" Sonny asks, taking in the mess before him.

Mav takes my hand and starts to lead me through the room, forcing everyone into the hall. He doesn't stop until we're out of the house. "No. Let's go back to Deac's. I'm done being here." Nodding in agreement, I climb into the back of the truck and sit quietly, allowing them to recount the last hour.

"Pop and Guy are getting in touch with the EWF right now. Let's get the Princess home," Sonny says softly, closing the door as Mav and Reggie agree with him.

It feels good to let them take charge for the moment so that I can think. I know that Deacon doesn't want me to put anyone in danger, least of all myself, but he has to know that I'm prepared to do anything to get him back. Now I just have to decide how to do that.

AFTER A SLEEPLESS night, I walk downstairs feeling like a zombie. I'm completely numb. We have nothing and they have everything. They have *everything.* The ache in the pit of my stomach is nothing compared to the hurt in my heart. I don't know what to do. I only know that I have to get him back. That's the only option. Wandering into the empty kitchen, I walk over to the Keurig and pop in a decaf coffee. What I wouldn't do for a regular right now. As the machine sputters and hisses, I walk over to the glass bowl on the counter that holds all of our keys, change, and extra little bits. Deacon's dry cleaning slip is sitting there with a note reminding him to pick it up as well as "flowers for the pregnant one." A sob from somewhere deep within bubbles to the surface. Letting out a cry, I throw the bowl against the wall and watch in fascinated horror as it shatters all over the floor, the glass glittering in the light like hundreds of little stars scattered about. I watch them, mesmerized. By their ability to be so pretty though so broken.

"Princess?" Sonny says from somewhere behind me. The concern in his voice makes me sad that I wasn't able to keep it together.

"I'm okay, I'm sorry." My voice is flat with remorse.

"Nothing to be sorry about. This is hard on all of us. You're entitled to be upset." He walks up behind me and lays a hand to the middle of my back. "Your coffee is ready. We'll get this cleaned up later." His tone is soothing, steady. So Sonny. That's all it takes. I lean into him, clutching his shirt as I start to cry silently.

Sonny rocks with me in his arms, talking softly to calm me. Finally my tears subside, leaving me a hiccupping, tear-stained mess. "I am so sorry. Again." I do my best to give him a smile, but I just can't manage it. He takes my arm and leads me over to the island, helping me onto a stool.

"Cream and sugar, right?"

I nod.

When he's finished doctoring my shitty excuse for coffee, he sets it in front of me.

"Everyone okay in here?" Reggie asks as he enters the kitchen. It's obvious that he witnessed my little breakdown by the sympathetic look on his face.

Sonny answers him so I don't have to. "We're fine now, Reg."

Reggie walks by us, patting my shoulder as he does. Crunching through the remnants of the bowl, he goes to the closet and pulls out the broom and dustpan. "Please don't. I'll get all that in just a minute."

"I got it. You're too pregnant to be cleaning," he teases,

pulling a slight smile from me.

Reggie pauses in his sweeping, bending to pick something up. "These your keys, Frankie?" He holds up my keys, the heart locket popped open, the picture askew.

"Yes."

"What's up, Reggie?" Sonny asks, walking over to him.

Leaning the broom against the counter, Reggie taps the heart against the counter and something falls out. I can't see what from where I'm sitting. "Who gave you this locket?"

"Drew did for my birthday," I answer puzzled. "Why?"

Between a thumb and forefinger, he holds up a tiny little chip. "Did you put this SM card behind the picture?"

"No. He must ha—Oh my God. Is that what they're looking for?" I ask, hopping down and going to where they stand.

"I think that it might just be," Reggie tells us.

With trembling fingers, I pluck the tiny chip from him. My throat is raw from crying, my voice barely a whisper. "It was in my locket? It's been there the whole time?" I cry, covering my hands with my face. "Why didn't he just tell me?"

"Probably because he was worried that your house, your cars, the phone lines were all bugged. If he'd told you and they were, they would have come looking for you harder than they have." He grunts out, "Don't get me wrong, he's no fucking hero because he should have never planted shit on you in the first place, but I believe that's why he didn't tell you."

That bastard.

CHAPTER
Twenty-Six

DEACON

I'M NOT SURE how long these fuckers have had me here, tied to this damn chair, but it feels like forever. And not because one of them thinks he's the next Conor fucking McGregor and gets hard off sucker punching me every time he comes in the room. Nah, he'll get his. It feels like forever because I'm worried about my girl. This is a lot of stress for one person to take on. She's a warrior, my warrior Princess, but this is life or death shit and she's pregnant. My brothers and Reggie will help her, but I also know Frankie and that she's carrying the weight of this and won't rest until she wins the war.

"Rise and shine, bud. Time to call yer bleedin' bird. Best hope she listened and didn't call the coppers," O'Reilly warns. "I would love to finish what I started at her gaff. Make ya watch before I kill ya both," he cackles.

I spit at his feet, the stream of blood hitting its mark, leaving a coppery stain. "You keep me tied up because you know I'll fucking kill you if you don't. Be a man. Untie me and then say some shit like that, yeah?" I snarl.

We're interrupted by Kiernan followed by the aspiring McGregor himself. Living up to my expectations, he walks

208

straight up to me and smiles, just before delivering a solid right hook that connects with my nose, blood spurting instantly. He chuckles gleefully.

"Hard to look rough and tough when yer nose is broken and yer covered in blood," he chortles.

"Even harder to look like a badass when the only way you can break someone's nose is if their arms and legs are tied to a chair." I smile at him, the blood dripping down my face and off my chin. It's not the first time I've broken my nose and it definitely won't be the last. These hits are nothing I'm not used to. This is simply training for me.

"Fuck you, you bleedin' arsehole!" he shouts, kicking the legs of the chair, trying to topple me but not succeeding. I laugh at his failed attempt. I shouldn't goad them, I know, but I can't help it. This little motherfucker is begging for an ass whippin.' He better pray that they keep me tied up while he's around.

"For fuck sake, are ya done now, Rayo?" Kiernan asks the young punk in disgust. "If yer looking for a pissin' contest, look somewhere else. I don't have the bleedin' time to scrape ya off the ground when he's done with ya." He shakes his head. "I wanna get what we came here for and get back to The Pale. I don' have time for yer bleedin' shenanigans."

Turning to me, "I apologize for me brother. He fancies himself a fighter. Boys a bleedin' spanner," he says in a bored tone. "You would do well to be nice to the man, Rayo—he's probably mates with your idol," Kiernan calls over his shoulder, snickering.

I look over to where the fucker stands sulking. His brother obviously has the same thoughts about his aspirations as I do. Spitting in his direction to clear my mouth of blood, I smile, "He's no McGregor. He hits like a pussy." Incensed, he rushes forward, but Kiernan catches him up before he can get to me. "That'll be enough, ya eejit. I can't have you manglin' him anymore than ya have." Setting him aside, he turns to me. "Ya ready to call your bird? Hopefully she's come through or else I'll let me brother here have at ya," Kiernan tells me cheerily. "Ya keep changing the bleedin' digits on us so I can't dial her, the fuckin' cheek of ya," he tsks. "Best be giving it to me so we can call her up."

Eyes narrowed, I recite my own telephone number to him and listen to it ring when he switches it over to speaker. My fingers are throbbing from how tightly the ropes are tied, my feet have long since gone numb, and my shoulder is a constant ache from the bullet most likely still lodged there. They were kind enough to pour whiskey over that to make sure it didn't get infected once they got me strapped to the chair yesterday. Upset with my unwillingness to cooperate, they'd pistol whipped me and trussed me up while I was unconscious. None of that matters though because Frankie is safe.

Sonny picks up on the third ring. "Hello?"

I look at Kiernan, waiting for instruction. He lifts his chin in my direction, indicating for me to go ahead.

"Sonny, it's me. Can you hear me? Put the Princess on for me."

"Hey, brother, I hear you. Are you okay?" Jameson asks, the worry evident in his voice.

"Yeah, bro, I'm good. Getting a little bit of training in with this kid who doesn't like my face too much," I try to joke, glancing at Kiernan when he kicks at my ankle, motioning with his hand to move it along. "Sonny, is Frankie there? They want to speak to her."

"Yeah, she was afraid to answer. She's right here beside me, Deac."

"D—Deacon?" she stammers in a raw voice.

"I'm here, baby. You doing okay? The baby?"

"Yes, we're fine." Her voice cracks and I just want to reach through the phone and hold her.

"That's enough of the chatter. Did youz find what we're

lookin' for, darlin'?" Kiernan asks. "Better be sayin' yeah, otherwise yer fella here is gonna get battered."

"No! Don't hurt him. Please. I found something that was hidden, a memory card. I didn't look at it. Andrew had it well hidden though so it must be what you're after," she rushes to say.

"Good, good. You meet us at the lake where we picked ya up in an hour. Come alone and if in fact you have what I think ya do, I'll hand over yer fella."

"Frankie, don't you dare come alone! You bring Reggie and my broth—oomph." I'm knocked stupid with the butt of a gun, my head lolling forward, skull feeling as if it's on the verge of exploding.

"You bring the law and I'll flat line ya both quick as ya please. Don' be testin' me, darlin'. One hour, not a minute past," he orders and disconnects the call.

"Yer a fuckin' eejit. Tryin' to get yer lady killed I reckon. You better hope that she's smarter than you are."

ARMS ZIP-TIED BEHIND me, pulling at my shoulder, I wince as we drive over the uneven dirt road that leads out to the lake. They didn't bother trying to clean my face of all the blood; I'm sure I look like I just went three rounds in the Cage. As we come into the clearing, the SUV rocks to a halt, the engine idling as the three other vehicles following pull up beside us. Across from us, I see my Rover parked, but can't see who's in it, the glare from the sun shielding the tinted windows.

Kiernan is sitting in the front seat, same as when we left this peaceful place just a little over twenty-four hours ago. He turns to me, gun in hand, "Now don' be goin' doin' anythin' stupid. Me mate will check the card that yer bird has and if it's good, we'll cut ya loose. Ya go actin' mad though and I'll fuckin' shoot ya right between your fuckin' eyes and piss off to The Pale without a care." I nod my understanding and follow the burly fucker they brought along out of the backseat. I don't believe for a second that they're going to let us just leave after this transaction is done. They're the fucking mob—they don't make deals. They dig shallow graves.

I straighten to my full height, my feet set in anticipation. I have no clue what to expect, no idea how this is gonna play out, but I need to be ready for shit to get real . . . and quick. Doing my best to get my blood-matted hair out of my face, I give my head a shake, ignoring the pain that rockets around my skull. It takes a second for my vision to clear and my eyes to adjust to the bright sunlight. When they do, I see Frankie, my brothers, and Reggie all standing beside the Range Rover. Frankie still has on her clothes from the day before, her hair a messy bun on top of her head.

I'm prodded into motion by Wannabe McGregor and his Glock digging into my spine. "Let's go, bud."

As we close in on them, I see the anger on my brothers' faces, anguish on my girl's. Reggie's mask is in place; he's in "mission" mode. I try to smile reassuringly at Frankie, but I can't quite pull it off. My gut is screaming at me to act. To start doing harm any way that I can and run like hell with my girl. Making eye contact with Reggie, it's clear that he's thinking the same thing. He nods imperceptibly. Just that one signal and I know that no matter what he'll put Frankie and her safety first.

Kiernan stops and holds up a hand for them to do the same. "That's far enough. Where's this chip ya have?" When Reggie steps forward to give it to him, every one of Kiernan's goons raises their arms, guns cocked. He shakes his head. "I don't think so, big fella. Hand it over to the lady and stay where ya are." Reggie stands where he is, the indecision flitting across his face. Frankie makes the decision for him when she moves

around him, both of my brothers directly behind her. Watching her every movement, I feel every one of my muscles tensing, readying for battle just like before a fight. She reaches Reggie's side and takes the card from him, and with a hand cradled under her swollen belly, walks to the devil himself.

"Such a brave girl ya are," Kiernan says as she nears him, arm outstretched with the tiny little chip pinched between her fingers. It's all surreal and in slow motion with the birds chirping happily in the background, the gentle lapping of the waves on the shore. All so serene and peaceful. Such a lie.

Kiernan takes her offering and hands it off to O'Reilly. As he turns back to Frankie, he draws his weapon. "Brave or just stupid, just like yer dead fella." Stock still, I watch in horror as Kiernan points his Glock at Frankie's head. At that moment, I don't think, I just act. Stomping on the foot of the asshole behind me, I throw my head back with all of my strength and connect with his face. Cursing, he drops to the ground, writhing in pain. A cacophony of yells and screams fill the air right before shots ring out and echo all around us Not sure where they're coming from, I barrel my way through mobsters with guns to my girl, noticing that the clearing is now full of cops, all adding to the melee. With Frankie in my sights, I wade through the chaos. Just as I near her, I see a flash out of the corner of my eye. I turn to see Kiernan, the sun glinting off the muzzle of his gun, a smile of pure evil across his face as he pulls the trigger. I flinch with each shot.

One. My heart stops beating. *Two.* I'm frozen in terror. *Three.* I lunge toward the mad man set on taking everything from me. *Four.* I tackle him to the ground, my arms still tied behind me, his weapon flying from his murdering hands at the impact. The birds now squawking in panic as I throw all of my weight on him. Screaming Frankie's name over and over, no way to stop it as it echo's in my ears, invading every space in my mind, I pin him to the ground with my body, heavy with the adrenaline running through my veins. I'm just about to slam my head into his face, just like I did to his brother, when I'm hauled up by the arm, but not before I get in two swift kicks to his head and one to his ribs as I'm dragged away.

"Deacon, it's Detective Adams. Please, stay still, let me cut your restraints," I recognize her voice as thick arms hold me steady. Stilling, I allow her to free me. Once my hands are unbound, the arms holding me loosen and I drop to my knees. Not allowing myself time to recover from what just took place, I stand and start searching frantically. Calling out for Frankie and my brothers, pushing my way through the hoards of people now clogging the banks of the lake. I see Reggie crouched down covered in blood and come to an abrupt halt. "No, no, no, no, no, no." Over and over, falls from my lips as I take in the scene in front of me.

Sliding across the grass and sand, I scramble to where Reggie sits. The guttural sounds coming from me rip from my very soul. How? How will I ever learn to live without the one person who believed in me the most? Loved me at my worst? Who I love more than I love myself?

I won't.

I can't.

I fucking won't.

CHAPTER
Twenty-Seven

I EXPLODE THROUGH the emergency room doors of the hospital, startling the people milling around with my haste and my appearance. I wouldn't allow them to treat me at the lake, my need to get here far greater. The three of us skid to a halt in front of the treatment room doors when we see a blood-stained Dr. Ashley push through them. Grim-faced he greets me, "Mr. Love, I'm sorry that we're meeting like this again." A part of me is hopeful. Everything turned out all right last time I saw him. It would this time too, right? I mean, it fucking has to. All hope is dashed when he shakes his head no. "I'm just so sorry that the outcome isn't the same." I knew. I knew, but having him confirm it is too much.

"No. No!" I yell and storm past him, pushing my way through the doors, searching every bay I pass, my eyes darting frantically until I come to the one I'm looking for. Collapsing to the ground, all my strength leaves me. Gone. All of it. Gone, as a nurse pulls a white sheet over my brother's face. "Don't. Don't put that on his face. He can't fucking see like that." Staggering to my feet, I move to his side. "He can't see. He needs to see," I demand, tugging at the sheet that she won't let go of.

"Sir, please. Sir, he's gone. I'm sorry," the nurse says to me gently, carefully removing my shaking hands.

"He can't see . . ." My words are lost on a sob. Sonny hates the dark. I've always made fun of him for it.

"Deacon?" I whirl around to the sound of my name. The haggard face of my dad bringing all the pain to the forefront. The nurse makes her way past him, giving us time alone.

"Pop." The moment he's beside me, I fall into him. His arms band around me, holding me up. "Why Pop? Why Sonny?" I can't catch my breath, the pain in my heart is too much. "It should've been me. It always should've been me. I'm so sorry, Pop. So sorry. He was the good one. He was so good, Pop." My voice catches on the words as my dad does his best to console me, even when his world is imploding.

The door opens and Maverick steps in tentatively, "They're wrong, right? He's not g-gone?" he asks hopefully, brokenly.

My chin hits my chest as another sob is dragged from me. I can't. I can't do this. Refusing to look at the bed that holds my now lifeless brother, refusing to meet the devastated eyes of my father, refusing to acknowledge my only living brother. My only. Living. Brother. I stumble into the hall. I have to find Frankie. I need to find Frankie.

Limbs like lead, I wander out to the waiting room, searching for my girl. My anchor. Not seeing her, I spin in a circle, frantically seeking. Please no. She was fine, wasn't she? I saw them put her in the back of an ambulance. She was sitting up and talking to them. Right? I dart for the door and run right into a brick wall.

"I got ya, bro," Reggie says, steadying me.

Eyes wild, I look behind him. "Frankie?"

"She's okay. They admitted her to the maternity ward though for observation because she was grazed."

My heart trips, trying to find a rhythm that isn't quite so painful. "Does—does she know?" I ask.

Reggie drags a hand down his face and shakes his head no.

Nodding, I look away, his pain more than I can handle right now. "Take me to her. Please."

I STAND OUTSIDE of Frankie's hospital room with my forehead pressed to the wood, tears falling silently and steadily down my face and dropping to wet my shirt as I ready myself to face her. She's going to know as soon as she sees me. I'm incapable of hiding the pain I'm suffering right now. I don't even have the energy to try really. I just want to spare her of it for another minute. Our lives are never gonna be the same. We're never gonna be the same. With one last fortifying breath, I push through the door.

She's sitting in bed, eyes closed, hooked up to monitors beeping and tracking what I assume is the baby's heart rate. I open my mouth to say something. Anything. But nothing comes out. Just then her eyes open slowly and land on me. One look and she sees everything, just like I knew she would.

"Nooooooo. Nooooo, Deacon! No!" she wails. Burying her face in her hands, her whole body convulses from the power behind her anguish and tears.

I start for her, my steps faltering when I see Guy stand from a chair in the corner. He brushes tears from his face, my dad's name falling from his lips as he heads for the door knowing that Frankie and I need each other right now. Turning back to the Princess, I reach over my shoulder and pull my shirt over my head as I walk to her bedside, wincing when it sticks on the dried blood of my wounded shoulder. Gently, I slide my hands under Frankie's legs, moving her over and crawling in behind her. She turns into me, burying her face in my neck, her tears dropping onto my chest.

"It's all my fault, all m-my f-f-fault, Deacon. I'm s-so s-sorry," she sobs. I hold her to me, doing my best to stay strong for her when, really, I'm on the verge of breaking again.

"Don't say that, Frankie. It's not your fault. It's not, baby," I demand, rocking her gently.

"It is! I brought him into our lives. I did that. I k-killed Sonn—" She can't even get his name out before she's crying so hard against me that it shakes us both.

There's nothing that I can say that she'll listen to right now, so I don't. I just sway her from side to side, letting my hands sift through her hair, over and over, letting the monotony of the motion calm me as the tears fall with hers, mingling before they leave a trail down my chest. I've never felt pain like this. It's all-consuming and heavy. It's so heavy. Like I'm lying beneath a ton of bricks and can't find the strength to get out from under them. May never find the strength to fight my way to the surface. I may never want to.

CHAPTER
Twenty-Eight

FORTY-FIVE DAYS. THAT'S how long I've been walking around in a haze. One thousand and eighty hours since my brother left this world and me to fumble my way through it. I'm barely living right now. I don't really know how. Sonny was always telling me what to do, and now . . . nothing. My pop isn't much better. Mav has himself so buried in work he doesn't have time for anything else. They got the fight postponed. I don't even know for when. Don't really give a fuck. The trial was over and done with as well. Those of the bastards that weren't killed at the lake that day are now behind bars. Better than they fucking deserve.

I come to the gym every day, work myself until I collapse. My shoulder almost completely healed. Most days I don't even bother to go home. I think a part of me feels Sonny here in the gym. Within the walls or something. Nobody bothers me here; they don't know what to say. I'm glad they don't try. Frankie is worried about me. Fair, since I worry about her too. Every time I see her, she's crying. I'm not sure if she even realizes it anymore. It kills me to see her like that. I know me staying here at the gym hurts her, that she doesn't understand it. I just can't find it in me to explain it to her right now.

How do you explain? I've been to war. Lost brothers. I've held them while the life seeped out of them in a country a world away from home. I've watched them be blown into the atmosphere by cowards not willing to even look you in the eye when they take your life. But never my own flesh and blood. Never *my* brother. It wasn't supposed to happen like this. I left the battlefield behind me; my war, my fight, a totally different beast now. Death wasn't supposed to invade my soul here. It wasn't supposed to take from me what it wanted with bullets and violence. Leaving me with gaping holes, soulless. Anger and anguish a constant companion instead of my beautiful girl.

The sound of the door catches my attention.

"What are you doing here?" I ask, confused.

"I called him," Frankie says, moving out from behind Leo.

Widening my stance, I look to them for some kind of explanation. Frankie walks into the weight room, closing the door behind her. "I called him, Deacon."

"Yeah, you said that. Why?" Eyes narrowed, I watch her cross her arms over her chest, Leo leaning back against the closed door, content on letting us have this out.

"Do you blame me for what happened?" she asks in a controlled voice.

"No, of course not. I've told you that," I say, agitated. We've had this discussion more than once, and I'm over it. Tired of telling her that it wasn't her fault. It simply wasn't.

"Then why don't you come home?" The hurt in her voice cuts right through me.

I glance at her then away.

"Leo, did you know that we're having twins?" she asks with a hint of sadness and wonder.

Whipping my head to look at her, I ask in astonishment, "What? We are? Why didn't you tell me? What the fuck, Frankie?" How the fuck could she keep something like this from me.

"I tried calling you. When I was in the hospital, Dr. Dean came to check on me and said they were picking up two heartbeats. He scheduled an ultrasound. You missed it. Indie took me." Her voice catches. "You didn't come home that night. I drove here to tell you, but you were sleeping." She shrugs her shoulders. "You haven't been home since, not in weeks really, figured you didn't care." There are tears glistening in her eyes. I shoot a look at Leo who is still against the door, head down. I still don't get why she called him.

"Of course I care, Frankie. You're all I've got left," I say to her softly. "I just—I just . . . fuck." Thrusting my fingers through my hair, I yank until I can feel the burn in my scalp.

"It should've been me, Frankie. He was a good man, honorable, fucking perfect, the bastard." I laugh, full of regret, squeezing my eyes shut. "Should've been me," I choke out.

I'm not sure when she moves, but when I open my eyes, she's standing in front of me. Her blues travel over my face slowly before they settle on mine. Black eyelashes spiky from her tears, she reaches up and trails her fingers down my face. "Sonny didn't deserve to die Deacon, but neither did you. You, you're a good man. The best man I've ever known. I don't ever want to hear you say that it should've been you again," she states firmly. "It shouldn't have been any of us." Flicking a tear from her cheek she continues, "I miss him too, Deac, every day. I also miss you. I feel like I've lost you both." Her voice is thick with emotion and it breaks me.

I give no thought to looking like a pussy in front of Leo. With tears streaming down my face, I scoop up my girl and bury my face in her coconut-scented hair. Immediately I feel a weight lifted. Not completely, but enough to let me breathe for the first time in over a month. This right here is all I have left—I can't forget that. "I'm sorry, baby. I didn't realize," I say into her neck.

"I know, Deac."

I pull back, a small smile all I can muster even though I'm happier than I've been in longer than I can remember. "Twins?"

I ask in awe.

Frankie nods, smiling sadly at me. "Yes. Dr. Dean says that sometimes one hides behind the other or their heartbeats are so in synch you can't tell that there are two." She fingers the chain at my throat. "I didn't know if you wanted to know the sex so I told them not to tell me."

"Baby, I'm sorry I missed it. Did they give you those picture things?"

We're interrupted when Leo clears his throat. He raises his hand in apology. "Sorry. I know you're having a moment. I didn't mean to interrupt," he says sheepishly. "But I practically had to suck my Commander's dick to extend my leave. We need to get to work."

Glancing between the two, I ask, "What do you mean 'get to work'?"

Leo sighs dramatically. "Your fight is in less than three weeks. You look like hell. You probably won't even make weight right now," he tells me shaking his head.

"I've been hitting it hard, dude. I'm in fucking fantastic shape. I've never not made weight," I spit out.

"Hitman, you've lost weight. You need to bulk up. You're not taking care of yourself, bro. Just being here in the gym going through the motions isn't cutting it," Leo chides. "If you're gonna be ready, we gotta get you on track."

I don't want to listen to his shit. I don't even want him here. I know that's hateful as fuck since he's my friend, and Frankie obviously called him, but Sonny is my trainer. "Tomorrow. I just want to go home with my girl right now. That's the track I need to get on." Wanting to change the subject, "You staying at our place?"

"Not tonight. I'll probably stay here tonight."

"Call me if you change your mind, Yoda," I say as I take Frankie's hand and lead her to the door.

She stops as we pass him and places a hand to his arm.

"Thank you for coming, Leo. I appreciate it."

He bends and gives her a peck on the cheek. "Any time, sugar."

Leo holds a hand out for me to shake. "Tomorrow, Hitman. You and me," he says pumping my arm.

"Talk to you then, Yoda. It's good to see you," I lie. It's not good to see him. I now know why he's here and I'm gonna have to break it to him that it's not gonna happen.

LATE THAT NIGHT, lying in bed with Frankie curled into my side, my mind is racing. My thoughts all over the place. I sigh deeply. "You asleep?"

"No, I'm up, Deac," she says as she begins to softly trace her name inked into my skin. She does it when she's lost in thought.

"Why did you call Leo, Frankie?" Pretty sure I've figured it out.

Her hand stills for a second and then resumes its path. "I'm scared for you. Usually I'm the one who is able to pull you out of whatever you're dealing with, just like you're it for me. Nothing I'm doing is working though. I couldn't even get you to come home." Frankie's voice is pitched low, but I hear all she's not saying. It's always been either her or Sonny able to keep my shit straight. I run hot a lot of the time, always have, and Frankie has been my anchor since forever. If it wasn't her, it was Sonny. "I couldn't watch you slip away any further than you already had. I called Leo a couple of weeks ago. He said he was about to go on leave and that he'd be here the first chance he could."

"What's he gonna do for me that you couldn't, Princess?" She sits up, so I stack my hands under my head.

"Train you. Help you find some purpose. Make sure you

don't step in that Cage with Rude Awakening unprepared and get hurt," Frankie says in a matter of fact tone. "I see you, Deac. I know you and I see you. You're hurting so bad and you won't let me in." Her voice hitches. "You're a hair trigger right now. I keep waiting for you to go off. It won't be long before you do. I'm afraid for you. For us." She reaches out and runs her fingertips lightly over my lips. "I need you. *We* need you."

Taking my hands from behind my head, she places them on her round belly, lacing our fingers. "We need you, Deac. I love you, let me in. Let me try to help you," Frankie says to me gently. With tears in her eyes, she takes my face in her hands. "I can't bring him back. God, I fucking would if I could. But we have to try to learn to live without him. Not forget him, we never could, but he would want us to live. You're not living, baby." Leaning forward she places a kiss to my lips, her own salty from the tears trailing down her cheeks and over our fused mouths.

I tangle my fingers in her hair, cradling her head and pressing her tighter to me. I've needed her. Maybe I was afraid to let her help me through this because that would mean forgetting my brother. She's right though. We don't have to forget him— we just have to live. Living's not forgetting.

I pull back and let my eyes roam over her face, every beauty mark, and smile line. With the pad of my thumb, I rub away the moisture our kiss left on her bottom lip. "Okay," I vow, releasing my hold on the silky strands of her hair and tucking it behind her ears.

She watches as I throw my legs over the side of the bed. I can't have her hands on me if I'm going to get through this next part. "I'm going to grab a drink. Do you want something?" I ask, placing a kiss to her wrist.

"No, I'm fine, thanks."

"Be right back, baby."

I go into my office to the bar and pull out a tumbler, filling it with Scotch. I need a moment to get my thoughts together.

Glass in hand, I walk back into our room, over to the window. Sipping slowly, I welcome the burn of the liquid. "Would you still love me if I gave up fighting?" Frankie is bewildered by my question, I can see it on her face reflected in the window pane. It's something that I've thought about a lot lately though and I need to see where she stands.

"I don't love you because you fight for a living, Deacon. I love you because you're a *fighter*," she says calmly like I'm supposed to know what the fuck she means.

My brows drawn in confusion, I turn so that I'm facing her and lean against the sill. Ankles crossed, I watch her over the rim of my glass as I sip. Assessing her words and trying to decipher them. "Isn't that the same fucking thing?"

"Not at all." After a few seconds of watching me and expecting me to pick up on her damn riddle, she stands and places her hands where her hips should be. "Where is this coming from, Deacon? Why now? Fighting inside that Cage is all you ever wanted. You've been training since you were just a little damn kid. Why now?"

"He was my team. My coach, my brother. He was wrapped up in all of it. I don't know how to do any of it without Sonny," I admit, throwing back the rest of my drink. Saying it out loud makes me feel weak, like a quitter. But I feel hollow. I have this huge void and fighting isn't filling it right now. "I don't know if I want to."

Watching me closely, she says, "You asked me if I would love you if you gave up fighting. Well, you can't give up fighting because it's who you are. You're full of passion and heat, determination and honor, and that's what makes you a fighter. You're fighting whether you're in that Cage or out. It's what I love about you most. You fight for everything you believe in. You never stop fighting." Smiling sadly she continues, "So, yes I'd still love you if you never fought on a stage again. If you never stepped foot in the Octagon. But you'll never *not* be a fighter.

225

And I'll never not love you." Still smiling she adds, "You're kinda stuck with me, Love."

"No one else I'd rather be stuck with, Princess," I say honestly. Maybe, just maybe, with her in my corner I can do this. My girl will help me. No more trying to do it on my own. She's my team too.

CHAPTER
Twenty-Nine

"CHIN DOWN, HITMAN! Get your fucking feet under you. Where's your power?" Leo's frustration is evident. "What the hell are you doing? You're not following through with your hits. You're giving me 'tap, tap, tap.' I need 'BANG, BANG, BANG!'" he shouts, slapping his mitts together. "Come on now."

His voiced raised, he goes to the middle of the Cage and puts his hands back up. "Let's go," Leo demands, waiting expectantly.

My chest rises and falls in exertion and unwanted emotion. Inside is all fucking turmoil and crashing waves. All of it way more taxing than the drills he's putting me through. "No," I say quietly, walking away, yanking my gloves off. Mav is standing off to the side with his arms crossed over his chest. Frankie sitting in a chair beside him. Exactly where she's been since we spoke the other night. Silently cheering me on and supporting me.

"No, what, Deacon?" Leo calls after me. "No, you don't want to spar? No, you don't want to hit me harder? No, what, man?" I hear his mitts hit the canvas. "I've been here for nearly a week and you've given me this half-assed shit. We leave for Vegas in two days, bro. In two weeks you're going to be fighting the most important fight of your career, and honestly, I don't think you're ready."

On the other side of the ring, I fold my arms and lean against the top rope. Chin resting on my forearm, I let what he's saying sink in.

"He's right, bro," Mav adds. "Your form is off; you're not giving even fifty percent right now and you need to be going at one hundred and fifty if you're going to beat Rude Awakening. It's all about that fire right now, Deac. Time to bring it."

My eyes on the Frankie, I search her face, looking for strength, the words, for the answers to explain. She smiles and nods in encouragement. "It feels wrong. All of it just feels wrong," I admit quietly. "I don't want to do this without him." I grab a hold of the ropes and straighten. "There's no fire left. I keep searching for it, waiting and hoping that it'll show up. But it doesn't." Pulling my hair free, I gather it all back up and tie it into a bun, my hands needing to be busy.

"You know I get that, bro, I do. But you're not the only one who lost a brother. You think that it doesn't kill me every day to walk in this gym and know that he isn't here to talk shit over with. To bitch about your ass to?" Mav snorts out a frustrated breath. "This isn't only about you. I need this too, Deacon." He slaps his rolled up notebook against his leg. "I need this to feel like I'm not letting him down. He would never let you give up like this. So I won't either." I can hear the emotion clogging his throat.

I clear my own, trying to rid myself of those same feelings. "How? How do I do that?" The clack of Frankie's heels against the hardwood has me turning to face her. She makes her way toward me; climbing the steps of the ring, she hugs the post in the corner, her blues locked on me.

"You fight. From the inside out, you fight," she says simply.

Leo moves to stand beside Frankie. "Men aren't made into fighters, Deacon. Your brother didn't make you the incredible warrior that you are. He helped to mold you, taught you how to respect the art, honed the skills that you were born with. You

can do this. I know that you feel like you can't win without him, but you were born a winner. You were born to wear that belt, and Sonny knew it. Don't quit on him because you think he's not here, that none of it matters without him. He is here," he says slapping a hand to his chest, holding it over his heart. "And it matters more now than it ever did. You do this for you and you do this for Sonny. Let's win this thing, together. For your brother."

I glance over to where Mav is standing, his baseball hat pulled low over his face, trying to shield his hurt from the rest of us. "For my brothers," I say past the lump in my throat and nod.

SINCE FRANKIE'S ALREADY been cleared for travel, we leave a day earlier for Vegas. All of us. My pop and Guy included. I just want to get there and start training hard. It always takes me at least two days to get acclimated to the climate change there, plus we have a lot of promo stuff going on. Mav and Leo were right—I haven't been giving it my all and was ready to throw in the towel on my whole career. My heart still hurts, my chest heavy with a shit ton of sadness that I think will always be with me, but I need to channel all of that shittiness into my training.

To save some time, and to get me into the gym sooner, we decided to take the private plane. Besides, the Princess is so wicked pregnant, it'll make travel a little easier on her. Once word gets out that we're here, it's gonna be a total clusterfuck. We've lain so low since we lost Sonny that the media is gonna be in a frenzy now that we've resurfaced. They all smell a story and like the vultures they are, they'll do anything to get it. Mav and I went over everything earlier. How much we're willing to talk about, what answers I'll give, and when he'll interject. I won't have Sonny's death made into a circus. I'll have to keep my head with the media. Having Frankie there will help though.

As we start our descent, I look over at my dad lost in thought, watching the lights come into view below us.

"Pop? You okay?" I keep my voice down so I don't wake my girl just yet.

"I'm okay, just ready to get in the gym with you, son." He smiles sadly at me and goes back to looking out the window. He's been quiet, handling his grief in his own way. Being in the gym training has helped. Like Mav, I think just being submersed in work makes the loss of his eldest son a little more bearable.

"You awake, Princess?" I ask, taking her hand and flipping it to pop a quick kiss to her wrist.

Frankie smiles sleepily. "Yes, I'm hungry though," she tells me, running her hands over her belly. I can't believe that I missed so much. Not being able to see past my own grief cost me a lot of memories that I can't get back. I'm gonna have to work double time to make new ones to make up for it.

I place my hands over hers. "I really am so sorry I wasn't around for the last six weeks. Hopefully we can do another ultrasound of the *girls* when we get back home." Just saying that out loud is scary. Two babies. Two. It's not even the thought of more than one baby that scares me. It's the thought of more than one teenager that has me ready to buy an island to live on until they're forty-five and I might think about letting them date.

"I've already made an appointment for you to get a look at the *boys* the moment we get back." Smiling cheekily, she leans forward and presses a quick kiss to my lips. "It's good to see you smile, Deac. We're going to get through this. We all are. Right after you kick the shit out of Saul 'Rude Awakening' Ares."

"So violent you are. It's because you're so small, right?" I tease. It does feel good to smile, and she's right—we will get through this.

Stick and move. Stick and motherfucking move.

CHAPTER
Thirty

Francesca

THE HEAT HERE is oppressive. I feel like I've been thrust into a fire it's so damn hot. Of course that could just be because I am extremely pregnant, a little swassy and a whole lot swooby right now too. Clearly been hanging around Indie too much, making up words for sweaty boobs and whatnot. Or maybe it's the fact that I'm in the air-conditioned gym, looking like a sweaty mess I'm sure. Like I said, swass and swoobs, while Deac is looking like a ridiculously gorgeous god of fighting or something, flipping a tire the size of an SUV around outside. It's honestly not fair for any one man to be that beautiful.

I place my hands on the small of my back, lean my head against the glass and just watch. The muscles in his back and shoulders ripple with every flip. The waistband of his gray sweatpants black with his sweat. I would die if I had to wear pants in this heat. Leo insists that he has to sweat, a lot. Something about impurities and maintaining healthy weight. Honestly, I stopped listening after he said "sweat." It's the end of August, in Vegas. Just thinking about it has me sweating.

"Stop eye fucking your man out there. It's gross and I'm

pretty sure your kids know what you're thinking," Indie says with a little hip bump. I asked her to come with for moral support, though she said she had been coming anyway.

"Oh my God, shut up," I sputter. "I was not eye fucking him." I bust out laughing at the lie. "Okay, I was. But I was also thinking hateful shit about the heat."

"Stop being such a baby. Go and bake by the pool," she suggests.

"First of all, hell no. Second of all, I want to be here for Deacon."

"How's he doing? Mav is doing better now that they're back to training," Indie says, glancing over at me.

Lips pursed in thought, I answer. "He's better. Sometimes he's just going, doing his thing, completely engrossed with whatever it is he's doing right then, and then a minute later I look at him and he looks lost. Like he's ready to bolt first chance he gets," I confide sadly. "It seems to get a little better, day by day though. Leo being here helps. He sees what I see, and when Deacon gets that look on his face, Leo pushes him harder. So far it's working." I smile softly watching Deacon roll the tire right into the back of Mav who is on the phone, probably with Carter dealing with the press and promo. Mav stumbles, flips Deacon off, and then goes back to his call.

"And you? How are you holding up, mama?" There's a gentleness in her voice that you don't get often with Indie.

"I'm surviving. I'm sad and I cry a lot, but I try to make sure he doesn't see it. I still feel guilty about the whole thing, even though I know it wasn't my fault. My doctor suggested that I see a therapist when I get back. I think I'm going to. Maybe I'll see if Deacon wants to go too." I haven't mentioned the therapist to him yet—one thing at a time, and right now, this fight is everything.

"Ha! Deacon isn't going to lie on a couch and pour his heart out to a complete stranger unless you're blowing him," she laughs. Snarky bitch.

"Whatever. He might." She's totally right. "Thanks for coming, Indie. I needed you here with me," I say to my friend, switching gears.

"I know it. I wasn't going to miss this. I mean, this is a big fucking deal, but you and the babies do need auntie Indie too. Everyone has someone to unload on, depend on, except you right now." She turns her back to the glass, leaning against it, facing me. "All jokes aside, Frankie. I'm here for whatever. You stay strong for Deac, and I'll stay strong for you."

"You're busy staying strong for Mav," I tell her coyly.

"I'm a multitasker; I can be strong for all you cunts."

"Ahhhhh, there she is. There's my ride-or-die chick. All that sweetness and I was getting worried that you'd been abducted by aliens," I laugh.

"Dude. It might be fun. As long as they keep their weird Martian dicks and anal probes to themselves, I'm down," she deadpans.

"Stop, Imma pee." I'm laughing so hard now a snort slips out which makes me laugh just that much harder as she stands there calmly watching me.

"You're the one into anal probing now, not me," she teases.

"Just the tip, right, Princess?" Deacon says from behind me.

I jump, covering my face in embarrassment as Leo and Mav stand there with looks of fascination and terror, respectively.

Indie snickers beside me, "That's not what I heard."

"Holy fucking fuck. Someone make this stop, please?" Mav pleads.

"Seriously, you guys are such asses." I try to sound pissy, but I can barely contain my own laughter.

"You're lucky we have a press conference to get to, otherwise we might have to discuss this further, Princess," Deac jokes, taking my hand and guiding me to the door.

"I have never been so grateful for one of these things in my life," Mav mutters, leading us all out of the gym.

"Don't think we're not gonna talk about this more later, baby," Deac whispers in my ear. Laughing at my embarrassment, he gives my ass a slap as I walk ahead of him. I glance back at him to find him staring at my ass.

"Eyes up here, Hitman," I taunt.

"Not my fault. You girls started it," he insists as he helps me into the truck. "I can't wait to finish it though." Deac winks and closes the door.

A COUPLE OF hours later and we're all headed to the press conference in a limo. Not because we're that important, but because there are so many of us. It seems to make Deacon more at ease if we're all together, so I've been doing my best to make sure that we all go wherever he goes.

Deacon slides out first, holding out a hand to help me. I take hold of his hand and pull myself across the seat, maneuvering my burgeoning belly and doing my best to keep my ass covered in my dress at the same time. It's no easy feat. Finally out, I smack Deac on the chest when I see him smothering a smile with his hand and a laugh with a fake cough.

"You got it, Princess?" he asks, beaming at me. I can't even be mad at him. I'm just so thrilled that he's happy tonight. I know that this press conference is going to be a nightmare for him. We've done extremely well evading the news teams, so he's prepared for mayhem as soon as he sits behind the mic. As we walk, Deacon puts me between him and Reggie, Indie between Deacon and Mav. Everyone else following behind us, Trent bringing up the rear. We make our way through the crowd that's formed outside of the MGM Grand for the press conference. Since it's open to fans as well, there are quite a few people already here.

"Stay close, Princess. Don't make me knock heads, yeah?" I nod and tuck myself into Reggie's back, while Deacon boxes me in. "I just don't want you to get jostled or anything, okay?"

We make our way through the crowd, Deacon stopping to sign autographs and take pictures with the kids yelling his name. He makes me smile from the inside out when he turns down the women asking him to sign their cleavage or calling out to him to marry, date, fuck them. More than one woman screams out to him, "Hitman, I want to have your baby!"

Smiling he pulls me into his side. "I already have two babies on the way, don't need any more," he calls out to her cheekily. "Only one baby mama for this guy. I'll be lucky to survive this one." Deacon grins wickedly at me and ushers us through the doors.

Once inside, he has to go and meet backstage with the rest of the guys on the fight card. He grabs up my hand and kisses my wrist. I hope he never stops. The butterflies that fill my belly every damn time rival these two future MMA fighters taking up residence in there. "Reggie, take my girl to the front row; they have seats waiting for you all." Reg nods and steps aside, holding out his arm for me to go ahead of him. Before I leave, I feel the need to reassure my Fighter. I'm more nervous about this than I am the fight itself. There's a lot of shit talking that goes on at these things, which is usually right up Deac's alley. Talking about Sonny is going to be difficult though, as well as everything that went on over the last year with the trial and me. Derek will be up there to field questions, and he said he'd keep them as professional as possible and redirect all of the personal shit. He agrees with the Love team that it's nobody's business.

I reach up and brush my fingers over his half of the Mizpah charm dangling from the chain on his neck, smiling softly at him. "I love you, Deac. This part will be over soon." On tiptoes, I place a kiss to his jaw then allow Reggie to lead me away.

We get settled in our seats and wait in anxious anticipation for the fighters to come out and the questions to start. I like how they've started doing these, allowing fans to come in and ask questions as well as the press, and hopefully it means the questions will stay neutral, more about the fight, rather than devolve into ugly dirt-digging.

The room explodes into applause as the fighters and Derek come from behind the black curtain. I can't take my eyes off of Deac as he stalks confidently across the stage to his seat on the far side of the podium, directly in front of where we're all sitting. His hair is completely unmanageable in this desert heat. I just want to bury my fingers in it. It's wavier than usual, escaping the messy bun he has it all pulled into at the base of his skull. All the men on the panel are required to wear suits, but Deac being Deac had to be a rebel and instead is wearing a black dress shirt, black pants and black suspenders. He looks dapper as hell all blacked out. I don't get to see him in anything other than sweatpants and workout clothes very often, and although I love seeing him in those, it's nice to see him dressed up every once and a while too. Deacon catches me admiring him and throws me the "I love you" sign as he takes his seat. Once all of the men are seated, the fun will begin.

AFTER TWO HOURS of trash talking from both sides and some of the most ridiculous questions—"Will you make Saul shine the belt in front of you before handing it over when you win?"—the press starts to get more comfortable and more personal. Asking questions about me, the babies, all of the broken hearts he's leaving along the circuit. Deacon answers each with a smile and his "no fucks given" attitude that I love so much. Until a guy from one of the sports networks stands up and asks about the Brazilian models who tweeted about sleeping with him. Deac picks the microphone up from the table and points over at me, "Have some fucking respect for my girl, bro. Those chicks and that question hold absolutely no importance in my life. One woman. That's all I need and she knows where she ranks with me." Deac tosses the mic down, the muscle in his jaw ticking. I can see that this is all about to go south, so I pull my phone out and shoot him a text.

Me: Who loves me more than you do?

I hit send and watch as he glances down at his phone and then up at me, a smirk on that gorgeous mouth of his.

Deacon: Nobody.

Me: I know that. No one else matters

Tucking my phone back into my purse, I blow him a kiss and settle in for the rest of the questioning. Does it hurt my heart? Hell yes. But, that's all behind us now. I only want for us to move and grow. No going backwards anymore.

Just as they're wrapping everything up, they allow one more question.

"This one is for Deacon. Mr. Love you didn't waste any time replacing your brother, your trainer from the beginning of your career. How are you and the new trainer working out? Is having a new trainer a weakness that you think Mr. Ares can benefit from?"

My breath held, I look at Deacon and watch as that one question takes its toll. It's as if he's been punched, the pain evident on his face. Derek leans into the microphone to thwart the question when Deacon puts a hand on his arm stopping him.

"First of all, my brother is and always will be irreplaceable. He didn't quit, or get fired, he was killed. Something that

I'm struggling with as a fighter and as a man who just lost his brother. Is it a weakness? I'm sure it can be viewed that way. Will I give Rude Awakening a chance to use it to his advantage? Absolutely fucking not. That fight is with me. No one else," he states firmly. "Secondly, Leo isn't just some random guy that I found to join my team. He trained me while we served together. He's the only other person I trust to have in my corner. My team is my family, my core. We're missing a big piece of our unit, but we're rallying together and that's how you win shit." I see how much that took out of him, but he sits tall in his chair, proud. And I know that no one else can see the anguish just under the surface. His eyes are full of sorrow and a weakness he's not accustomed to even as his body is pure strength. But he's right—he won't allow anyone to use that against him.

The room is quiet, nobody sure how to respond at first, and then hands shoot up all over, people yelling questions, one more personal than the next. It's like this guy opened a floodgate. And that's when Derek puts an end to it, turning the mics off and bringing the guys to the center of the stage to face off for the cameras.

CHAPTER
Thirty-One

DEACON

AFTER THE CONFERENCE, we go right back to the hotel, each going our own way, agreeing to meet in the morning for the pre-weigh-in. With one hand on the small of Frankie's back, I raise my other in farewell, following her into our suite.

"I'm so fucking glad that's over," I mutter, tossing my coat over the chair and going over to the bar in the corner.

"You did good, Deac. You didn't let them beat you. I'm proud of you. I can see that fire again, and it makes me happy. You're light's not made to be snuffed out, baby." Her voice is like a balm to my soul. Just hearing her say the words makes me feel it. Believe it.

"If it's back, it's because of you. I get through it all because of you, Princess. I'm sorry I pushed you away. Never should have; I know better. I'm through with that. I've got my head in the game and I'm ready to fight. Inside and outside of the Cage. I'm ready . . . because of you."

"No, because of you. I'm just here to love you. The rest is all your doing. My Fighter. Always fighting, even if it's himself," Frankie says to me as she toes out of her heels, an affectionate smile touching her lips.

Just that simple move has my focus shifted. "How in the fuck do you wear those? You're about to pop and yet here you are walking around in six-inch stilettos. Not that I'm complaining; you know how much I love your shoes." I wink, smirking at her around the rim of the water bottle pressed to my lips.

"That's why I wear them, and they're only three inches. Plus, I'm so used to being in heels all the time that I don't even notice. Since you did though, I'm rocking my Chucks tomorrow," she teases. As she climbs onto the bed, she pats the mattress. "Now come here. I've wanted to get my hands on you ever since I watched you get dressed to leave," Frankie orders in her sexy rasp.

"Is that right?" A wicked grin splits my face. I bury my hands in my pockets and lean back against the bar. "Well, what're you gonna do about it, Miss De Rosa?" Eyes dancing over her, I can feel my pants getting tighter. She has her hair up and off her neck in some messy bun thing that makes her look like she's got "just fucked" hair, the diamonds on her necklace catching the light every time she moves.

I amble over to the bed and sit next to her. "I really am proud of you. This is all a lot to take in right now and you're handling it like a champ," Frankie says as she maneuvers so that she's kneeling behind me. With her belly pressed into my back, she begins kneading my shoulders, breaking up the tension that's been resting there for weeks.

"I'm sorry that they got so personal. I don't ever want that shit to be brought up again. It was inevitable though." My head falls forward to give her better access. "Princess?"

"Hmmm?"

"I promise to never put you in that position again. You're all I want. I'm done with the rest of them. You understand that, right?" Almost afraid of her answer, I glance over my shoulder at her when her hands stop their soothing motion. "Frankie?"

"I believe you," she says softly. "Let's not talk about it

anymore though, okay? I'm over it, forgiven you, but I won't ever forget. So for now, I just want to focus on us. Only ever us here." Her hand makes a sweep of the bed.

"Okay." I nod, standing at the foot of the bed, looming over her.

My finger traces her pouty bottom lip, smiling when she nips the pad and then soothes it with a swipe of her tongue. Gaze traveling over her face, across her bare shoulders, I land on her superb fuckin' rack. "Whatcha got on under that little dress, Princess?" Need making my words sound rough. It's been too long. How did I stay away from her for so damn long?

"In this heat? Nothing." It comes out like a purr, a promise. My girl is a seductress; she knows how to work me over. Up on her knees, she slips her fingers underneath my suspenders, yanking me as close as her belly will allow.

With hooded eyes, I watch her, waiting to see what she'll do next. I'm the dominant one in our bedroom. All she has to do is look at me and I've been properly seduced. Open that pretty mouth of hers, drop a few dirty words, and I'm fucking done. This right here is more than I usually allow, because I'm incapable of waiting when I want her. And I always want her. So I take charge, take her. And she lets me. This time though . . . this time is her show.

Hands flat against my chest, she runs her hands over my pecs, trails them over my shoulders to lock behind my neck. Head cocked to the side, she tangles her fingers into the hair at my nape. My heart is stuttering in anticipation, yearning as I fight the urge to take over. Frankie pulls my head down to meet her mouth, taking my bottom lip in between her teeth and tugging. I growl low in my throat. Fighting the urge to flip her over and bury myself in her right now. "You want me, Deac? Will you let me love you? I want you to let me fuck you." The words are no more than a breath against my mouth, but their impact is what has me tightening my hands on her back.

"Is it—" My voice is like gravel. I clear my throat and try again, "Is it okay? Did you ask the doctor?" Concern for the babies gives me pause.

"All cleared with Dr. Dean. Apparently dancing keeps me in great shape. He said no restrictions other than no sparring with you. I'm sure this wasn't what he meant though," Frankie says with a cheeky grin. A wicked glint in her eyes.

"Fuck me, Princess." It's an order. A plea.

Silently she pushes the suspenders off my shoulders, and once they're hanging at my side, she begins slipping buttons through my black shirt one by one. With every disc she slides through, she places an open-mouthed kiss to my skin leaving a path of fire behind. Tugging the tails of my shirt out of my waistband, Frankie pushes the tailor-made shirt down my arms, letting her fingers caress every bit of exposed skin before dropping it to the floor. I grab her wrist when she reaches for my pants. "No fucking around, I want inside you, you feel me?" I demand.

Frankie just shakes my hand off. "Not yet I don't, but I will." Her voice affects me as much as her touch. As my pants hit the ground, I fist my hands into the gauzy material of her dress ready to rip it from her body. Literally. I draw in a breath when she reaches into my boxer briefs, cupping my sac with one hand as she strokes over my cock with the other. She releases me and pushes the briefs down over my hips. Helping her get them past my thighs, I kick them away the moment I'm free. The Princess lets an appreciative sound slip past her lips, making me smile. "Have I ever told you how perfect you are? How magnificent every inch of you is?" she asks, dragging a pink-tipped fingernail from the base of my cock to the crown, causing it to jump.

"I don't think you have. Right now I would rather you show me."

Without hesitation, she reaches for the hem of her dress

and pulls it over her head, flinging it to the side. Not one to lie, she's completely bared to me, nothing on underneath, just like she said. I love how she isn't self conscious about her body. On her knees in front of me, her tits full, rose-colored nipples tight, begging for my attention. I crack a smile at the size of her belly. She's so petite everywhere else, except for this perfectly round and wicked distended Buddha belly. It's fucking beautiful. She's beautiful. Stunning. "You're fucking gorgeous. Inside and out. I've never seen a more beautiful woman." My words light her up, just like the vision of her, naked and pregnant with my children, does to me.

"Only you could love me like this," Frankie says slightly amused. "But only you matter." Placing a kiss to first her name and then the charm dangling against my neck, she sits back, her knees spread. "This is going to be soft and slow. I promise I'll make you feel good, Deacon. But I'm the one fucking you tonight, and I say soft and slow.

I can't see her pussy, but I don't have to. I can smell the sweet scent of her arousal, see it on her flushed skin as she pulls me onto the bed, guiding me to my back. With my hands gripping the headboard, I let out a groan when she slides my cock into her mouth. In and out, working me farther down her throat. My head thrown back, neck exposed, I hiss out a breath through my teeth when Frankie swallows my entire length. Immediately, my instincts kick in and I jerk my hips forward, hitting the back of her throat. She pulls back and lets me fall from her mouth with a pop, laughing softly, "Greedy."

"Can't help it, baby," I grit out.

"Help me?" She holds out her hand for me to take. I steady her as she carefully straddles me. Her pussy glides over my cock as she teases us both by rocking back and forth, over and over, until the friction sets off a trembling in her legs. My teeth sunk into my bottom lip, I grab her thighs and help her torture me until she comes all over my cock before I can even get inside her.

"You're fucking killing me, Princess."

With a look of pure sin, she lifts up. Meeting my eyes, she gives me the go ahead with a smile. Sliding a hand in between us, I guide my cock into her, moaning as she stops midway down my shaft only to lift back up to the tip and back down again. Finally, her ass is resting against my thighs, her hands planted on the headboard for balance, giving me access to more of her. I lift my head and take a puckered nipple into my mouth, scraping my teeth against it, then blowing as I abandon it to drag my mouth down one, then the other tit, nipping the sensitive flesh as I go. She has us both panting now as she rolls her hips in a sensual figure eight, over and over. I run my hands over her stomach in wonderment, with love and a desire that burns through me like nothing ever has. Not even fighting. I might keep her pregnant forever.

A trail of goose bumps is left in my wake as I fist her hair and snake an arm around her to palm her ass, spurring her on, but still not taking control no matter how bad I want to. I growl into her ear, "Whose cock is this, Princess? Who owns me, huh? Tell me." I flex my hips, holding myself rigid to apply more pressure to her clit with every rotation of her hips. "Tell me," I demand, tightening my grip in her hair.

"Mine. Mine. Mine. All fucking mine," Frankie moans out. Her movements become a little less coordinated and she slaps an open palm against the headboard. That's my breaking point.

"That's right, baby. This cock is yours. Can I give it to you now? Please, let me give it to you? I've reached my limit. Don't even care that I'm begging." The nod she gives me is all the encouragement I need. Remembering that I have to treat her more delicately than I normally would, I sit up with Frankie still straddling me. Nearly chest to chest, I run my hands down her thighs to delicate ankles and pull her legs to wrap around my back one after the other, locking them at the base of my spine. "Okay?" I question as I settle her further onto my lap, putting

me even deeper. Her belly resting against me as I rock gently and deeply.

"Mmmm, yes. Perfe—" her words are cut off by her gasp, her nails digging into my shoulders where she hangs onto me. "Again," she cries out in pleasure.

"Greedy." I throw her words back at her, even while I thrust my hips forward at the same time as I pull down on her shoulders, pressing her tighter still. "Your pussy is fucking perfection, Princess. Tight, wet, fucking perfection." The words tumble from my lips. I feel almost delirious with the need I feel for her. My heart is racing, pulsating, electric. Like it's own living entity everywhere we touch. My fingers spearing through her hair, my arm anchoring her to me, the silky smoothness of her thighs rubbing against mine, my cock buried in her sweet, flawless, fucking cunt. My whole damn body in flames from the heat being with her like this creates. I rest my palm against her chest and apply pressure, tugging her hair so that she's leaning back, her hands planted on the bed for support. "Ahhh, there's that pretty pussy," I murmur, bringing my thumb to her clit, strumming over it. I'm so close. I need her closer. Want her coming with me, all over me. Frankie throws her head back, exposing the long column of her throat, her tits moving in time with my thrusts. I know she's close when she begins working against me as much as her position and belly will allow. "You ready, baby? Take me with you, let me feel it." Without breaking our rhythm, I grasp her hips, taking control again and thrust, soft but sure, flicking my hips with every thrust, making sure I hit her spot with every stroke. Her eyes squeezed shut, Frankie's breaths come out in gasps, my name mingled in between. Her muscles contracting around my cock in waves, each one tighter than the last. "That's it, Princess. You know what I want. Give me what I want—come all over my cock. Then I'll dirty this pretty little pussy up," I grit out through clenched teeth. There's no room for finesse now, I'm too close. When she goes rigid in my hands, her thighs falling wider apart, I grunt out in relief as my control snaps and I'm coming. Long and hard. Shudders racking my body every couple seconds from the intensity.

We both sigh in satisfaction, making her giggle. "Laughing after I've just fucked you senseless is not cute, Princess," I groan, pretending to be hurt. Pressing into her one more time, I groan again, this time because I don't want to leave the wet heat of her pussy. I would like to just stay like this forever, but I have to get her in a more comfortable position. "Let me get you all cleaned up, baby." Once I slide out from beneath her, she rolls to her side, a content smile on her pretty lips. I can feel her eyes on my ass as I make my way to the bathroom. "Keep that up and you're gonna get fucked . . . again," I toss over my shoulder at her, whistling all the way.

All cleaned up and tucked into bed next to my girl, I pull her tight against my chest, my arm draped over her hip, tracing letters and words on her skin, across her belly. "Thank you," I say softly, pressing a kiss to the back of her head.

"Thank you? For what?" Frankie asks me drowsily.

"For that. I needed that. Needed you. Always will."

"Then you'll always have me," she whispers, bringing my hand to her mouth and kissing my wrist.

"Yes, I will," is my answer, along with a kiss mimicking hers to my spot on her wrist.

CHAPTER
Thirty-Two

THE PRESS CONFERENCE yesterday took its toll on me, but having the chance to be with Frankie after so long was exactly what I needed. That connection. Her. To make me feel alive. If even for that little while in her arms, nothing and no one but us and those kicking ass babies. Shaking my head and smiling, I bring my focus back to the here and now.

Today is the weigh-in and tomorrow the fight. The. Fight. The biggest one of my career. It doesn't matter how many times I'll defend the title from here on out once I win it. This first bout to take the strap and the title that goes along with it is the most important. In the two weeks that I've been here training, I've gotten myself in a better place. I'm focused, dedicated, and though I'm missing Sonny, feeling his absence deeply, I can hear him. When I'm training, I can envision him standing there with his arms crossed shouting orders at me. My mind instantly picks up on things that Leo says that I've heard Sonny say to me a million times. Before all of this, I never realized just how much alike Leo and my brother were.

I see the two of them off to the side discussing strategy and I feel Sonny's presence. I was afraid to leave the gym in Chicago because it felt like I was leaving Sonny behind. Like those walls held all of the things he's ever taught me, and as long as I was there, so was he. It was me grasping at straws, I see that now, but I still find myself searching for signs of him in everything I do. I'll never let the memory of my brother go. I'll take him with me always. I'm just slowly learning to live again and I have Frankie to thank for so much of that.

"Where you at, bro? You look like you're a million miles away," Mav says, slapping me on the shoulder, sitting down next to me.

"Nowhere. Just thinking about Sonny," I admit.

He looks away, lost in his own thoughts. "He was so damn proud of you, Deac. He rode your ass hard because he knew." Mav puffs out a little laugh. "I think you were about seven, in the gym just messing around with Pop, when he first realized. We were standing there waiting on Pop to finish with you, and Sonny said to me, 'I betcha ten bucks Deacon goes pro. He's way better than you and me. I'll be his trainer. You can be the towel boy, Maverick, because you hit like a pussy.'" We both laugh at that. "He was eleven and already bossy as hell." My brother shakes his head, the sad smile on his face mirroring my own. "He never gave up on you. You were always the one angriest about mom leaving. I think you invented trouble to get into just so you didn't have to be so mad at her. And every time you got yourself in a scrum outside of the Cage, Sonny would tell Pop, 'Go easy on him; he'll learn to control it, Pop—we'll teach him.'" Mav looks over at me, "And they did."

My eyes a little watery with the onslaught of emotions, I look up at him with a cocked brow.

"Well . . . kinda," he teases to lighten the mood. "Now let's go weigh your ass in so that we can eat. I'm fucking starving."

"Between you and the Princess, I'll be lucky to make weight. You must be having sympathy cravings or whatever the fuck they're called," I joke as we walk over to where Pop, Guy, and Leo are talking.

My dad looks up as we join their circle and grins, "You boys ready?"

"Yeah, Pop, we're ready," I answer.

"Are we stopping at the hotel so that you can change first?"

"Nope. Why?"

"That's what you're wearing?" He flicks his hand at me.

"Sure am, Pop. Why change now?" I say as I run a hand down my "God wears a manbun" shirt.

"I hope you have children as ornery as you are, son." Pop walks away chuckling, like the mere idea thrills the shit out of him, which makes my brother and I smile at each other. My dad hasn't had a whole fucking lot to smile about.

"That's just mean, Pop. I'm telling Frankie you put that evil on her," I call after his still-laughing ass.

THE AMOUNT OF people in the room where the weigh-in is being held is staggering. I'm not sure how many people, just that there are a fuck-ton. Derek doing the best he can to accommodate Frankie, whom he has a soft spot for . . . not that I blame him, makes my life a lot easier. Under normal circumstances, I like to have her in my sights. Now with her being pregnant and with my emotions all over the fucking place, I need her around more than ever. As long as I can put eyes on her, I'm good.

Standing at the side of the stage with Mav, I watch as Saul makes his way out to a cheering crowd. He has a massive number of followers here today. No surprise since he's had an incredible run, especially lately. He has taken down every opponent he's come up against in the last year. I smile to myself when I think about how I'm gonna end that streak.

"Dude's cocky, but he has a right to be, Deac. He's a shit talker too, but it's good for publicity, so let him do it. Just makes it that much sweeter when you beat his ass in the Cage," Mav tells me.

I nod in agreement, scanning the crowd for Frankie. She's sitting, hands rubbing her belly, listening to something her dad is saying. They call my name and she turns her attention to the stage and then to the stairs when she doesn't see me. Smiling, she blows me a kiss and gives me two thumbs up. Her smile could light up a fucking room. It wrecks me and puts me back together every damn time. I throw her the sign language symbol for "I love you," just like yesterday, as I make my way to the scale, and watch that smile brighten even further. My girl's a sucker for sweet shit like that—I'll have to put that one in the "get you laid" column.

"Stop making googly eyes at Frankie and give me your damn clothes, lover boy," Mav tells me, holding his hand out.

Reaching over my shoulder, I yank my shirt off and toss it to him, followed swiftly by the rest of my clothes. The cheers in the room drown out everything else as I step onto the scale. They quiet when they announce my weight of two hundred and forty-two pounds, exactly where Rude Awakening weighed in. Mav meets me at the scale and starts handing me articles of clothing to put on as I amble over for my photo op.

Derek shakes my hand and then places an arm in between Saul and I as we faceoff. All is fine, his shit talk not fazing me in the least. I let him work himself up into a frenzy and smile for the cameras, pissing him off even more. This just might be my favorite part of all this. Well, except for getting that win.

Stick and move. Stick and motherfucking move.

CHAPTER
Thirty-Three

TITLE FIGHT:

Deacon "The Hitman" Love vs. Saul "Rude Awakening" Ares

THE MOOD IN the locker room before the fight is somber. Everyone feels the loss of Sonny, more now than ever. It's in the little things, like Leo doing my prefight rubdown, talking me through some of the things that we've been working on over the last couple weeks. All things that Sonny would be handling. Leo knows I'm with him, paying attention, but also that I'm missing my brother. He's not expecting me to answer, he just keeps rubbing and reminding. Not allowing me to get inside my head too much. That's where shit gets murky.

There's a light knock on the door and Frankie walks in, a tentative smile on her face. Without a word, I hop down, putting a halt to Leo's ministrations and pick her up. Carefully I set her on the table and climb up to sit next to her, placing her hand on my thigh after laying a kiss to her wrist. Not missing a beat, Leo goes right back to what he was doing and saying. We're all perfectly content to let him.

The closer it gets to fight time, the more at ease I become. The tension slowly letting my insides go. I glance up when I feel eyes on me. Pop gives me a small smile and nods. Almost as if he feels it too.

"I'm ready," I say to the room as a whole.

Mav comes over and helps Frankie down, handing her the tape.

"Thank you, Mav," she says as she steps in between my legs to start wrapping my hands. Tucking her phone in her pocket, her ear buds are firmly in place. Apparently she has to find her zone as well.

"Finally ran out of that pink shit, huh?" Maverick asks, amused from the corner of the room he retreated to.

"Oh, don't worry, I'll get him some more," Frankie teases.

With the hand she's not wrapping, I tuck the hair falling into her eyes behind her ear. "You special order that shit or what, Princess?" I ask, plucking the bud from her ear to place in my own.

"Nope, I have a supplier," she tells me, winking.

As I get the headphone nestled into my ear, I hear the chords of the song she's listening to. Eyebrows raised, I grin at her bent head, waiting for her to look up. When she does, she asks, "What?"

"Fight of my life and you're listening to some chick with pink hair? This *is* the pink-haired chick, right?" I ask in mock indignation.

"Yup, sure is. And she broke your favorite ginger's heart. Her hairs not pink anymore though and this song reminds me of you, so shut up and stop ruining it. Would you rather I start praying in Italian?" She slaps my thigh in reprimand.

"Nope, I'm good." I do as I'm told and shut up, letting her repetitive movements work their magic on me, a smile on my face. The next song begins and I bark out a laugh startling her. "You are so fucking random, Princess. Does this one remind you of me too?" I ask, nudging her with my knee, singing along to "Thriftshop." "You're not allowed to be in charge of the pre-fight music anymore."

"Speaking of fight music, are they all set up for the live performance out there?" Mav questions. I'm not sure how he did it, but he got Imagine Dragons to perform "Radioactive" live as I walk out.

"Yeah, it's insane out there right now. Amazing," Frankie says reverently, her hands stilling. "You did good, baby. Be proud. I am." She gives my wrapped hand a squeeze. "How does that feel?"

"Perfect." Frankie nods her head and then starts in on the next hand. This time I sit quietly until she's finished and listen to her odd playlist, chuckling quietly to myself as "Beast" queues up.

"Okay, Deac. You good?" she asks expectantly.

I flip them over, flexing my fingers and making a fist. "Yep. Good." Frankie steps aside and lets the Federation come over and inspect her work, signing off on the white tape.

"May I?" she asks one of them, indicating for the sharpie. He passes it over and she moves back in between my knees, head bent over my hands, writing on first one and then the other. Placing a kiss on each when she's finished, she hands him his marker back and turns to me.

"You never fought for Sonny; you always fought with him. Today will be no different because he's with you here," she says softly placing a hand over my heart. "And he's here." Frankie taps a finger lightly to my temple. "This is your dream, your fight. You fight for you, *with* him." I glance down at my taped hands and see that she wrote "Sonny" on the right, "Love" on the left, her lipstick staining each in a perfect imprint of her lips. "Go out there and show him how bad Love hurts, Deac." Her hands cradling my face, she brushes her thumbs over my bottom lip. "This is your fight." Frankie replaces her thumbs with her mouth. A press of her lips to mine that carries as much meaning as her words do.

I'm unable to speak past the lump in my throat or the fire

in my heart. This woman lights my ass up. She's my mother-fucking everything. And this is why.

SHOWTIME.

I stand at the mouth of the tunnel, my hood pulled over my head, Frankie's hand tucked in mine, Pop, Mav, and Leo at my back. Rocking from left foot to right and back again. The energy in the arena is palpable, I can feel it pulling at me, calling me down that path to the Cage. It's electric, a force that I let wash over me. I look down at Frankie, and she smiles up at me and nods, gazes locked, mouthing my mantra along with me. *"That's my Cage. I'm a warrior. I dominate because this is who I am. I will win. There is no other option. I am a warrior."* I didn't even know that she knew it. Never realized I said it out loud. If I had time, I might be embarrassed.

Head lowered, eyes squeezed shut, my head bobs in time with the music. Letting it settle over my bones, I concentrate on loosening every one of my taut muscles. The moment I hear the live drums of "Radioactive," it's like someone breathes air into me, power, *fight*. I begin moving forward toward the darkened arena, the lights flaring to life as the music hits a crescendo. It's like a motherfucking rock concert. We're flanked on both sides by Reggie, Trent, and Bo as well as MGM's security detail. I warned them we would be walking slowly because of the Princess. There was no way I was entering the arena without her by my side. Never again.

The cutman greets us as we reach the Cage. I slip out of my hoodie, handing it to Leo as Mav hands me some water and my mouth guard. Before slipping it in, I lean down and kiss Frankie. "I love you, Princess," I say against her lips so that she can feel it, since there's no way she's going to hear it in here. She pulls

away, smiles, and flashes me "I love you" in sign language just like I did to her. Winking, I work my guard in and face my pop who pulls me in for a hug. Tightening his arms around me, he thumps me on the back and kisses my shoulder. It's an emotional fucking moment. He releases me, his eyes shining with pride. Next, I'm grabbed up by Leo and my brother and then handed over to the cutman. I close my eyes as he applies the Vaseline to my face, the adrenaline singing through me, building at being forced to stand still. Finished with my face, he slaps my leg and moves aside for the doctor who gestures to my mouth for me to show him my mouth guard and then knocks on my cup. Once cleared, he waves me into the Octagon.

Bouncing on my toes, I surge forward and bound up the two stairs. Stopping just inside the Cage, I lower my head and let my thoughts go to Sonny and what he would be telling me right now. My heart thudding in my ears, I kiss my fist and raise it into the air, saluting my brother because Frankie was right—I'm doing this for me, *with* him. That's the only moment I can give to him though because Sonny doesn't belong in the Octagon with me. Inside the Cage, everything and everyone else disappears.

Off to the side, I block out the crowd as Saul enters the arena. Standing with my back to Leo and Mav, I focus on what Leo is saying to me as I bounce and rock, shaking out my limbs. "You keep off the ground. Rude Awakening is a grappler first. Hit him hard and fast; he won't be able to take the heat behind your punches," Leo yells over the crowd. I nod my head letting him know I hear him. "You have more power than he does, use it. Take your knees to him. He won't see them coming. He gets you on your back, stand the fuck up. Stand the fuck up and put him against the Cage," he insists. I turn to face them both as Rude Awakening dances around the Octagon.

"Don't let him wreck that pretty face of yours," Mav says smiling. I give him a thumbs up and turn back to the center, concentrating on the feel of the canvas under my feet.

After what seems like forever, we're introduced by the announcer with much fanfare, and moments later, the referee points at us both and claps indicating it's go time. Not paying attention to anything Saul is spewing, I look right through him and wait to see what he's going to come at me with. If he wants to wrestle, I'll wrestle his ass. My wrestling guru took me to school. I'm ready to go all five rounds with him if I need to. I smirk at him when he starts talking shit, telling me that I'm fucked if he gets me on the ground. I motion for him to fucking bring it. I'll let him take us in one more circle, and then I'm taking him to task.

Halfway through a turn around the Cage, he charges me, going for my waist. I let him get his arms around me, but hold steady when he tries to bring me down. He tightens around me, trying to cut off my airflow, so I stun him by dropping elbows on his back one after another until he's forced to release me. The second he's upright, he catches me with a jab to the face, which lands solid and splits my cheek. The blood warm as it trickles down my face. It feels fan-fucking-tastic. It's been too long. The surge of adrenaline it gives me makes me soar, makes me feel invincible, when it should do just the opposite. I beckon him closer and let him throw two more punches before I get him with a spinning back kick that staggers him enough for me to move in and get him with an uppercut just as the bell rings ending round one.

Leo is already vaulting over the top of the Cage, the cutman waiting for me to sit so that he can check my face. Assuring him that I'm fine, I listen to Leo, the excitement in his voice contagious. "You liked that shit, Hitman? You crazy fuck. I saw that smile. That's it now. No more. You take his ass, motherfucker. Don't you let him land one more fucking punch, you hear me?" he demands. "This is your show!" Nodding my head enthusiastically, I push the cutman off me and get to my feet,

waiting for the next round.

I don't listen to Leo and let Rude Awakening land a few more punches. Just until I remember that my girl is here and that she would not be impressed. One minute and eighteen seconds into the third round, I decide to play him at his own game and take him to the mats. Rubbing my bleeding wounds across his face to blind him with my sweat and blood, I get him twisted into an Americana, shocking the hell out of him. Putting pressure on his shoulder until I feel it start to give, and just before it pops out of joint, he taps out and I release immediately, allowing the referee to pull us apart. Spread eagle on the floor of the Cage, I stare blankly at the bright lights overhead, in a complete and utter daze. Scrubbing my hands over my face, I ball my fists and press them into my eyes, trying to reel in my emotions, which are now a living, breathing thing racing around inside of me.

We just won the motherfucking belt.

CHAPTER
Thirty-Four

HELPED OFF THE canvas, I stalk over to the corner and drop to my knees, overwhelmed with emotion and the consuming need to celebrate this victory with Sonny. The noise around me is electric; it's a pulsing that I feel in my soul. Pressing my head against the padded post, I breathe deeply to slow my racing heart. "We did it, Sonny. We did it, brother," I shout, knowing that he's there, he's with me and he'll be with me 'til the end. My team is holding everyone back letting me have this moment, and that's all I allow. Sonny wouldn't want more than that.

Standing, I stride forward and make it to the center of the Cage. I'm swarmed by people, bombarded with congratulations, hands slapping at me, reaching out from every direction, and I push my way past all of it, all of them, with Vince the emcee trailing after me, shouting questions and thrusting the mic in my face. I don't stop until I reach the chain link of the Octagon. There she is, front and center, right behind the surprised announcers, hand on her swollen belly as she stands on her chair, Reggie watching to make sure she doesn't fall. The smile that lights up her face sets me on fire. This moment, right here, is what I've been waiting for, fighting toward. I couldn't claim her completely until I had my belt. I promised myself that I wouldn't give up on all that we had worked for, even when what I wanted most was her. Well, I've got my belt. Now it's

time to get the fucking girl. I look down at Vince who is still trying to get me to answer his questions and take the mic from him. He nods in agreement as he relinquishes his hold on it. A wicked grin takes over my mouth—she's going to kill me.

Raising the mic to my mouth, I point at her, "Princess!" Her eyes widen, as she shakes her head no at me. I just laugh, "Woman! You see this?" I ask as I hold up the belt that Vince passes to me. She nods, tears streaming down her face. "I told you, one fight to go, and then I was coming for you. You re-member what I said, Frankie?"

If I thought that her eyes were wide before, I was wrong. The blush creeping up her cheeks at the thought of what the text messages said is evident even from here. Dipping my head and smothering my laugh with the back of my hand, I take a moment to rein my shit in before focusing on her once again. "I sent you a text message that said I was going to do something to show you that I love you. I can't do *that* now, but I promise I will later, repeatedly." I can't help but chuckle at her obvious embar-rassment as she glances around to see who is paying attention to the show I'm putting on and the answer is . . . everybody. Every-damn-body is watching and I couldn't give a fuck less. This is my girl, my time, our moment. "Since that's off the table for now . . ." I shrug, my head cocked to my shoulder and hand my belt to Vince who looks absolutely perplexed as to what in the fuck I'm doing. Clapping him on the back, I turn back to my girl, her hands covering her mouth, the smile peeking around her steepled fingers.

Slowly I drop to one knee and the roar that rips through the crowd is deafening. The catcalls and whistles bouncing off of every wall in the stadium making their way back to me. I raise my hand to try to quiet them, my eyes glued to Frankie, no hope of controlling the tears rolling down her beautiful, stunned face. The first happy tears either of us have cried in a while. Once our audience has quieted, I raise the mic to my mouth, "Princess,

I've loved you for too long now. I didn't tell you until I almost lost you. I won't lose you again; you're mine and I'm yours. Nothing will ever come between us again, Frankie. Living without you isn't an option, you feel me?" She nods slightly and I go on, "Marry me." It's not a question. I'm not asking. I give her a second to let that soak in. For her to hear me. "I'll take care of you, of my family. I'll keep you safe, always."

The lights in the arena shine down on her, making her tears glisten like rows of tiny diamonds marching across her cheeks. My throat works at swallowing down the moment of panic that takes over when she doesn't say anything. The silence around us is as loud as their cheers were. How thousands of people can be so quiet is beyond me. Slowly she reaches her hand out for Reggie to take and he gently helps her off the chair she was perched on and walks protectively behind her as she makes her way to the Cage. Rising from my knee, I meet her at the black fence of the Octagon, hooking my fingers in the links as she presses against them from the other side. The mic hangs at my side forgotten as I take her in. She's the most beautiful woman in the world, and regardless of what her answer right now is, she is mine and she will be a Love, *my* Love, always.

The rapidly beating pulse in her throat and the way her skin is starting to flush that pretty shade of pink that it does when she's hot for me makes my lip kick up in a half smile, "You want something, Princess? You only turn that color when you need fucked, baby." Probably not the most romantic thing for me to say at the moment, but that's what she does to me. If the smile taking over her face is any indication, she doesn't mind.

"Oh, I need something, Deac," she says in a raspy emotion-laced whisper.

"Yeah, what's that?"

"You." Simple. Sure. Honest. "Just you. Only you. Yes!" my girl yells as the crowd explodes around us, rivaling the chaos inside me.

Got my girl, got my belt. Stick and move. Stick and motherfucking move.

THE END

Epilogue

One Year Later . . .

"MAVERICK!" I SHOUT as I walk into JR's room and reach to scoop him from his crib. Jameson Rocco Love, this one is gonna be trouble. I already know it. No less than his twin sister, Gianna Isabella, though. Gigi is a fucking rebel. And gorgeous like her mama.

"Dadadadadadadadaaaaaa," JR says, bouncing like a crazy man when I hold my arms out for him.

"You ready, little man? Today is a big day, yeah? We gonna marry the mama?" My face buried in his dark curls, I press a kiss to his head.

"Mamamamamama." The smile that splits his face when I mention Frankie has one just as big spreading across mine.

"Let's go, stud. We have to get ready or we're gonna be late, and then we'll both be in trouble." He squirms to be put down. Little dude has been walking since he was only nine months; at eleven months he's booking it. My dad said all of us boys were early walkers and once we started running, we never stopped. "Nope, no way. I don't have time to scoot down the stairs. I have to get us both in suits and make it to the church in less than an hour," I tell him, squeezing him tight and pretending to gnaw on his cheeks and neck.

"Yo. What the hell are you screaming about, Deac?"

Maverick asks from the doorway, hands outstretched for JR.

Not relinquishing my hold on my boy, I ask, "Why aren't you dressed? You know we all have to be there soon, right?"

"Bro, relax. Do you need help getting him dressed? Pop is downstairs, ready and waiting."

I'm sweating. Not because of nerves over getting married or anything, just over what it all actually means. She'll finally be mine. I mean, she's always been mine, always will be, but this is it, man. She'll be my wife. My. Wife. That's as good as it fucking gets. Plus, it'll make Guy happy. I'm pretty sure he's been putting curses on me and shit since he found out Frankie was pregnant and that we weren't getting married right away.

Guy wasn't happy that we had children out of wedlock, old school Italian and his only child and all, but Frankie wanted a real wedding. In a church, with the dress and flowers and dancing. The whole fucking thing. He wanted Italy, she wanted to be married where he and her mom were married, in her mother's dress. There was no way to get that done before the twins were born. But she immediately started planning so that we could get married soon after, only this is Chicago and everything is booked years in advance, so I was forced to fucking wait a year. We got lucky because she enlisted Indie, who of course as an event planner has a ton of connections and was able to get Frankie whatever she wanted. I can't wait to see that fucking bill.

"Nah, I got him. You go and get your shit on though," I toss over my shoulder at him as I enter my bedroom. Maverick going the other way to do my bidding.

Once in the room, I sit JR down on the bed next to his little tux that matches mine and go into the bathroom to start the shower. Humming a little Van Morrison, I go back to my boy. "Let's clean us up, stud. We gotta smell good for this. We can't put monkey suits on all stinky," I coo. Fuck me, I fucking coo. It makes him happy though, and that's all that matters.

Twenty minutes later, me, my son, Pop, and Mav are heading out the door. Our moods bordering on somber because we're a man down. Sonny's loss is felt every day; it just isn't as suffocating as it was. JR and Gigi help with that though. There's no room for sadness with them around. They're hell on wheels, keeping us all on our toes.

"You have the ring, right?" I ask Maverick expectantly.

"Was I supposed to bring that?" he deadpans. Smartass.

"Don't make me kick your ass on my wedding day, fucker." Punching him in the arm and smiling, I turn to Pop. "Guy is with the Princess?"

"He's at the church with the family, making sure everything is set there," my dad says, tickling JR under his chubby, little chin.

"Indie is with Frankie. Trent said they're getting ready to leave in a few minutes," Reggie chimes in from the front seat. Pulling up in front of Holy Name Cathedral, he turns around. "I'm gonna park and then I'll be in there, okay?" We all agree and exit the SUV, my pop handing JR over to me.

"Let's go get married, boys," I say to them and lead the way inside.

STANDING UP AT the altar next to Maverick, I look out over the mass of people in attendance. It literally looks as if we're in the middle of a Godfather movie. Frankie's entire family is here from Italy. Rome has invaded Chicago. Chuckling, I go to say something about it to Mav, when the music starts playing, signaling the beginning of the rest of my life. My brother elbow's me, grinning like a damn fool, both of our eyes trained on the back of the church. We watch as Indie walks down the aisle slowly, holding a small bouqet of flowers in one hand and

Gianna's little hand in her other. Gigi is all smiles in her tiny ballerina dress, a fistful of feathers I'm pretty sure they thought she was going to toss. I grin as Indie passes Gianna over to Pop and he sits her next to him. JR is alongside Reggie, and Trent for backup, I'm sure.

Frankie wanted Ave Maria playing instead of the traditional Wedding March, so when the first strands of the song fill the room, I take a deep breath, my heart thundering in anticipation of seeing my girl. When she finally steps into view on Guy's arm, I feel the first prick of tears. I swore that I wouldn't cry like some kind of fucking pussy, but looking at her now as she stops and places a flower on the table set up with pictures of her mom and Sonny, I've lost that battle.

The sun coming through the stained glass windows casts a glow over the church, the light reflecting off of everything it touches. Watching her glide down the aisle toward me is the most humbling experience of my life. It's ethereal. Everything I've ever wanted but never deserved is coming to join me in front of God and all of our friends and family to marry me. It's more than I ever dreamed.

Overcome with the enormity of it all, my chin hits my chest as I blow out a breath, the tears I had been fighting rolling down my face. Not wanting to miss a second of this, I raise my head, dashing the wetness from my cheeks. Frankie beams at me through her own watery gaze as she gets closer. I let my eyes wander over her. She's stunning in a handmade lace gown and matching veil. It meant the world to her to be able to wear her mom's dress and judging by the pride on Guy's face, to him too. Finally they're standing in front of me and all I see is her. I don't hear anything the priest says as I stare at her in awe.

When Guy starts to speak, I turn to him, taking his hand in mine when he offers it. He pulls me into a tight hug, patting my back, "Nobody but you would I give my Francesca too. Take care of each other. Always," Guy says to me, emotion choking him. Placing her hand in mine, he kisses her cheek, saying something to her softly in Italian before going to sit beside my dad.

I shake my head, ghosting my fingers down the side of her face. "You're gorgeous," I murmur, raising her hand to my mouth and placing a kiss on her wrist.

"And you are the most beautiful man I've ever seen," Frankie says through her tears, her smile infectious.

Turning to the priest, I ask, "Is it time to kiss the bride yet?"

CANDLES. LITTLE CANDLES. Big candles. Candles every-fucking-where. We probably have the Chicago fire department right outside of the museum, just waiting for the call that we've set the fucking place on fire. None of it matters to me though when I look down at Frankie, wrapped in my arms, swaying to the sound of Noah Guthrie singing.

"You happy, Princess?" I watch the fire from the thousand candles flicker over her skin. Brushing the hair out of her eyes and tucking it behind her ear, my hand settles on her bare back. The delicate gown of her mom's replaced by some fuck-hot backless lace dress that I'm dying to get her out of. Or just get around her waist. If I don't stop, the fire department will be putting out a totally different kind of fire.

"No." Stunned out of my thoughts by her answer, brows drawn, a quiet laugh escapes me.

"No? You're not happy?"

Her smile spreads slowly, the pink staining her lips drawing my attention. "Nope. Not happy, Deac. That's too simple of a word." Bringing my eyes back to her blues slowly, I gather her even closer.

"Tell me," I whisper. My hand splayed against her skin, tingling with the need to roam. "Should we get out of here so you can tell me?"

Frankie giggles low in her throat. "We can't—we haven't even done cake yet."

I sigh. "Fine, you better tell me what I need to hear then," I chide in mock seriousness.

"I'm more than happy. I'm ecstatic. I'm thankful, so thankful," she says in quiet sincerity. "I'm right where I want to be, need to be. I'm completely . . . yours." Her raspy voice hits me straight in the chest. Right in the spot that she consumes with her very being.

"You're my wife." Raising her hand I place a kiss over her wedding ring before flipping it and laying my mouth on her wrist. Tears shimmer in her eyes as she nods her head, smiling that smile at me. My own wicked grin creeping across my face I ask, "So, can we please get out of here? I need that dress out of my way and I need to be buried deep inside my *wife's* sweet little pussy."

Steps never faltering she manages to raise on her tippy toes as she dances and brushes a quick kiss to the exposed skin at my throat. "Whatever my husband wants," Frankie murmurs.

"Damn right," I praise, patting her ass.

Francesca

WATCHING MY HUSBAND—MY. Husband. My big, bad, manbun wearing husband—buckle our children into the back of the SUV, kissing both of their heads tenderly, my heart swells. Never in my life could I ever have imagined loving someone this much. He shuts the door and taps the roof of the vehicle and turns toward me, a wolfish gleam in his moss-colored eyes.

He has long since abandoned his tuxedo jacket, the snowy white dress shirt rolled to his elbows, his muscled arms and ink gloriously on display. His newest addition, a tattoo he got for me and the twins, a crown encircling his wrist with our names in cursive along the bottom, makes me smile longingly at him.

"What?" he asks, bringing me into his body. Arms wrapped around me, he settles one big palm on my ass. Pressed tight, cuts to curves, just how he likes.

"Nothing, I just love watching you with them," I admit as I pull his head down for a kiss.

"Mmmmm, you know what's gonna happen if you keep looking at me like that, don't you, wife?" he asks huskily.

"Why don't you tell me, husband?" I tease, knowing full well what it's going to get me.

Deacon scoops me up in his arms, carefully navigating the steps to our home and carries me over the threshold like the romantic he is but pretends not to be.

Smirking down at me, he leans in and says against my lips, "It's gonna get you fucked."

"That's what I was hoping."

"Just the tip?" he asks slyly.

"I think I've earned more than that," I say pouting.

"Yes, you have, Princess. You've earned it all." His voice resonates with his love for me, something I'll never get tired of.

"Show me."

"Every fucking day for the rest of my life, Mrs. Love."

"Stick and move?" I chide with a smile.

Deacon's teeth sink into his plump bottom lip and then the most wicked grin takes over his beautiful face. "Stick and motherfucking move, baby."

Acknowledgments

IN CASE YOU feel overlooked please know that you have not been. It takes a village to write and publish a book. An army of friends, blogs, readers, writers and every single person in between. They call it self publishing but they're wrong. None of this would happen without you. No matter how big or small a part you may have played, it mattered more than you know.

I'm acknowledging people in alphabetical order again because it's probably my best shot of not forgetting someone. Before all else though, I need to thank the readers. Without them this would be just another journal entry instead of a story someone cared enough to read.

To My Readers:

It is still a surreal thing to say. To know that you love my characters and their story humbles me so much. I will never be able to put into words what that means to me. You've left the writer . . . speechless. This book was a long time coming, I know it was. Thank you so much for sticking with me. For being patient, mostly, and for encouraging and talking about this series and convincing others to read it. My cup runneth over. Stick and Move!

Addy:

I could say nothing or just do this whole thing in hashtags and you'd get it. You'd get it and laugh because you're my easy friend. I love you and your feels. I cannot thank you enough for all that you do just by being the love to my filth and I will always make room in my boat for you. #ELC forever #Factasfuck

#Yahtzee

Beck's Beta Babes:

Who, Tamsin, Thistle, Goldie, Stephy, Nini, Jilly Bean & McKinley

I would never in a million years be able to do this without you. Thank you for letting me torture you and spoon feed you my story word by word. You're support and dedication mea the world to me, just as you ladies do. I love you.

Breathin' Easy:

BITCHESNACHOS!!!! Need I say more? My You three are my rocks and I would be just a stumbling fool without you! Love your faces, each and every one of you. #timezones

Corinne:

My friend my LP! I love you and value you more than you could ever know. Simple as that my stabby friend. You're my people and you're stuck with me so get used to it. I couldn't do this without you, wouldn't even want to try. Love you big.

Coco:

My Inide! I'll love you for as long as we share a ridiculously awesome love for even more ridiculously awesome music! We may not have books, but we have Brit bands and skinny jeans! Love you, cuntasaurus We shoulda been Brits!

#DEACSGIRLS:

My IG QUEENS! I can't tell you how much all of you have come to mean to me and how much you've made IG one of my favorite places on the planet! You ladies are the bomb.comb and I love your faces!

Deacon Originals:

You're always in my corner, and forever in my heart. I love you more than you'll ever know.

Dirty Love girls:

You ladies make my day. My happy place, because of you. Love your dirty little souls.

Elites:

Near or far we'll always have RT and each other! Love you to the moon and back

FYW:

Thank you so much for taking me in and making me feel like family. I've learned so much from you incredible ladies. You're an invaluable, wonderful group of women whom I am honored to be a part of. Bring on the pink!

Get your Makeup Did Ladies:

We sure did! I love you dirty girls so much it hurts. Thank you for always having my back.

Jodi:

JUDE! My fisty friend. I made a life long mate in you. I wouldn't trade you or your rants for a million Franggy's. Well . . . maybe. HA! There can never be another you for me. Love your face!

Kari:

Still and always my graphics queen always coming to my rescue. Thank you friend. I love you to bits!

Lauren:

No plan B needed this time my friend! Thank you for always humoring me and doing things my way just so we can turn around and do them your way, the right way. Your friendship is invaluable. Love your face ad your crazy dog stickers.

Lisa:

Editing queen and Saint. Thank you for believing in me enough to not change my story but to make it the best that it could be. Because of you and your love for traveling, I'm an international author! Grazie.

Mandi's Lovers and Fighters:

You ladies. I can't thank you enough for all of your leg work and sharing and teasing and suggesting and encouraging. I'm humbled and so incredibly lucky to have you in my corner. Thank you from the bottom of my heart. Thank you.

My Family:

Thank you all so much for all of your support and encouragement, your bragging and somewhat awkward selling tactics. I love you to the moon and back.

PCVPPC:

My family, my sisters. This wouldn't be as magical as it is without you. I love you.

Perfectly Publishable:

Christine, my Canadian queen. Not only are you amazing at what you do you've turned into a wonderful friend who shares my love for hockey. That makes you the dopest. Thank you so much.

SFAB:

You ladies make my world right. I can't thank you enough for all of the work you put in. Thank you for always putting me first and making me feel like I'm your only client. I love you ladies big.

Stephy poo:

I don't know how I ever survived without you. You're my official, unofficial assistant and I love and treasure you more than you'll ever know. Your friendship and ability to be awesome all of the damn time humble me beyond words. I love your face so so much. Thank you. For everything. Literally.

Tammi:

Woman. You have a heart of gold and never fail me. Thank you from the bottom of my heart.

The Bloggers:

Thank you so much for the long arduous hours you put in to share your love of books. It's not always fun and it's never easy and yet you do it anyway. Thank you for helping me to see my dream through. I couldn't do it without you. And a special thanks to A Book Whores Obsession, Smart and Savvy with Stephanie, Angie's Dreamy Reads and my girls at Schmexy.

About the Author

MANDI BECK HAS been an avid reader all of her life. A deep love for books always had her jotting down little stories on napkins, notebooks, and her hand. As an adult she was further submerged into the book world through book clubs and the epicness of social media. It was then that she graduated to writing her stories on her phone and then finally on a proper computer.

A nursing student, mother to two rambunctious and somewhat rotten boys, and stepmom to two great girls away at college, she shares her time with her husband in Chicago where she was born and raised. Mandi is a diehard hockey fan and blames the Blackhawks when her deadlines are not met.

She is currently working on the next in the series along with trying to keep up with whatever other voices are clamoring for attention in her mind.

Connect with Mandi

www.authormandibeck.com
Facebook
www.facebook.com/authormandibeck
Twitter
https://twitter.com/authormandibeck
Goodreads
www.goodreads.com/book/show/23367669-love-hurts
Instagram
http://instagram.com/authormandibeck/
Spotify
https://play.spotify.com/user/manranbeck